CLARE LITTLEMORE

Flow

First published by Clare Littlemore in 2017

Copyright © Clare Littlemore, 2017

ISBN: 978-1-9998381-0-2

This book was professionally typeset on Reedsy.
Find out more at reedsy.com

Contents

Dedication	i
Brit Alert!	ii
Chapter One	1
Chapter Two	12
Chapter Three	21
Chapter Four	27
Chapter Five	35
Chapter Six	42
Chapter Seven	51
Chapter Eight	57
Chapter Nine	66
Chapter Ten	74
Chapter Eleven	86
Chapter Twelve	96
Chapter Thirteen	105
Chapter Fourteen	113
Chapter Fifteen	122
Chapter Sixteen	128
Chapter Seventeen	136
Chapter Eighteen	145
Chapter Nineteen	154
Chapter Twenty	163
Chapter Twenty-One	171
Chapter Twenty-Two	177

Chapter Twenty-Three   186
Chapter Twenty-Four   194
Chapter Twenty-Five   205
Chapter Twenty-Six   215
Chapter Twenty-Seven   227
Chapter Twenty-Eight   236
Chapter Twenty-Nine   246
Chapter Thirty   255
Chapter Thirty-One   262
Chapter Thirty-Two   270
Chapter Thirty-Three   279
Chapter Thirty-Four   287
Chapter Thirty-Five   295
Author's Note   297
About the Author   298
Reviews   299
Acknowledgements   300

Dedication

To my family, the most important people in the world.

Brit Alert!

If you are reading this book and not from the UK, a brief warning that I am a British author and use British spellings throughout the book. In The Beck, there is a 'harbour' instead of a 'harbor', characters wear overalls of different 'colours' (not 'colors') and may, on occasion, have to apologise (rather than apologize). Happy reading!

Chapter One

When I woke it was well before dawn. I could hear the rain pattering on the pod tarps, a sound I had long ago learned to tune out. Usually in the dark I could hear the comforting sound of the other girls' slow, sleepy breathing, but not today.

For a long time, I refused to open my eyes. Lying still, I tried to prolong the moment when I would have to admit that I was no longer asleep. Of course, the only day we were allowed to take a break from duties was the one time we could never stay asleep. All non-essential tasks would be suspended, for the morning at least.

Ours was an Agricultural pod. Growing the produce which fed the entire Beck was a vital task, and there were more than two hundred workers assigned to man the fields and greenhouses. Heavy flooding and regular storms meant our community fought a constant battle against rising floodwaters, so protecting the growing areas was paramount for our survival. But the fields and greenhouses could manage a short period without our labour force. The Supers would man any crucial stations for the earlier part of the day.

Usually our pod slept until the very last moment, and then became a frenzied chaos of activity before we all headed out to face the day. We grabbed our undershirts and pulled on dark green overalls and boots, the creaking of camp beds echoing throughout the near-silent pod. Every day we headed out the door as one just before 5.30am.

Not today though.

A dramatic sigh from the bed next to mine interrupted my thoughts. Reluctantly I opened my eyes to find a pair of alarmingly blue ones staring back at me, as I had known they would be. Cassidy. Her regulation cropped hair was white-blonde and stuck out in every direction. I tried to smile at her, knowing that the occasion and the early hour would turn the expression into a grimace even as I tried to seem optimistic.

"Hey."

"Hey yourself."

Our voices were a whisper. Anything above that would earn the entire pod a reckoning. Nobody wanted that, especially today.

"You ok?"

I shrugged, not knowing how to reply.

"Quin!"

"I'm ok."

"Really?"

Now it was my turn to sigh. "No. Not really."

"Harper?"

I nodded and rolled quickly on to my back, staring at the tarp above my head. The pod was filled with muffled whispers now, and we were in danger of being overheard. Grady, our Super, was the only one still sleeping, but she wouldn't be for much longer. We were better off not talking, not making any noise. I wondered as I justified it to myself whether it was simply an excuse not to discuss the subject any further. I had been awake for hours the previous night, dreading today. Not for myself: for Harper. But talking about it wouldn't make any difference.

"Quin?" This time the voice came from my other side and was softer, less insistent.

I turned to see Harper staring at me. Her thin face was ghostly in the early morning light, and I sighed as I took in her sunken cheeks and the listless expression in her pale green eyes. Forcing a smile, I tried to sound confident.

"You ready?"

"You know I'm not. Barely scraped through last time."

"But we worked on it."

"Not enough Quin."

Harper's eyes filled with tears but they did not fall. Fear lanced through my chest at the defeat in her tone.

As I turned away, I noticed that the whispering had stopped. Grady was awake and had climbed out of her bunk to begin dressing. Eager not to anger our Super unnecessarily, others followed suit. Today the rush to haul on overalls and boots was not chaotic. Instead our actions were slow and measured. We had time, and no-one was eager to embrace the day's events. Despite this, within a few minutes our group had gathered at the mouth of the pod and lined up. Her usual grimace in place, Grady unzipped the tarp and a dim, grey light spilled through the entrance. I shuddered as we marched outside in silent unison and headed towards the canteen.

The rain had stopped but the sky was iron grey above us. This was not unusual, but the looming clouds seemed angrier today. As we passed the other Agric pods in silence, different units emerged, our numbers growing steadily until the area was filled with the sound of rhythmic marching that propelled each line, like automatons, towards the hilltop path.

Glancing left I could see down into the fields which stretched away before us into the distance, empty for now. The dark, protective fencing round the Hydro Plant, where The Beck got much of its power supply. Then the wall. Tall, strong, protective, manned by Patrol guards as always. Beyond the wall were the floodplains, their waters seemingly still from this distance, reflecting the steely sky and encircling the entire Lower Beck. Sometimes the level of water was barely visible. After a storm it increased and everyone got twitchy for a while, until a spell of better weather beat it into temporary retreat. But the huge body of water was always there, a silent threat that nobody in The Beck could ignore.

Moving beyond the Agric Compound, we skirted the edge of the LS pods, deserted at this time of day, and then passed by the Dev Compound, where the staff would not yet be awake. In the distance I caught a tantalising glimpse of the woods leading to the Upper Beck, and in the distance I could just see the pass between the hills that provided a fourth wall to our valley. Finally our line snaked sharply left towards the Lower Beck canteen. Steam rose softly from the rear of the building and the unmistakeable scent of baking bread filled the air. The Sustenance Crew would also not avoid their duties today. We all had to eat.

Marching a few steps ahead, I watched as Cassidy turned her head slightly towards me. Usually she did this when she wanted to direct a whispered remark at me, or snort with suppressed laughter at whatever she had found amusing. We had perfected the art of communicating in near-silence after years of practice. Only essential, work-related communication was permitted in The Beck. We had learned fast that the easiest way to survive was to exist unnoticed, under the radar. But today Cassidy's speech seemed to die in her throat and she merely glanced strangely at me before spinning back to face her destination again as though she had thought better of it.

Our lines came to a halt at the flagpole just in front of the canteen. Usually we were eager for food and this was tangible, even in the silence. Now the lines were filled with grim expressions and no one seemed eager to hustle in and eat. A solitary voice, whichever Sustenance Super was on duty today, called out pod numbers from a clipboard. One by one, the lines trudged inside the tent.

I found myself willing the process to take longer to delay the inevitable, but too soon our line was filing in behind the others and queuing for the daily bowl of porridge and rough hunk of bread. Today's portion was made with milk, a rare treat. The usual watery substance which lurked in our bowls was replaced by a creamy, filling warmth. It was only a pity that we couldn't enjoy it.

Collecting my allotted bowl, I walked to the pod's usual table and slid on to the bench. A moment later, a small, cold hand slid inside my own underneath the table. I couldn't believe how small the hand inside mine felt, how feeble. I turned slightly to my right and managed a small smile for Harper, squeezing her hand in return before turning my attention to the meal.

I had little appetite, but the porridge was thick and creamy and I knew my body needed the strength it would provide. Forcing down spoonful after spoonful, I wished we could be afforded this kind of nourishment on a day when we could actually enjoy it. But it was tradition, to provide us all with a filling meal before the trials which awaited us.

The room was eerily quiet for a building which housed so

many people. All female at the moment, the canteen contained row upon row of benches which housed a never-ending stream of hungry workers. A large, barn-like structure with whitewashed walls and stark, simple furniture, the canteen never stopped, and every pod was carefully assigned two meal-time slots each day. The portions we received were meagre and barely kept us going, so anyone missing a meal really suffered. In our world, there were very few justifications for missing out on food.

I watched as table after table of girls ate, heads bowed, our silence more severe than usual due to the tasks which awaited us. The table at the top of the room was elevated slightly and contained the Supers. Their portions were slightly larger than the rest, which was why Super positions were so sought after. Both Cassidy and I would be considered for Super positions today, and Cass was looking forward to the prospect of a slightly better diet, but I knew that being promoted also came with its down sides. Being separated from friends I had known from the moment I was assigned to the Agric Compound was one. The extra responsibility was another. I wondered again if I had the stomach for it. But what else was there?

I glanced at Cassidy sitting beside me, consuming her breakfast with a grim determination. She too was sneaking looks at the Supers between swallowing, as if making vital mental notes about them. After a few minutes she stared directly at me, her eyes burning fiercely.

"Three," she hissed.

"Three what?"

"Places up for grabs," she raised an eyebrow, "I think three of them are going up."

I thought about it. Of the twenty Supers currently at the top table, Cassidy believed that three of them would be promoted to positions in other fields today, leaving their places free for others to take. There were at least thirteen girls I knew of being considered for elevation. Competition was tough. Cassidy was desperate to become Super. I wasn't quite as enthusiastic. My main reason for wanting promotion was Harper. If she could only get through today, and if Cassidy or I could make Super, we might protect her. Without that, we all knew she couldn't go on for much longer.

A tap on my thigh brought my attention back to my friend sitting on the bench next to me. I realised I was being handed something else. Harper was determinedly pressing something into my hand: the hunk of bread she had been given by the Sustenance worker. I stared at her fiercely.

"Take it back."

Harper shook her head.

"Take. It. Back!" I hissed.

The Super on duty was looking our way. I bowed my head rapidly, pushing the bread towards Harper, who was now staring in the other direction. I noticed that her porridge was barely touched.

"But you need it," I pleaded, "more than I do."

"I can't."

Finding sudden tears in my eyes, I had to bite my lip to keep them from falling. Harper was desperately skinny already, she had been for months now. She had struggled to collect her share of crops in the fields and Cassidy and I had been helping her out, collecting extra and slipping it her way when no one was watching. The additional work had almost killed us, but we had agreed it was worth it for Harper. It had also had the unexpected effect of strengthening us both, building real muscles on our wiry frames, and was one of the reasons that we were eligible for Super promotion today.

Harper, on the other hand, had only grown steadily weaker. I suspected that she was ill, but admitting that was far more dangerous than trying to hide her weakness. There was no option of medical treatment for her. We could only help her out where possible and hope time would help her to heal. Over and over again, I had offered her a share of my rations, hoping that the extra food would allow her to grow stronger, but more often than not she had refused to take it. Even when she did accept a small amount of food, she struggled to eat it. Whatever was the matter with her seemed to have killed off her appetite and her spirit, and she struggled even to consume The Beck's paltry rations.

Watching Harper struggle to finish the tiny bowl of porridge, I remembered the way she used to be. I had known Cassidy and Harper for a long time, but three years ago, when we all passed out of Minors and were assigned to the same Agric pod, our friendship had really taken root. The three of us had quickly become inseparable. The Beck was a restrictive place: the work hard and the hours long once you moved into a compound at the age of fourteen, but between the regulations and the hardships there was room for friendships to grow. The relationships we developed with our pod sisters were what kept us all going.

Where I was quite thoughtful and quiet, Cassidy was loud and boisterous, a character trait she was mostly forced to stifle. Cass regularly made fun of me for being uptight, which had led to several arguments between us in the past. But Harper was loving and gentle and funny, the perfect connection between us and she diffused our regular spats with an easy understanding of both our characters.

She was also by far the most suited to the Agriculture compound. Even in the very early days she had shown herself to be extremely adept at planting, nurturing, and gathering the crops so essential to the continuation of life in The Beck. She was the one who understood exactly how to make things grow and thrive, and she was looked upon as an unofficial Supervisor well before the age of sixteen due to her capacity for understanding exactly what was required to ensure the healthiest harvest.

Realising that the rest of the table had finished eating, I thrust the bread at Cassidy underneath the table. I knew she would accept it, where I couldn't swallow my friend's quota of food without feeling a keen sense of betrayal. Moments later, we rose and began filing out of the large room, the Sustenance staff already sweeping in to clear the bowls from the tables and begin again with the next sitting. Leaving the canteen, our line turned out of the exit doors and wound its way back round the path which took us within sight of the entrance again. Now, a similar sized group of young men from the LS pods was hungrily awaiting their turn to eat, having already chalked up several hours of work with The Beck livestock.

Usually plenty of glances passed between the groups, even from this distance. The Lower Beck's male and female citizens were separated from a very early age, when they were still Minors even, and most of the pod assignments at the age of fourteen were single gender. Only in certain compounds were male and female citizens permitted to work together. That didn't prevent curiosity though, in fact it probably made us even more inquisitive about the other group. The Agric girls always looked across at the boys, and were occasionally rewarded with a sly wink from one of the more confident among the group.

Few people were looking today though. The lines of girls marched forward resolutely. We knew what was awaiting us and no one was looking forward to it. Behind me, I heard Harper gasp as she tripped and I automatically shot out a hand to catch her before she hit the floor. She stumbled for a few paces before regaining her balance and I let go, knowing that Grady had not missed Harper's near fall. She was so clumsy these days. I was certain this fact was known by all the Agric Supers.

Around a year ago, I had begun to notice the gradual change in Harper. Cass wouldn't accept it at first, but I saw the early signs. She was quieter, less likely to chat, found it more difficult to complete the long hours required of an Agric worker. Where previously she had joined in the whispered chatter between us, and the stolen glances at the boys as we passed them, now her head remained permanently bowed and she didn't so much as glance in their direction.

While Cassidy and I had grown stronger, Harper had only seemed more sluggish and depleted in energy by the day. Eventually we had to support her on her return from the fields each night, and tried to switch our greenhouse allocations with her as often as we possibly could, so she could work where it was warmer and duties were light.

Today was Assessment day. It happened every six months without fail, and its purpose was to test the ongoing durability of The Beck workforce. We kept the place running, and without all staff being in prime condition, The Beck risked a complete breakdown. The series of tests we underwent each time included a gruelling physical, a mental health test, and a written examination which tested our knowledge of life and work in The Beck. All three were graded and the results defined what happened to a citizen next.

Promotion to a higher position within your own pod was possible, and carried with it some benefits. Reassignment to an alternative Sector was also possible. Citizens were sometimes moved between the different areas if the Supers felt we were better suited to another role, or if we had gained the necessary experience and knowledge to work at a higher level. In an environment where floods had destroyed huge parts of the country and land was scarce, overpopulation was not an option. Those failing the tests risked demotion to a lower level Sector, or even assignment to Clearance. This was my biggest fear for Harper.

Clearance was the place where citizens ended up when they had outlived their usefulness. It was saved for the elderly, for people who were not able to maintain a useful position in Beck society, for those who were seriously ill and unlikely to get better.

Situated across Black Hill on the far side of The Beck, none of the ordinary citizens were ever permitted to visit Clearance. Only the Governor's officials and Patrol members on duty were allowed over there. Whatever went on, it all took place over the other side of the hill, completely hidden from view. There was only one thing I knew for certain about Clearance.

No one ever came back.

Chapter Two

What I resented most about Harper's position was the lack of respect for her when she had played a huge role in Agriculture since she had been first assigned. Cassidy and I managed to complete our assigned tasks daily, but Harper had a real talent for cultivating crops. She had begun over time making small changes to the accepted methods of growing and reaping. This had massively improved their pod's productivity and gained them praise from Governor Adams himself. The experiments she had tried with a number of the core crops grown in The Beck had worked, and her methods had since been adopted throughout the entire system.

But however significant her contribution to our way of life, I knew that nothing could protect Harper if Beck rule decided that she was no longer fit for service. A citizen who could provide nothing, who could not work, was useless here, and no amount of reasoning or pleading would save her from Clearance.

As our group continued along the path towards the Assessment Compound, I steeled myself for the trials ahead. I could see determination in Cassidy's stride and was aware of its contrast with the slow drag of Harper's feet behind me. Cassidy would pass with no problem. She was strong and agile and capable of much more than our current position demanded of us. She was the most likely candidate to make Super too, her ability to identify a problem and see a simple solution without allowing her emotions to take over was a quality I admired and feared in equal measure.

I was pretty sure that I would pass too: I had consistently demonstrated my growing strength through the amount of work I was able to complete, even when I was helping Harper, and I had always been able to single-mindedly focus on a job until it was completed. Harper was a different matter. Six months ago she had been struggling, but we had somehow managed to coach her through most of the physical. Her intellect had never been in question, and she knew so much about the Agric culture that she had aced the written paper. Her mental health test had also been passable, so she had scraped through despite her physical exam results being below average.

But now she was far weaker. Occasionally, we had to actually carry her back from the fields in the evenings, ensuring that we were out of sight of the Supers, and they couldn't have failed to notice that Harper's crop quota was often lower than the average, despite Cassidy and I topping it up whenever we could. I also doubted her ability to complete the written exam effectively this time. Lately her concentration was poor, and I often had to repeat myself when I spoke to her. If she scored just below average on two tests, she stood a chance. Three, and she was history.

The line halted abruptly as the path levelled out and we reached the large gates of the Assessment Compound. Lost in my thoughts, I bumped into Cassidy before I could stop myself, and earned myself a dirty look from the Dev Super who was standing expectantly in front of us, brandishing a clipboard and barking instructions.

"Agric Sector pods 1 through 10, move forward into the Kennedy Building. 11 through 20 to the Lincoln Building and 21 through 30 with me."

She moved off rapidly, not waiting to check whether the hundreds of girls in front of her had followed. It had begun to drizzle again, and I was glad that we were not completing the physical assessment first. My line moved forwards when our turn came, marching around the side of the forbidding Kennedy Building in front of us to the Lincoln Building behind. The psych test was first for us then. I wasn't sure if this was a good thing or not. At least it would be over with quickly.

The Lincoln Building was not impressive. Similar to the canteen, it was built from rough wood which had been whitewashed, but had been fitted with dividers to create lots of smaller subsections. It was a practical space, like all of the buildings in The Beck. Mostly unfurnished, the room echoed more than the canteen did and our marching footsteps were amplified until the room was filled with a dull roar like distant thunder.

Our lines were met by ten separate Supers in white overalls. The Dev staff were ruthlessly efficient on Assessment Day. Each one took a single line and directed it immediately into a different section of the space. Our pod was taken to the very back of the building where we huddled in a group, awaiting individual instructions. Another Dev citizen in white sat behind a desk to the side of the area and the Super who had guided us over drew a curtain across to create some kind of privacy for the psych test, before calling the first name.

"Cooper."

The tall, rather shy member of our pod separated herself from the group hesitantly. We watched, until her regulation-cropped jet black hair disappeared behind the curtain. Harper shot me a look of terror and I forced a smile. Slowly the room began to fill with noise, a dull drone assaulting the ears of all the waiting Agric citizens. This was not the sound of voices sharing conversation, but the monotonous buzz of questions asked and answered, with brief pauses in between while potentially life-changing judgements were recorded.

Reaching out, I grasped Harper's hand on one side and Cassidy's on the other. The density of our group now hid this frowned-upon contact from Grady, who seemed busy trying to eavesdrop on Cooper's progress. Both Harper and Cassidy returned my gesture with a squeeze. I felt rather than saw Cass and Harper's hands connect on the other side. Cassidy's connection was firm but momentary: she released my hand quickly after the initial reassurance of the gesture, but Harper's fragile contact remained, and I felt glad that I could be of some comfort to her. The circle was a ritual we had kept up at every Assessment Day so far. It had always got us through in the past. Perhaps it would again today.

Minutes later, Cooper emerged from behind the white curtain and rejoined the group. Another girl was called forward, and then another. I examined the face of each pod member returning from the psych test, trying to decide from their expression how successful they believed they had been. It was useless, I realised. I knew each of these girls well, and their facial expressions were only a reflection of their ability to mask their real feelings from those who might condemn them. In a community where testing was constant and rejection a permanent threat, trust and honesty were hard to come by.

After judging three faces in a row to have failed the test I gave up, deciding I should focus on my own performance instead.

"Cassidy."

My friend strode forward and quickly disappeared behind the curtain. I knew that others in our pod thought Cassidy to be arrogant and over confident, but I understood her better. Cassidy was one of life's survivors and she understood the need to show the world a brave face. That didn't mean she was without feeling. Having spent the past year watching her give up so much in order to support Harper, I understood that the strut was simply a front to mask her inner feelings, which she would rather die than show to the world at large.

"Quin?"

My name was a hissed whisper. I turned to see Harper shooting me a quick glance before looking deliberately in the other direction. It was a technique we had perfected months ago which allowed us to communicate without drawing attention to ourselves. I too looked away from Harper.

"Mm-hm?"

"What if I…"

"What if nothing. Focus. Do what we practised. You'll be fine."

"I'm dizzy though, and I feel a bit sick."

I risked another glance at my friend, who seemed paler than she had been before, if it were possible. The hand in my own was clammy too.

"Shh. Deep breaths – remember?"

Harper nodded imperceptibly. It was easier to talk in Assessment situations because there were only so many staff in charge and they were less likely to notice a single pair of girls chatting. Still, I didn't feel I could risk anything more, and turned instead to face the curtained area again. Cassidy was just emerging, and from the look on her face, I decided I could have been wrong about all three of the previous candidates: for once even Cassidy looked as horror-struck as the rest had.

"Quin."

This time my name was spoken loudly and clearly. It was my turn. Trying to stride forward with Cassidy's confidence, I managed a few steps before tripping over my own feet and stumbling sideways. Hurriedly I caught myself and rushed behind the curtain, my face burning. Not a good first impression. Opposite me was a small, wiry woman with close cropped flame-red hair. She motioned for me to take a seat on the chair opposite.

"Good morning, Quin. How are you today?"

"I'm...um...well thanks."

Great start. It was always strange when we were actually permitted to speak out loud. My voice sounded like that of a stranger. I wasn't surprised that I had stumbled over my first few words. I hoped that the small error wouldn't count against me. Clearing my throat, I readied myself for more questions.

"Can you tell me how old you will be on your next birthday?"

"Seventeen."

"And you've done the test," she consulted her notes, "six times before?"

"Yes."

"Ok. Let's begin."

She folded her hands on the table in front of her and leaned back, clearly knowing the questions by heart.

"How well do you sleep at night?

"I sleep fine – usually straight through until the morning,

though I'm often awake a little before the others."

"Why do you think that is?"

I shrugged, "I don't know."

"How do you find your work in the Agriculture Sector?"

"It's fine. I don't find it difficult. It's physically tiring, but I cope with it."

"Have you been feeling irritable lately?"

"No."

"More tired than usual?"

"No."

"Happy?"

"Yes, I suppose."

The expression on the operative's face changed. I cursed myself. Why had I felt the need to add the 'I suppose'? Basic answers. Simple. That was the way to go.

"Can you clarify? What do you mean, by 'you suppose'?"

"I mean yes. I'm happy. Not every second of every day, but generally, I am happy."

"Are you able to keep your focus on one task at a time, or do you find your mind jumps around?"

"I can stay focused."

"Alright. Now, I'd like you to look at these pictures and tell me what they make you think of."

The Super opened a folder and brought out a sheaf of papers which had been poured over many times previously. Clutching them to her chest secretively, she took out one and laid it on the table between us. The paper had a stark white background and a random grey shape printed on it. A nondescript shape which resembled a map, or a squashed insect. I had seen it before, in the previous psych tests, and I never knew what response would be the safest. I suppose that was the point.

"I see a map."

"And this one?"

"I see a butterfly."

"And this one?"

"A fish."

She continued with the pictures, revealing them to me one at a time at a pretty rapid rate as I continued to give my answers. After each picture, she ticked a box on a form in front of her and moved on until she had shown me around twenty. Eventually she stopped and scrutinised me closely.

"One final thing, Quin."

"Yes?"

"Are there any other Sectors you feel you might be suited to? Other than Agriculture, I mean?"

"No! I mean... I've never really considered—"

"Really? Surely you must have thought what the other Sectors might be like?"

I stayed silent, unsure of what the safest answer would be.

"Never?"

"Well yes, of course I've wondered about life in other Sectors. Doesn't everyone?" I paused, again, fearing I had said too much. "But I don't have any ideas that I would be better placed elsewhere."

"Alright then. You're done. Off you go."

She looked at me expectantly. I got to my feet, rather more slowly this time. Once I had taken a step away from the table she started scribbling notes again and didn't look up as I backed away.

Joining the back of the line, I heard the operative call out Harper's name. I watched with trepidation as she jumped slightly before walking slowly forwards, looking more insecure than ever. I willed her to appear more confident as she disappeared behind the white drapes.

"How'd it go?"

The voice was Cassidy's, taking advantage of the changeover between tests.

"Fine, I guess. Did she ask you anything unusual?"

"No. Same as always. Why? What did she ask you?"

"No. I was just curious if the format had changed, that's all."

Cassidy looked puzzled, but was unable to reply as the Super had returned to her prior position and was staring directly at us. We shifted our positions slightly and when I glanced back at her a moment later, the Super was studying her clipboard intently again.

A chilly breeze swept through the Lincoln hangar and I shivered, wishing that my overalls were made of thicker material. As I turned back towards the curtained area the white drapes fluttered in the wind, for a second revealing the people sitting in the assessment area. I froze, even as the curtain fell back to its original position, transfixed by the stricken expression on Harper's face and the tears that were streaming down her cheeks.

Chapter Three

Never show weakness. That was our mantra. We had spent weeks training Harper to keep her face guarded, expressionless. It was the key to maintaining a secure position in The Beck, and we all knew it. There was no place for vulnerability in our society. The Beck began as a saviour society, set up by a group of people determined to re-establish order after flooding had torn the country apart. It was governed by an extremely strict code of conduct. It had to be, to ensure the survival of its citizens in what were often extremely dangerous surroundings.

As inhabitants of The Beck, we did not receive much in the way of formal schooling. Beck citizens were taught a trade from the age of fourteen and, before that, efforts were focused on preparing us for life outside of Minors, the junior Sector of our society. In Minors we received only the education that was necessary to make us into useful citizens, and this was mostly focused on the various skill areas which we might be apprenticed into, as well as instruction on the general workings and laws of society in The Beck.

But all citizens were required to take a history course warning us of the extreme threat posed by the flooding and the risk of ignoring it, as our society had done in the past. It was drummed into us how challenging our world was, but we were repeatedly told that if we learned to live by Beck rule, we could remain a sustainable society. There was no room for rebellion. Citizenship here was not a right, but a privilege, and there were those who would take it away as soon as look at us.

So we learned from an early age to be vigilant, to guard against those who would judge us unfit. We all knew the consequences. And now Harper was sitting in the psych test, the *psych test* for God's sake, silently sobbing, revealing to the Dev operative who had so much power over her just how weak she was. I cursed her inability to control her emotions.

Harper stayed behind the curtain for a long time. I began to panic that they might have escorted her out of the building by a separate exit without us noticing, but in the end she stumbled out, her face starkly white. I heard some of our group gasp as she returned, ghost-like, to the relative safety of our group. I worked my way next to her and grasped her hand, which felt even colder than before. Squeezing it gently, I felt her entire body trembling and forgave her tears instantly. I had only been angry because I was so frightened for her. I knew how much she risked by revealing her weakness, her illness, to those in charge.

The rest of the psych tests passed in a blur. I remained by Harper's side, her hand in mine, until we were ordered back into our line again and marched out in the direction of the Kennedy Building. The written examination was longer than the psych test, but we all took it at the same time, so in a way it was less intimidating. The Kennedy Building was laid out as always, with rows of rickety desks and chairs filling the gigantic space. We filed in and were directed to a row near the back. As I slid into my place, I glanced up at Cassidy who was passing me.

I nodded at her, raising my eyes towards Harper. Cassidy winked.

"Distraction."

For a moment I didn't understand what she was getting at. Then she stretched a hand towards me and I could see the hunk of bread from breakfast concealed inside it. She hadn't eaten it. And it finally dawned on me what Cassidy had immediately understood. Harper was far more able to consume smaller amounts of food at regular intervals. She simply couldn't cope with the two assigned mealtimes per day. We had discovered this over the past few months, when she was unable to consume the full ration on a regular basis. If we could sneak food out from the canteen and save it, she was far more able to eat it, in smaller portions, throughout the day. This kept her going for longer and she had been more capable of making it through the day with this kind of diet.

Saving the bread was a genius move on Cassidy's part. How she had managed to conceal it during her psych test was beyond me. But if we could get Harper to eat at least some of it now, she would be able to tackle the written paper with more focus. But we would need a distraction to achieve our goal. I looked around for the Super in charge of us. She was busy guiding other pods into the row in front of us. Shifting slightly in my chair, I twisted the leg of the table sharply before overturning it. The crash echoed the length of the Kennedy Building. My heart hammered as the eyes of every citizen in the room turned towards me. Surely I couldn't be judged harshly because of an equipment fault? I took a deep breath as our assigned Super hurried over, a questioning look on her face.

I motioned to the table, pointing at the leg which had bent easily in my hand before it fell. She understood instantly and signalled to some of the Dev staff at the front of the hall. Within minutes a replacement table was being brought forwards and set up. As I slid into my chair, feeling the blush finally start to fade from my cheeks, Cassidy nodded at me. Turning around on the pretence of checking that my chair was sturdy enough to hold me, I saw Harper's head bowed low over her table. No one else would have noticed anything was amiss, but I knew what I was looking for. Ever so slowly, her jaw moved, indicating that she was chewing.

Breathing a sigh of relief, I turned back to my desk and glanced at the paper in front of me. It looked the same as it always did. An off-white booklet, thick and rough to the touch. There was the usual space to include citizen details, and the questions set out over the following pages. I felt them burning through the test paper, demanding answers.

The room had already been quiet, but I felt a sudden change in the atmosphere and glanced up from the paper. At the front of the room stood a figure who had not been there previously. Superintendent Carter. Second only to Governor Adams, Carter was an important figure in The Beck. She carried out trials, delivered judgements and reckonings, and generally had the role of bad cop to Adams' good cop, who liked to paint himself as a symbol of unity throughout The Beck.

"Before you begin, I would like to remind you of the severe consequences of trying to cheat. I know that the majority of you take the test as you are supposed to, but there remains a small minority of citizens who continue to believe they can flout the system and escape retribution."

She stepped sideways and grabbed the collar of someone

sitting close to the front, hauling the girl to her feet. She was tiny and her cropped hair was a mousy colour. I wouldn't have looked twice at her if I had passed her working in the fields or in the canteen. Her face was drained of colour and she looked like she was about to collapse. Carter stepped closer to her and leaned down until she was staring directly into the girl's face, their noses only inches apart.

"Miller, what are you hiding?"

The girl shook her head fiercely. I could feel the fear emanating from every pore of her body, even at this distance.

"Tell me or I will find it myself, and that will be far worse for you."

Carter almost spat the words into Miller's face. I felt a growing admiration for her when she managed not to blink.

"Last chance."

There was a short pause before Carter nodded towards two of the Supers who grabbed hold of Miller's arms. Carter lunged at her as if she concealed a deadly weapon, ripping at the sleeves of her overalls. Miller put up more of a struggle than I had expected from someone so tiny, lashing out several times with her feet in Carter's direction, but with her arms fixed behind her and two large Supers holding on to her, she was pretty much helpless. Moments later it was over. Carter stood victorious, Miller's skinny arm clutched firmly in her fist. She lifted it and Miller's torn overall sleeve fell away, revealing tiny figures inked in black on her forearm. The answers.

Lord knows how she had got hold of them, but there they were. The answers to the written test, printed on her body for all to see. I winced as a smile spread over Carter's face. Pausing for dramatic effect, she slowly lowered Miller's arm before dragging the young woman towards the doors at the front of the hall. Before she swept out of the room, she turned around to face row upon row of terrified girls.

"Be warned. You cannot and will not defy Beck rule."

A strange smile crossed her face.

"Best of luck, citizens."

Chapter Four

A feeling of dread swept the room, but I couldn't repress a sense of respect for Miller. How brave, to boldly carry the answers to the test on her skin. My thoughts went to Harper. She could have done with a set of answers to help her through this. Perhaps Miller was like her, weakening and in desperate need of support to get her through the assessment. The idea had backfired, yes, but at least she had tried something. She couldn't have done it without help though. I glanced around, willing to bet that there were a couple of Miller's friends in the room, biting their lips to hold back the tears which would give them away as co-conspirators as they mourned the loss of their friend.

Because Miller had sealed her fate. It would be Clearance for her now, whatever her performance in the tests had been so far. The Beck did not give second chances. Anyone guilty of rule-breaking was immediately assigned to Clearance with no chance of appeal. I wondered which pod she was from. She hadn't looked familiar, just one of the many faces I passed every day. But she mattered to somebody in the room.

"Agric Sectors 1 through 30, your written test will begin now. You have thirty minutes."

I found myself wasting valuable time glancing around the room before I opened my paper. Almost as one the rows of girls picked up their pencils and opened their tests. Carter's visit had created the required effect. We were petrified. It kept us working, that fear, made sure we were obedient. I sighed softly as I opened my paper to the first page.

Part One focused on general skills awareness. Twenty questions on Beck regulations to test our general knowledge of how life in our community worked and ensure we knew the rules inside out. Part Two was divided into sections, one on each of the different Sectors. Citizens were required to answer on two. It was usual to select your own Sector, which most people passed with ease, and then an additional one.

The second would be far less familiar, containing questions about an area which we were unfamiliar with. This meant drawing on memories of general studies of the apprenticeships in Minors, or our observation of another area. Most chose something obvious, like Sustenance, which could be seen in operation at every meal time, or an area which had some crossover with our own. Many of the Agric workers selected to answer the Livestock section. The LS barns were situated right next to the Agric greenhouses, which meant we were able to watch workers tending to the animals on a daily basis.

I managed to answer the Part One questions with relative ease. There were only two I was unsure of, and I took an educated guess at them before moving on. I had twenty minutes left for Section Two. Having taken the test six times now, I found the Agric questions simple. Even though they varied slightly, the general information required was the same, and after three years of Agric life, I knew pretty much everything I could possibly know. Pausing before beginning my second section, I considered my choices.

Sustenance was an easier option, as was LS. I had successfully answered the questions on both those areas before and passed. Repair, known as Rep, didn't interest me in the slightest. Development was not an area I felt drawn to at all: the Dev staff were specially selected and their work was pretty secretive, making it a difficult area to know enough about to secure a pass. Many of the decisions made by the Governance Sector baffled me, and I knew that section of the exam would be a poor choice because of this, especially if I let my frustration with Beck Law show.

This only left Patrol. With fifteen minutes left, I made my decision and began reading the relevant questions. I didn't really know why. Patrol was an ever-present group, but I had never actually spoken to a Patrol Officer, and had little experience of their role. Still, I had always found Patrol fascinating. They got to move around The Beck far more freely than any other unit, and this appealed to me. Even though I enjoyed the outdoor lifestyle of Agriculture, it didn't give me much scope for movement. Once we were in our allotted field for the day's work, we weren't required to go any further than the storage pods and back to fetch equipment, or to the canteen once the day was over. Beyond that, we didn't go far.

Patrol workers by their very nature guarded the whole of The Beck. They saw areas we never could and guarded the borders of our community day and night. Whilst I was respected within the Agric Compound, I had experienced a growing feeling of discontent over the past year. I had adjusted to the demands of the Sector and begun to tire of it. I felt that much of Beck Law was grossly unfair, yet the Governance department seemed to do little to improve things.

But Governance employees seemed to do little other than sit in their administration building and hold meetings, which bored me.

Patrol got to see how those laws were broken, and witness the sentences given to those people who broke them. The rest of us were fairly naive in that respect. I saw Patrol as having freedom and power, at least more power than we Agric workers ever seemed to have over our lives. Burying myself in questions about Clearance duties, guard duties, and Hydro Plant maintenance, I managed to write what I felt were fairly suitable responses to the ten Patrol questions before the time was up.

A bell sounded at the front of the room, signalling the end of the written test. Cassidy straightened up in front of me, stretching her long limbs after the prolonged time spent hunched over her paper. In Agric we were used to being far more active. I heard a small sigh from Harper behind me, and hoped that she had managed to gather sufficient focus to get through the paper, and that she had answered the Agric and Sustenance questions as we had discussed the previous day. Playing it safe was definitely the way forward.

And then I thought about the choice I had just made on my own paper. Patrol. What had driven me to choose a department I knew so little about? My skin went cold at the thought. I had drummed it into Harper: play it safe. Select the options we know you can pass on. All day in the fields for weeks Cass and I had been testing Harper on every Sustenance question we could think of, from the five times we had selected the Sustenance section of the paper between us. Day after day of quizzing each other, remembering the key sustenance duties, the dos and don'ts of life in the canteen.

Only in the fields did we find ourselves with the freedom to talk to one another. Not openly. There was always a Super on duty close by who kept an eye on our production rates and our communication, but given a lenient Super, we were able to talk fairly fluently and actually feel more human than we could in the pods or the canteen. One Agric Super, Riley, was particularly easy going and we knew she would turn the other way and allow us to engage in the communication we so desperately needed. She was older than us, around twenty, but seemed to understand the necessity of us letting off some steam whenever possible. Life with no communication was lonely and miserable. Riley let us talk. She warned us of the approach of other Supers who might judge our chatter more harshly. She even joined in occasionally. She was a far cry from Grady, and we respected her style of leadership far more.

The weeks in the fields running up to Assessment Day had been filled with conversations about all the different Sustenance information we could remember, with a view to getting Harper as high a pass level on the written paper as possible. Only time would tell whether she had managed to score enough. Or if my own decision to answer questions about Patrol was as foolish as I feared it might have been.

The bell rang for a second time. It was over. Nothing more could be done to improve our written test marks now. There was only the physical left. I stood up slowly, stretching as I had seen Cassidy do, and slipped back into our pod's line. The silence felt heavier now. We all dreaded the physical more than any other part of the assessment. Even the strongest and most well prepared citizens worried that the physical might be the one section that let them down.

The Dev Super who had first greeted us had reappeared

31

and was guiding groups towards the exit. The marching had become automatic now; the sound of the hundreds of feet pounding on the concrete floor took on a nightmarish quality inside my head. I could barely follow Cassidy's figure in front of me, and just focused on keeping the back of her head in the centre of my line of vision, and putting one foot in front of the other.

Within moments we were outside and had begun the short march to the arena where the physical took place. The rain had eased, and Cass and I exchanged relieved glances. This was the one element of the test I had never known to change, but it was as daunting as ever. The arena was a large field close to the wall itself, and was filled with a range of obstacles which citizens had to successfully tackle to pass the assessment. I had never known anyone to overcome every single obstacle in the allotted time, but the more we managed to conquer, the higher our score. Every point counted towards our chances of avoiding Clearance.

As we approached, the last group was just finishing. We stood and waited, lined up along the side of the main arena. There were several girls clambering over an eight-foot-high wall to the right, and a number of others were scrambling under a section of netting suspended above a muddy ditch. More were running around a circular track, while the central area was filled with the last few girls stretching to warm themselves up.

As I watched, my attention was caught by a small girl who had just emerged from the tunnel closest to us. She was covered in mud from head to toe and there was a large open cut across the side of her cheek, which was pouring blood. She headed for the wall and grasped a rope, pulling on it to begin the arduous climb. I had to admire her stamina. She was injured, bleeding, yet refusing to allow anything to get in the way of her progress. If she forfeited the wall climb, she would lose major points. If she got over it, even slowly, her final score stood to be far better.

While stronger, taller girls powered past her, she struggled valiantly to scramble up the wall's smooth surface. There were ropes dangling down from the top and some cleats which you could jam your feet into on the way up, but they were small and spaced quite far apart. The girl reached for the rope above her head, stretching an arm as far as it could possibly go. I could see the strain etched on her face. The rope was just out of her reach, and her grip on the cleat below looked shaky. Another girl thrust ahead of her, almost knocking her sideways, but she hung on and waited.

When her route was clear, she stretched up one final time, the tips of her fingers just managing to hook on to the rope. I found myself breathing again without having realised that I had stopped. Relief surged through me as she secured her grip and began to haul herself up the wall. She hadn't fallen. She would make it.

On the far side of the arena, a couple of Supers hurried towards one of the cargo nets. I shifted sideways to see what was happening. The participants on that side had been halted for some reason. Squinting against a pale sun which was struggling to appear from behind the clouds, I watched in horror as the Supers dragged something out from under the cargo net.

Caked from head to toe in mud, a figure was hauled to the side of the course. Face down. Motionless. The two Supers rolled her on to her back and briefly checked her face. Then they walked away, leaving the still, silent body of the unknown girl on the ground behind them.

I felt a shudder ripple through the entire pod as we waited to begin the course. This wasn't an unusual sight, in fact we should have been used to it by now. Participants collapsing during the physical was not rare, so challenging was the course and so small our food supply. We often had little enough energy to complete our tasks in the fields, never mind finish a demanding assault course. But every time we were horrified.

No one would come to this girl's aid. She would recover by herself or she wouldn't. It was that simple. Passing The Beck physical was an essential requirement of life here. Even if she did recover, she could hardly expect to have passed the test. It was over for her. I glanced quickly at Harper. Thinking about her crawling through the mud pits, attempting to scramble up the sheer walls, even continuing to put one foot in front of the other, made my heart ache.

It was small comfort when the girl who we had watched struggling to scale the wall closest to us finished the course last and stumbled out of the arena, tears streaming down her ashen face and her legs giving way beneath her. She had made it, barely. But others had not.

And now it was our turn.

Chapter Five

As we stood in line preparing ourselves, I found myself desperate for the comfort of our protective huddle. Citizens began the physical alone, each participant setting off at evenly spaced one minute intervals. That didn't mean no one could overtake. The course had many stages, and each one could take a different length of time for a participant. At least this way we didn't feel like we were competing directly against each other. We were of course. There was no avoiding the fact that we were being compared to see who could measure up. But it comforted us a little to have no one racing next to us the moment we began.

In front of me, Cassidy was already stretching, mentally preparing herself for the trial ahead. The course was not long, but it was gruelling. Most of the inhabitants of The Beck were not in great shape. Our everyday work was hard and kept us quite fit, but our rations were insufficient to build us up and provide us with the muscle required to really excel at such a physical challenge.

I felt stronger than usual. The porridge I had eaten this morning had clearly done me some good, as had the tiring job of providing more than the single person's required harvest levels for the past few months. I could feel my muscles, lean and wiry, and capable of so much more than they used to be.

Supporting Harper had pushed me above the average Agric inhabitant. At first I had found it extremely difficult to cope, but once my body had adjusted to the faster rhythms of the extra harvesting it had risen to the challenge, and the result was a leaner, faster body capable of more than most.

This fact should have comforted me as I prepared to begin the course, but instead I felt guilty. The additional labour had been meant to support Harper, to help her to survive and regroup. I had wanted Harper to regain her previous strength and become well enough to exist unaided in The Beck once again. But while my own strength had grown, Harper's had continued to drain away. If I made Super in our pod, I could try and support her more. I could look the other way while she failed to make her quota and adjust the figures to hide her failings, but if her illness continued to worsen, there would be nothing I could do in the end.

And being a Super meant a possible pod reassignment. While our own pod Super was quite likely to be elevated to another area, there were no guarantees in The Beck, and there were plenty of others desperate for the Super role. If someone else was assigned as our Super there was no telling what would happen to Harper. And if they reassigned me to another pod I would hardly see Harper at all, so there would be no chance of protecting her.

I looked up to see Cassidy setting off from the starting post, legs pumping furiously as she headed off around the circuit for the first time. She was fast, and I estimated that she would overtake the girl in front pretty quickly. She had been practising running any time she could. We didn't get much free time in The Beck, but Cass had been using any time we did have to race up and down, sometimes with a load on her back, for weeks now.

Cass was proud, and ambitious. From her first moments in the Agric pod at the age of fourteen, she had been planning her way out of it. She wanted a Super position, and then to be elevated to something better. She hated The Beck rules as much as I did, but her way of fighting them was to put her all into achieving promotion. She tried to excel in every area possible. She understood that strength and stamina were commodities The Beck valued, and went about making sure that she had both of those. The problem was her temper. While I was able to keep my mouth shut and quietly seethe about a rule which angered me, Cass found it difficult to mask her feelings, which often got her into trouble. She also deliberately went about defying Beck rule as often as she could manage to without being caught.

Cass had been breaking the rules for as long as I could remember. Not openly. She was the master of managing to defy authority sneakily, without anyone noticing, knowing that her chances of promotion were slim if she was branded a troublemaker. She did it to silently show those in charge of The Beck that she would not lie down and be trampled on. It was Cassidy who had worked out that, if we harvested enough crop to go over our daily quota, we could siphon off a little raw food and sneak it back to the pod for later. This had seemed like a defiant act of rebellion to begin with, but one particularly bitter winter our pod had been the only one to survive without a death because of these secret rations.

She was also the one who had worked out how we could sneak out of our pod at night and spend some time exploring parts of The Beck we weren't supposed to see. My thoughts drifted to the first night she had taken us to the wall at the edge of the floodplains and we had managed to scale it via a ladder between the Patrol Guard changeovers. From the top of the wall the view was amazing, and the three of us had spent an hour up there, gazing down at the shimmering water in the moonlight. We had almost been caught on the way back down, and had to hide in the Lower Agric fields for another hour whilst extra Patrol came through searching for trespassers. We had been so tired the next day that we could barely keep our eyes open, but it had been worth it for the momentary feeling of freedom and we had been to the wall on many occasions since.

The Super to my left tutted impatiently, and I realised that my turn had come. Indicating the stop watch around her neck, she jerked her head sideways and I began to run. I couldn't see Cassidy any more, and instead focused my energies on my own performance. I didn't feel too tired, and found that as I began to circle the track, my breathing evened out and I got into a good rhythm. The first challenge of the physical simply involved running around a track in the centre of the course. The track had to be circled three times. Not too much of a challenge, but it was no accident that it tired participants out for the more difficult obstacles to come.

I wondered if I was strong enough to hang back and encourage Harper without risking my own chances too much. The running she might manage slowly, but I was certain that the walls and the tunnels would defeat her if she had to tackle them alone. But supporting her without being noticed was a different matter. Even if I could manage a decent time whilst hanging back to help her, could I really assist Harper without being caught? Out here, so exposed, so visible? Unlikely.

I decided again that my best chance was to ace the course

and hope for the Super promotion which might allow me to protect Harper. With this in mind, I sped up and found myself passing the person in front of me: not Cassidy, but Cooper, the girl who had been at the front of our pod's line. She was not running fast, but was keeping a steady pace, and I knew that her strategy was to conserve her energy. This would mean that despite only managing a slow finish time, she would be able to complete the course, which would assure her more points for resilience. I passed without looking at her, not wanting to put her off.

Within a few minutes I had circled the track for the third time and set off across the obstacles. The first was a tunnel which I had to scramble through. I tackled this with ease, the long hours spent on my knees in the Agric fields paying off. After this came a large wooden frame which had to be scaled, and a plank across the top which required balance. Heights had never worried me, and my balance was good, so again I managed with little discomfort.

When I reached the third obstacle I hesitated. In front of me lay the cargo net. To the side, still motionless, was the abandoned figure of the Agric girl who had passed out face down in the mud. I couldn't look at her without imagining Harper. Taking a deep breath, I tore my eyes away from her motionless figure and thrust my shoulders underneath the net. It was heavy from the rain and weighed my shoulders down. I began the constant struggle to hoist the tangled net far enough above me to slither under it. I could feel it sapping my strength as I continued to struggle, my neck aching from the effort of keeping my face clear of the mud.

I could well imagine what had happened to the other Agric worker. It would take nothing at all to simply let go of the net and allow it to push my head beneath the hungry, sucking mud. I was tired, and I was stronger than many of the girls in the Agric Sector. For a moment I paused, my lips millimetres from the grime beneath me. Fighting to swallow my terror, I fought my way bit by bit through the rest of the netting and emerged on the other side, refusing to look back at the body I had left behind. Ahead of me was a series of trenches which I knew I would not be able to see out of once I slid into their depths. Then a set of monkey bars which led upwards to a high aerial zipwire. Many a citizen had lost hold before they reached the bottom, some fatally. Finally, there was the wall I had witnessed the young girl struggle to get up earlier. None of these obstacles would be easy.

When I hit the trenches I was usually shattered, but I found today that I could manage them better than I had in previous assessments. I scrambled in and out of them with relative ease after the terror of the ground level net. Here the strength developed during the extra hours of harvesting were paying off. The monkey bars had defeated me on my last attempt and I had missed out on the zipwire altogether, costing me valuable points, but somehow today I managed both of them without a problem. I reached the wall at the same time as Cassidy, who looked none too pleased that I had caught up to her.

"Last one."

She grunted something at me out of the corner of her mouth and set off up the wall with far more agility than me. She had always had the edge when we were completing any kind of climbing obstacle. I followed her, pleased that we would make it through together and vaguely amused by her annoyance. The wall was easy after the bars, with the ropes helping to ease our way up. My height helped me, while Cassidy's light frame allowed her to swing from one to another rapidly.

We reached the top almost together and slid down the ropes on the other side. Once we were running together on the flat, Cassidy's anger seemed to disappear and we completed the final length together, racing over the line out of breath, but more than a little exhilarated. Collapsing on to the ground, we crawled towards the support provided by the wall which edged the arena, where we could sit in relative peace. Breathing hard, we rested for a few moments, knowing we had completed the course in good time and happy that, for the time being, were not being observed or evaluated.

It was only when I glanced back towards the course that I thought about Harper. My eyes scanned the obstacles, knowing that she should not have been too far behind me. There were several girls coming over the line now, some running, some almost crawling, but no sign of Harper. Cassidy prodded my arm so sharply it hurt. I turned to smack her hand away and saw what she was looking at. A familiar figure was standing frozen at the base of the wooden frame near the start of the course. As we watched, helpless, she raised her face slowly towards the sky and collapsed.

Chapter Six

Panic rippled through my body. Visions of the body in the mud pit under the cargo net flashed into my head. I couldn't stand to see her lying there, ignored by the Supers and left for dead. I made to run forward to help her but was stopped by Cassidy's hand on my arm.

I glanced back and forth between Cassidy and Harper, shaking my head fiercely to clear away the tears, then sat back down. Cass was right as usual. Any move towards Harper now would mark her out as done for, and make me into a rebel who those in charge would want to watch. So I sat and stared at Harper's body, silently willing her to move.

It seemed strange, but the physical assessment was still going on around me as I watched my friend. Girls were running around the central track, scaling the obstacles, even stepping over Harper on their way up the wooden frame. I could feel the blood coursing through my veins as the injustice of Beck society hit me again, more keenly this time. How could we exist in a place where human life was given so little respect?

And then, somehow, Harper raised her head from the ground. Just a little. She looked up slowly, her eyes confused and unfocused, and pushed herself up on her hands. Like someone coming round after a nightmare, she blinked and shook her head. Finally she stumbled to her feet and took some deep breaths, planting her hands firmly on her knees just like Cassidy had shown her when we had practised. She looked around the arena, her eyes searching us out, and eventually fixed on us, both sitting bolt upright at the end of the course.

And she smiled. A beautiful, strange smile which told me she was going to be ok. A girl ran past her, almost knocking her over, and she staggered to one side, but she recovered herself and began to wander in our direction. I wanted to wave her back, to try and encourage her to complete the course, but I knew it was useless. She was exhausted just from the run. There was no way she could possibly attempt the bars, the zipwire, the wall climb. It had taken everything she had to complete the psych test, the written paper, and the first part of the assault course. At least she had come round after fainting. She was ok. For now, at least.

I welcomed her back with the tightest hug I could manage. Contact was frowned upon, forbidden most of the time, but overlooked on such occasions as assessment day due to the huge amount of endorphins they knew were coursing through our bodies. Today I took full advantage of this, holding Harper as close as I could, my grip on her so tight I felt I might squeeze some strength back into her. After I let go of her the three of us sat, our arms touching along the entire length from wrist to elbow. Waiting for the others to finish. Waiting to resume our Agric routines this afternoon. Dreading the moment our results would be published.

The rest of the physical passed without incident. There were no falls, no more slips or accidents. Many girls skipped one or two obstacles, a few didn't finish, but no one else collapsed and there were no other bodies left abandoned at the side of the track. As we lined up to head back to the fields, I glanced back at the cargo net once more.

The body had gone.

Returning to the Agric Compound, we were given half an hour to rest, recuperate and wash off the mud of the morning's assault course. Assigned rations of dry oatcakes were given out. Like the porridge this morning, these were a special added bonus meant to somehow make up for the trials we had gone through on Assessment Day. Cass and I consumed ours within seconds, and even Harper, who we had half carried back to the pod, managed to eat some of hers and recovered slightly. We were desperate to get to the fields, where we might manage a proper conversation about the morning's events, despite the hard work which awaited us.

When it was time to get back on duty, we marched out as one and joined the ranks of girls travelling to the Agric Compound. The fields had been manned by Supers all morning and there would be extra work this afternoon to make up for the shortfall. It was harvest time and we were busy. As we arrived, another pod Super, Riley, was just leaving. She paused as she passed me, all-business.

"Field two needs extra draining because of the overnight rain, knotweed is threatening the pea crop in the lower fields again, and greenhouse duty will be pretty light this afternoon, if you know what I mean."

She nodded at Harper. Her tone softened.

"How'd she do?"

I shook my head.

"Not good."

Riley sighed. She looked like she had expected this outcome, but nevertheless it did not make her happy. Bad news about Harper, plus she now had her own assessment to deal with.

"Just keep a close eye on her."

I nodded this time, managing a small smile for her, noting her shaking hands.

"You'll be just fine, ok?"

I squeezed her hand gently. She pulled away and walked quickly in the direction of the Assessment Sector before I could say any more.

I pulled Harper into the greenhouses as soon as we arrived. She was still looking a little dazed, but there were less Supers on duty because of the other Assessments, so I had to trust that she would be safe in there and manage to keep her head down for the afternoon while Cassidy and I worked outdoors.

We wandered in, skirting around two boys from Rep who were fixing one of the window frames which had come loose. They shot us a slight smile as we passed, but I ignored them. The greenhouses were damp and warm as usual, the steam rising up from some of the hothouse areas in thick clouds. I started to sweat the moment I entered. Switching my place in the greenhouses was never a chore for me, I preferred to be outside. Today, Harper desperately needed to be in here. I checked the rota on the wall. Cooper was on greenhouse duty this afternoon, and would maybe allow Harper to take her place if we were clever about it. We had beaten her there, so we had the advantage.

As she ducked her head in through the door of the greenhouse we were ready. Tall and willowy, she had to stoop in certain areas of the glasshouses where the roofing was low. She looked pale and tired, and I remembered passing her as she made her slow, steady progress around the running track.

I hadn't noticed her coming over the finishing line. Now, she wandered towards the assignment rota, looking as though her thoughts took her very far away. I sidled up to her, smiling and keeping my voice deliberately low.

"Hey Coop, any chance you could be our hero and switch with Harper for the afternoon? I'm not sure she'll manage to stay on her feet all day if you know what I mean."

Cooper scrutinised Harper closely, saying nothing.

"It'll be worth some extra rations if you do."

Cooper hesitated. I could see the wheels turning in her head. Giving up an easy duty on Assessment Day was no small request. But she was a nice girl, and staring at Harper, she couldn't possibly fail to see what a state she was in.

"Where are we outside today?"

"Various places, but I can get you on the team shifting knotweed from the pea crops if you like. I'll make sure you don't get stuck with the drainage going on in the lower fields."

Drainage was difficult. I knew I had just volunteered myself and probably Cassidy for the job, but if it made Cooper agree to help Harper, it would be worth it.

"Ok."

"Thanks, Coop. You'll never know how much she needs this."

I nodded at Harper, who had a dreamy look on her face.

"Go on then."

I gave her a gentle shove in the direction of the hosepipes and she floated, zombie-like, in their direction. As a Super I didn't know well entered the greenhouses, Cooper and I hurried outside to join the others, our heads bowed to avoid any eye contact.

"Thanks again."

"S'okay."

Cooper turned in the direction of the pea crop fields but turned to face me at the very last minute. Checking that there were no Supers within sight, she leaned towards me and breathed the words in my ear.

"The way she performed today, it might be the last thing I can do for her."

She turned and was gone before I could respond. Sighing, I headed after the group assigned to work on draining the lower fields, knowing that the trials of the day were far from over.

The afternoon passed with the exhausting task of digging trenches and installing drainage pipes to remove the excess floodwaters from the lower fields. This was a huge part of our work in Agric: nothing to do with cultivating crops, but an essential part of ensuring the survival of the food which sustained our society. We worked solidly for three hours, using spades to excavate a large area of land at the side of the fields and laying lengths of perforated pipe which would hopefully help to keep the majority of the crops in those fields from ending up underwater.

The lower fields were much closer to the wall, and as a result, often received more water than the plants within them required. The wall was fairly watertight, and the Rep boys worked constantly to repair any leaks, but the heavy storms we regularly experienced often led to higher water levels and pressure being placed on the structure. We were constantly working on new projects, all of which aimed to keep the fields close to the wall as dry as possible. Most of these schemes seemed to have only limited success.

The work was heavy and constant, and even when the Super

declared the levels had reduced enough to leave the fields for the day, there was still a harvesting quota to fill. We spent the final hours of the day digging up carrots, some of which Cassidy managed to sneak into her overall pocket at the end of the shift. She side stepped the Super on her way back to the pod as I engaged her in conversation about an issue with the knotweed spreading more rapidly than usual and we reached the pod safely without being caught. After giving Cooper her promised share, there were five carrots left. We immediately shared two of them between the three of us, Harper only managing a few bites. The rest were concealed beneath Cassidy's mattress for later.

The afternoon's hard work had mostly kept us from dwelling too much on the Assessment results, but at some point we had to face them. As we made our way to the canteen for our second meal of the day, we were too exhausted to mind the silence, most of us lost in our thoughts. Harper seemed to have made it through the greenhouse shift, but her small frame was bent almost double on the march to the canteen, and I worried that she might collapse at any moment.

We reached the canteen to find a group of Dev staff just leaving. Dressed in white overalls, they looked a lot cleaner than we did and had clearly been allowed to change back into their usual clothing after the Assessment. No one could complete the physical and stay clean. The Dev group were a strange lot. No one really understood how their staff were recruited. Just that occasionally following an Assessment, people would be reassigned to them and disappear into the Dev Compound, where no one but Development staff, high level Patrol Officers, and important Governance citizens were allowed to visit.

There were a lot less of them than other Sectors. Agric, Rep, LS, and Sustenance required a lot of staff and not much expertise. Clearly those in the Dev department had to have particular skills, but there was less in the way of physical labour to occupy them. I suspected their work was more mental than physical anyway: they oversaw all the Assessments, and none of them looked particularly strong, although they were still required to pass the physical like the rest of us.

There was far less interaction between the Dev staff and any other department. Contact between most of the pod areas was frowned upon, but the Dev staff seemed more reluctant to break rules than those of us in the other Lower Beck Sectors. Dev citizens were mixed though, so perhaps between them there was enough variety: boys, girls, old, young. The Rep and LS boys and Agric and Sustenance girls were definitely more starved of varied company.

A large board had been set up outside the canteen exit door. As we waited to be called into the canteen, we watched with interest as the Dev staff looked at their Assessment results. Some faces showed intense relief, others disappointment and, worse still, a few dissolved into silent sobs. Shuddering as one, our line shuffled closer to the canteen door, knowing that soon it would be us having to face the inevitable.

The evening meal was no different than usual: a small helping of potatoes and vegetables in a stew. No meat today. We generally only got meat once or twice a month. LS couldn't keep up with a demand of any more than that with so little land to graze the herds on. So some kind of vegetable-based mush was expected fare in the evenings. At least it was warm, but the portions were small considering the amount of energy we had all expended this afternoon.

I watched as Cass ate every morsel and scraped her bowl clean. I did the same. Harper managed most of hers, and slipped the rest across to Cooper when no one was looking. As the meal ended and the Supers rose, our cue to file out of the room, a kind of hush hung over us all. We knew that it was results time and that what waited for us on the boards outside could change everything. Tears stung my eyes before I even reached the doorway. Both my friends grabbed hold of my hands silently on the way across the hall.

This time, neither of them let go.

Chapter Seven

Outside, there was already a crowd of people gathered around the boards. Despite the silence, the facial expressions were enough to convey how each person had fared in today's Assessment. We waited nervously at the back of the group, desperate to know, but also desperate to delay the knowledge which awaited us. There was no point trying to look until we got closer.

Our pod reached the boards within a couple of minutes, but it seemed like hours. I watched Cooper's face, filled with relief as she staggered away from the boards and headed back towards the pod. Her slow but sure plan had worked then. The next two of our pod also seemed also to be ok, but I thought I saw one of them give me a strange look as they passed by.

Then it was Cassidy's turn.

I heard her tiny gasp but I wasn't sure what it meant. She walked backwards, stepping hard on my toe, before racing in the direction of the pod, her hand covering most of her face. I bit back a yelp of pain. Then, taking a breath, I stepped forward. Pod 19's list was close to the top of the board. My eyes skimmed it furiously.

I noticed Cassidy's name, the word 'Super: Pod 28' printed next to it. Not our pod then, but a Super at least. This, I had expected. I tried to be pleased for her.

The next two lines of the list contained a double blow. Next to my own name were the words, 'Reassignment: Patrol'.

Reeling, I managed somehow to read on.

Next to the name Harper, it simply said, 'Clearance'.

I wanted to wait for my friend but I knew I couldn't. There were too many Supers watching, and I was afraid one of us would openly break down if we even looked at each other. I completely understood Cassidy's rush to avoid my gaze as she left the notice boards and headed towards the relative safety of the pod. Numb, I retraced my steps towards the pod which had been my home for so long. When I reached it I hardly remembered the walk. I had expected that I would have to deal with Harper's fate, but not that my own would be also thrown into disarray.

Patrol. I didn't know how to react.

It was my own fault of course. A combination of me filling in that section of the written test and the Super in the psych test asking if I had ever considered another skill area. I should have been more definite. Said no with more power. But then I had chosen to answer the questions on Patrol. And presumably I had been quite successful in my answers. Of course, none of us had any real power over our fate in The Beck. Governor Adams made all the decisions and if he had decreed that they needed more manpower in Patrol, and I seemed a likely candidate for that area, there was really nothing I could do.

So tomorrow, I would begin again. In a new Sector. With a new set of people and a new set of rules. A shiver went through me as I considered how I felt about this. Something inside me had selected a different section on that test. I wondered for a second if I was actually excited.

Then I thought of Cassidy. And Harper.

The three of us would be divided. Not just one separated from the rest, but all three of us in separate places. Unknown places. Even Cass, who would remain in Agric, had been assigned a new pod. I would go to the Patrol Compound to begin a new discipline. Perhaps cross paths with Cass every now and again, but only in passing. And Harper would go to Clearance. And we would never see her again.

Clearance was a mystery to all of us. The citizens sent there were those who could no longer be of benefit to The Beck way of life. Yet they did have a role. They made and supplied clothing to all the different Sectors. Our pale green overalls, the blue uniforms of Patrol, the brown Rep overalls and Dev department's white ones: every single citizen dressed in clothing made by Clearance. I had a vision of large warehouses filled with Clearance staff constantly occupied with needles, patterns and cloth, day and night. It was merely a skewed version of what I knew: similar to life in Agric but with daily shifts at sewing machines rather than in the fields.

Yet if they were just like Agric staff, why had we never seen them? They didn't eat in our canteen, we didn't pass them around The Beck, we were forbidden to cross Black Hill. Very few citizens had access to Clearance. Why would Governance hide them away from the rest of us on the other side of the hill? It didn't make sense, unless there was more going on than we realised.

A thought occurred to me. Patrol were assigned to Clearance duty, at least according to the questions on the test which I had answered today. Perhaps as a Patrol Officer I might actually get to see Harper. In some way keep an eye on her. A tiny hope sprang up inside of me.

Cass's head was buried in her pillow when I entered the pod. I lay down on my own bed beside her.

"Cass?"

Nothing. I didn't dare speak any louder. Grady wasn't back from the canteen yet, but she wouldn't be far away, and now was not the time to break down and cause an issue. She wasn't known for being forgiving, even on Assessment Day. I glanced at the small, green sack lying on the bottom of my camp bed, then over at the one on Harper's and Cassidy's. These were standard issue for those citizens assigned to move to another pod or Sector. We all had to pack up and be ready to transfer over tomorrow. I shuddered at the thought.

The tarp was pulled back again and Harper entered. Her head was down and she looked thoroughly beaten. As she passed, I reached out a hand and tried to hold on to hers, but she resisted with surprising strength. Bending down next to her bed, she pulled a small box out from beneath it and began to go through its contents slowly. I admired her calm control. The thought of gathering my own things together sent a second shudder through my body.

We didn't have much here. Very little we could call our own anyway. We were allowed two sets of work overalls and undershirts; one pair of shoes; a bar of soap and toothbrush; a single book borrowed from the stock at the tiny library housed at the back of the canteen which we were permitted to visit once per month on a strict rota. Reading was one of the pursuits we were allowed to engage in, mainly because it was a silent occupation. But the supply of literature was meagre and anyone who read quickly found themselves finished long before the month was up.

Harper would have to return her book now. Clearance did not use the library, were not permitted in the Lower Beck at all. I wondered if there was any kind of library over in Clearance. Biting back painful tears, I watched Harper preparing her things to be placed into the tiny bag. In addition to the assigned equipment, she had several tiny packets of seeds and a variety of planting equipment she had brought here from the fields. Before she had become ill she had often occupied her time in the evenings planting out seedlings, playing about with the soil type, the fertiliser, and the amount of water each plant received.

This was an infringement of the rules, but had been over-looked by the Supers. They were well aware of how successful her experiments had been in the past, leading to a significant increase in crop yields and better rations for all Beck citizens. I felt instantly furious again, considering how unfair it was to simply sacrifice someone like Harper because she had become, in their eyes, a burden rather than an asset. A citizen who had spent time considering how to better sustain and improve Beck life. I bit back a sob as I watched her pack away her meagre belongings.

"Quin."

It was Cassidy, who had managed to bring her head up off the pillow and compose herself. Taking a deep breath and swallowing my tears, I forced myself to look at her.

"Later. Usual place."

Her voice was no more than a whisper, but I understood. She wanted to go to the wall tonight while the others were asleep. To sneak out and sit together where we had the freedom to talk without any fear. It was the last piece of support we could offer each other.

I was nodding in response when Grady stepped into the pod. She glared around the room, looking more fearsome than usual. Unable to cope with anyone else's emotions, I left the pod and spent longer than usual in the wash tent. Returning to the pod later, I buried my head under my bed and began to go through my own things in preparation for leaving Agric, which had been my home now for three years.

Chapter Eight

The rest of the evening passed in a blur. I eventually managed to pack my bag, though the tears were never far away, and the whole pod passed an hour reading or simply sitting quietly. We only had an hour of Rec time each evening and were limited in our permitted pursuits, and tonight no one felt like leaving the pod to exercise, our only other real option.

Tonight the silent readers in the pod seemed less engaged by their books. Most of us were literally staring into space, the pages of our books remaining unturned. Grady didn't seem to notice, or was ignoring the tense atmosphere in the pod, lost in her own frustration. Although I wasn't certain what was wrong with her, I was guessing that it was linked to the fact that she hadn't been promoted. It was no secret that she had been angling for an elevation to Governance or Patrol. She was one of the strictest Supers I had come across in my three years in Agric and her harsh attitude had earned her praise from those higher than her. Still, it didn't seem to have been enough.

She had been shooting particularly poisoned looks at me, and that gave away the true reason for her disappointment. I was now a member of Patrol and, whilst I would only be a foot soldier and not a Super, meaning she was still technically a higher rank than me, she still hated the fact that I had been assigned to a Sector she was desperate to join.

Bitterly regretting my decision to complete the Patrol section of the test, I wished I could trade places with her.

Darkness soon fell and Rec was over. Grady patrolled the pod, checking that we had all stowed away our books. She paused by my bed, staring at me.

"Book."

"Sorry?"

"Your book! I need to take it. You're leaving in the morning."

I reached underneath my bed and found the book which I had finished last week and pretended to read tonight. She snatched it from me, and then took Harper's from her calmly outstretched hand without even looking at her.

"I hope you're up to it, Quin. They have some nasty reckoning methods up in Patrol. If you can't cut it..."

Her voice trailed off, leaving the words unsaid.

I bit back my response: that they couldn't be much worse than those inflicted by Grady herself in Agric, who liked to push the limits of the permitted punishments as far as she could. I remembered an incident two years before when Cassidy had fallen in the fields, landing on a set of sharp secateurs and crushing a row of young potato plants. Grady had been more concerned with the fate of the crops than the nasty gash on Cass's leg, and had administered a reckoning of several shocks with the electric prod usually used on the cattle in LS.

Between the blood loss and the after-effects of the shock, it had taken Cass several days to recover and she had been very lucky she hadn't contracted an infection. She also wouldn't have been able to manage without a lot of secret support from myself and Harper, who had been far stronger back then. No, Grady's punishments were right up there with those rumoured to be used in Patrol.

Staring at Grady, I forced myself to simply nod, before turning over and feigning sleep. She sighed and strode away a moment later, clearly unsatisfied by my lack of response. It was agony to conceal my feelings sometimes, but ultimately worth it when I felt Grady's frustration at failing to get a reaction from me. Cass found it much harder to remain calm and resist talking back, but as a result she had earned far more reckonings than I had. It was safer my way.

Within an hour, everyone in the pod was asleep. On Cass's signal, I rose silently, collected my shoes from the base of my bed and pulled on my overalls. It could be very cold up on the wall. We moved almost silently, our stealth well-honed from many similar trips out at night. Harper had not joined us on our exploits for a while now, but there was no question: she had to come tonight. Outside the pod all was still. We padded to the edge of the Agric Compound barefoot, risking cuts on our feet to avoid getting caught. Once outside the fence, we pulled our boots on and moved with a little more freedom. Not much, we still had to guard against being seen out of bed, but we had made it past the first obstacle. Harper leaned heavily against me as we walked. Cass kept a keen eye out for any sign that we might be spotted.

We made it past the LS pods and into the Agric fields with no problem. There were Supers on duty at the entrance to the fields, but only at the main gate. We had found an alternative route in the form of a hole in the hedge which could easily be scrambled under. The Agric Supers hated night duty and didn't expect to have to apprehend anyone, so it was relatively easy to sneak down the side of the fields behind the shelter of the corn crop, which was quite tall now, and through into the lower fields behind. There would be no Supers there.

At the bottom of the lower field we stopped to rest. Harper was finding the trek difficult after the long arduous day, and Cass and I needed her to be able to make the ladder climb to the top of the wall. While we sat, Cass passed around the carrots she had taken from the field crop gathered that day. We sat and chewed on them for a while, deep in thought.

The night was still and silent. So silent that I could hear the waters swirling back and forth on the other side of the wall. The sky was unusually clear and the stars shone down on the fields around us. Under other circumstances it would have been a beautiful night. I watched the tips of the corn swaying in the distance, curving in mesmerising waves which rolled continuously down the field towards us.

"Okay?"

I was startled from my reverie by the question, but it was not aimed at me. Harper nodded shakily in response. She seemed to have found some strength from somewhere, but it was going to be a Herculean task to get her up on the wall. I noticed Cass's hand on her arm, comforting, reassuring.

"Come on. We can do this. Together. We have to."

Cassidy's voice was unusually soft and caught slightly on her final words. Out here, when we were able to speak more freely, her voice was usually strident, strong. But tonight emotion was getting the better of her and she seemed to be struggling. I found myself fighting tears again.

Glancing back up into the field above me, I fixed my eyes on the waving stalks, trying to pull myself together. But one particular area of swaying corn continued to move in our direction, and I realised now that this movement was not affecting the entire field. In fact it was not being caused by the wind at all. Something was moving in amongst the corn, advancing on us.

Slapping Cass's arm silently, I gestured towards the moving crop. Her eyes followed my finger and she immediately recognised the danger that had taken me several seconds to see. She froze, her hand digging into Harper's arm.

"What?"

"Ssh!"

As Harper too realised what was happening, the three of us instinctively shrank lower. We froze, clinging tightly to one another, hoping desperately that whatever was approaching us was not a threat. My mind was racing. It could be a cow escaped from the LS enclosures. That had happened before and caused much hilarity as the LS boys raced around trying to catch the poor creature. Harper and I had laughed so hard we needed to clutch on to each other for support, and Cass had whistled loudly at them as they raced past. Ours was not the only behaviour to earn a reckoning that night. We had gone without our evening meal, but most of us felt better for the moment of freedom.

But the escaped cow had moved in a chaotic way. Whatever this was made its way across the field gradually and almost silently. It had to be a person. A Super? I considered the possibility that Grady had woken up and seen us leave. The thought sent a shudder through my entire body. I glanced at Cass, whose eyes were fixed on the shaking crop. Harper was hunched down, her head resting against her knees, clearly waiting for the danger to pass, or to find us. I suppose it didn't much matter to her who this was: for her, the worst had already happened.

The hushed rustling of the corn grew in volume as the person or persons worked their way towards our hiding place, the stalks bending ominously closer. The punishment from a Super for being caught here didn't bear thinking about. The only other possibility was that there were other citizens moving around. Others willing to risk being found out of bed in the middle of the night. We had never met anyone else on our previous night-time expeditions. Few were willing to risk it. And the larger the group, the higher the risk of being caught.

The person was so close to us now that we risked being seen within the next few seconds. Cass and I stared at each other. The time to run was well past, but even if we had tried to, we would have been spotted. The moving corn gave anyone away easily. We would just have to see who approached, and deal with the consequences. Perhaps they would pass us by.

A second later a single figure emerged from the darkened field beside us and tripped right over Cassidy's outstretched leg.

"Ow! Damn!"

A tall figure in Agric overalls lay sprawled in the dust by our feet. I noticed the Super badge on her arm and my heart sank. As she sat up, she rubbed her leg and groaned painfully. But her short hair was light blonde in colour, not dark like Grady's. My heart leapt. Riley. But her face was thunderous.

"What are you three doing out here? You know what will happen if anyone else catches you!" She paused. "If Grady catches you."

"It doesn't much matter anymore."

"Huh?"

"Didn't you look at our list?"

She shook her head, her face softening as she realised. She glanced sadly at Harper.

"Clearance?"

Harper raised her head and nodded.

"There's more though. Quin-"

She looked horrified, "Quin?"

"Not Clearance. Patrol."

"Patrol?" She paused thoughtfully, "A lot of change today."

I glanced at her questioningly.

"Promotion?"

"Not exactly."

"Then what?"

"I'm being transferred to Meds."

There was an awkward silence. We all understood what that meant.

"I guess I'm the right age. And I'm strong. My Assessment clearly marks me out as good birthing material…"

She trailed off.

"It's supposed to be a privilege. So why do I not feel… privileged?"

"What does a birthing assignment… involve?"

It was Cass asking the question, but we all wanted an answer. Even Harper had raised her head and looked interested. Meds was an area few of us had experience with. Like Clearance, few people were allowed in. Since illness was regarded as failure, citizens were generally not treated. Occasionally, valued members of the higher-ranking skill Sectors were admitted to Meds because of an injury received whilst on duty, but they were given a maximum of two weeks in the Med Centre to recover. Any more, and they were dispatched to Clearance like anyone else. But lower ranking Sectors, like

LS and Agric were not allowed such privileges. The Med Centre was therefore mostly used for the process of birthing, vital to the continuation of our society.

The sole reason anyone from Agric would be transferred to Meds was if they were assigned to birthing. The Beck had very strict population controls. When there were sufficient deaths to warrant an increase in our population, a number of women were assigned to Meds ready to birth. They were always selected from the Supers, so those of us in the lower rankings didn't really have a concept of what happened to citizens called to birthing. We knew that some were never seen again. We knew that others returned to their original posts after a period of time, but other than that, the process was fairly mysterious.

Riley for one, looked uncomfortable about the whole idea.

"I'm not sure what happens really. I only know you spend around a year away from your original pod, and sometimes you don't come back. I only ever knew one girl who did, and she wasn't well. She was assigned to Clearance soon afterwards."

There was a silence. We could all see why Riley was nervous about the prospect. I sought some words of comfort.

"It might very well be fine. You're strong, Riley. They wouldn't have selected you if you weren't."

"I guess I'll have to be."

She shook her head sadly.

"I'm sorry about you, Harper though. I really thought... I mean I was hoping so much that you could pass again."

Harper shrugged, "It's not just me though is it? There are plenty of people who didn't get good news today." She looked away across the field. "What are you doing out here anyway?"

Riley shrugged. "Thinking. Trying to stay calm. I just wanted some peace before... before tomorrow. I'm often out here on my own."

"We're often out here together. We just talk. Really talk. We needed to do that tonight."

She nodded. "You're risking a lot you know, but I guess I understand it."

She stared off into the distance, thoughtful again. I stood up, stretching slowly.

"We'll leave you to it then."

I helped Harper up awkwardly. Cass followed suit.

"Well... best of luck then, Riley. I hope..." Cass faltered, "I hope we see you again."

I echoed her, "Yes. I hope so too. And thanks for your support. For everything really. Don't know where we'd have been without you. If Grady had always been in charge, well..."

Riley managed a weak smile.

"See you guys. When I come back I'll let you in on the big birthing secrets huh?"

"You do that."

Moving off across the field, we left her sitting amongst the corn, feeling very much like we were abandoning an ally.

Chapter Nine

Soon after leaving Riley, the wall loomed over us. Crouching in the nearby bushes for a while, we waited for the Patrol Guards to change over and then went to the base of the ladder closest to the lower Agric fields. The ladders were numbered, and this one had a large 17 painted beside it. The wall was guarded at all times, but we had worked out the timings and positions of the Patrol months ago. As long as the officers remained in position we knew we could get up the ladder at a point far enough from the sentry posts to avoid being seen.

Cass began to make her way up, climbing slowly enough that Harper could follow close behind and still keep up. I admired Cassidy's agility for the second time that day. Even at a slower pace she was fluid and precise in her movements. Harper, however, was weak and clumsy, and her hand slipped from the rungs more than once. I feared she might fall at any point during our ascent, but admired her determination.

Harper had not been out this far with us at night for months now. The only times she had been outside the pod at all at night were those when we had been trying to practise for her assessment. Usually she hadn't wanted to join us on our longer jaunts: we'd even had to persuade her to leave when we wanted her to prepare for Assessment Day. On the occasions when she had wanted to come with us on a more recreational expedition however, we had managed to dissuade her and made her rest instead. But we couldn't deny her tonight, on our final night together.

Climbing up close behind her, I noticed again how skinny she had become. We were all thin, our rations only just sustaining us, but Harper was almost skeletal. The calves and ankles which moved painfully from one rung to the next above me resembled those of a small child rather than an almost-grown woman. How she kept going was beyond me.

Reaching the top, Cass swung herself on to the narrow ridge which ran the length of the wall, staying low all the time. She stretched down an arm to Harper below, and helped her struggle up the last few rungs. As I joined them, I heaved a private sigh of relief. I hadn't been convinced that I could save Harper if she slipped. From our entry point, we began to crawl along the top of the wall to a small alcove where we knew we could crouch, hidden from view.

The ridge was flanked by a narrower section of wall on the floodwater side. Every now and again there was an alcove, jutting outwards, where a Patrol guard could comfortably stand and keep watch. Not all of them had guards assigned though. Our alcove, we had worked out by a process of elimination, was always empty and the farthest one from the other manned sentry posts. It also snugly fit three skinny Agric girls, shielding us from the weather and from view as long as we stayed low.

We packed ourselves in and settled, my arm running the length of Harper's and hers running the length of Cassidy's. Sheltered, warm, together. We'd made it.

For a moment we were silent. The flood waters lapped against the wall far below us and a light wind whispered through the cracks in the wall. Mingled with the scent of burning wood from the sentry's fire and the glow of the nearly full moon in a cloudless sky, the atmosphere was almost tranquil. Almost. But I couldn't push the horrible truth from my mind.

"This is it then."

Cass nodded. "We knew this was coming."

"Cass!"

"Well didn't we? Harper anyway. Sorry but... well you've been struggling for ages." Suddenly she looked shamefaced. "Not that I don't – well – care very much that you'll be gone tomorrow, but..." She trailed off.

"Harper, I..."

I too found myself with nothing to say that didn't sound trite or forced. I stared down at my hands. When Harper spoke, I was startled.

"It's ok."

Cass and I stared at her.

"No really – it's ok. I've been expecting this. Preparing for it. I've known for ages that there was no way I could pass this assessment."

"But – we practised!" Cass stumbled over her words, "We helped you. Didn't you even try?"

"Of course I did. But really – we've been pretending. I knew how much you wanted to save me, so I did try. But I did it for you – not me. I've had enough."

"Had enough?" This time it was me who was incredulous.

"You don't know what it's been like. I've struggled for months now. Months. I'm just so tired." She sighed. "I'm ready for whatever Clearance holds. Anything has to be better than this constant battle."

And suddenly I could see the pain she had been in, the fight she had been losing, the struggle she had hidden from us as best she could for so long now.

Cass broke the silence. "So what do you think will happen in Clearance then?"

"I don't know, Cass. Maybe I'll just make clothes. I don't think I'd mind that. At least I'd be able to sit down all day."

"Will you miss Agric?"

"I'll miss you two. And growing my seeds."

I tried to comfort her, "We'll try to get to you. Sneak over Black Hill – there must be a way."

"Don't. I don't want you to know."

"But…"

"Seriously," Harper's tone was terse, deadly serious, "You'll do nothing except get yourselves in trouble. Whatever happens over there can't be good. Why else would they keep it a secret? I'd rather you never knew."

I found myself biting back the tears again, unable to speak for fear I would be the one to break down. Harper looked serene, steady, strong even. I couldn't be the one to fall apart. I looked away, unable to hold her gaze.

"So, Quin. Patrol? Where did that come from?"

I stared down at my lap, guilt washing over me. I couldn't face telling them that it was my own fault. That I had chosen to answer on the Patrol part of the test. Harper might just about understand, considering how accepting she was being about her own situation. But Cass? Cass would never forgive me. Her two best friends being ripped away from her at the same time was hard enough. She would never understand my decision to answer the Patrol questions and voluntarily risk being torn from my home in Agric.

I took a deep breath, forcing my voice to stay steady. "No idea. Maybe–"

Cass interrupted abruptly, "I guess they need new Patrol recruits. That's all it can be."

"But why Quin though? No offence, but you're more of a climber than she is. You'd make a good guard, Cass."

"And I won't?"

"I'm sure you will, Quin. I just think Cass is the more obvious choice."

Cass was silent now. She stared down at her lap, constantly twisting her fingers into knots. Her knuckles were white.

"Cass?"

She looked at me, her face flushed. Her voice was almost a whisper, "I hate this."

"We all do." Again Harper amazed me with her calm acceptance. "But we're all in the same position. New places. New people."

"So all as lost as each other!"

She took hold of Cass' hand. "But *all* of us going somewhere different. I know it's selfish, but the one thing I couldn't stand was the thought of you two staying together while I was sent somewhere else. It will comfort me to know that we're all having to adjust to somewhere new."

I wished I could feel the same. But all I felt when I considered tomorrow was a cold, growing dread.

Harper continued. "Cass – you'll be fine. You've wanted a Super position forever. It's what you've been preparing for. All those secret jaunts at night? The training sessions every night during Rec? Did you think we didn't notice?"

"No. But I really believed that... that Grady would get promoted and I would take her place and you two would be with me and…"

"And you could save me and we'd all live happily ever after?" Harper snorted, "There's no such thing."

"But–"

"No." Harper's voice was more strident than I had ever heard it, "No, Cass. You got what you wanted. And you will be good at it. You'll find a whole new set of girls and you'll have them shaping up to be great Agric citizens in no time."

"But I don't want to be like Grady!"

"And you won't be. When you need to be tough, you'll be tough. But when someone in your pod needs you, you'll be magnificent. You'll help all those girls because… because…"

Cassidy's voice shook, "Because I couldn't help you."

"And Quin," Harper turned to me now, her eyes blazing, "it might take some time, but you'll learn what Patrol is all about. And you'll get to move around The Beck with more freedom than you ever got in Agric. Don't tell me you don't want that."

"No! Yes. I–"

She grabbed hold of my hand now too, cutting me off, "You hate working in one place all day every day. It bores you. And you have so many questions about The Beck that never get answered. Admit it!"

I nodded slowly.

"See! I know you. And I know that you're completely terrified right now. Completely. But that tomorrow you will suck it up and get on with it. And in six months' time you will fly through the assessment as an experienced member of Patrol with a ton of new skills and stronger than ever. And with a lot more answers to your questions than you'll ever get stuck down here in Agric."

She nodded triumphantly.

"And in the end, just maybe, you'll figure out what's wrong with The Beck and be able to change it."

"So you've got it all figured out."

"Yup. I don't get to live a better life in Clearance. We know that," she waved her hand at me impatiently as I tried to protest, "Deep down, we know that. But you two have a chance. And I have to know that to be able to get through whatever is going to happen to me tomorrow. So no giving up, right?"

Harper's fingernails were digging into my hand now, her grip was stronger than I had ever imagined possible from someone so thin. She shook with the effort of her speech. Cass and I stared at each other.

"Right?"

There was no other answer after a speech like that.

"Right."

A flashing light to my left distracted me and I twisted my body to the side to peer along the wall top towards the distant ladder. Something was moving. It was too early for the next changeover, so no one should have been walking along the wall yet. Up to now we had only witnessed the Patrol guards standing at their posts staring out at the water or back towards the fields. They only ever moved when a new guard arrived.

The purpose of the wall guard was to keep an eye on the floodwaters and watch for anything approaching from the water. Also, to watch over the external areas of The Beck and make sure no one was anywhere they shouldn't be in the middle of the night. There was no need to move *along* the wall. Unless we had been spotted. Or overheard. Unless the guard was bored and had decided to leave the usual post and wander along to the next empty alcove, just for something to do.

Only this time, it wouldn't be empty.

I felt sick. Being caught by Grady was one thing, but being caught by an unknown Patrol guard was completely unchartered territory. I had no idea what they might do. Alerting the other two to the approaching light, I indicated that we should shrink back further into the alcove. Perhaps the guard, if it was a guard, might only walk a short distance along the wall and then return to the sentry post. Perhaps they were just stretching their legs.

We could only wait and hope.

Chapter Ten

The guard was getting closer. I could hear the footsteps, slow but steady, moving along the wall. There seemed little we could do to avoid a confrontation now, and I couldn't stop my legs from shaking violently. Out of nowhere, Harper stepped right out of the alcove and directly into the path of the guard. The footsteps stopped.

"I'm sorry," Harper's voice was quiet but steady, "I know I shouldn't be here."

"Too right you shouldn't." The voice was deep, male and vaguely amused.

"It's just that – well I was assigned to Clearance today and–"

"Clearance huh?" The amusement had disappeared.

I saw Harper nod.

"That's tough." He seemed to reassess her. "Wait – you made it up here alone?"

Harper nodded again, and took a step forward, away from the alcove.

"It's just – no offence – but you look like a gust of wind would blow you away. I'm presuming you failed the physical? That ladder – it's no picnic."

"Well maybe I'm stronger than I look."

"Maybe." He didn't sound convinced. "Really? You climbed the ladder by yourself?"

Harper stepped forwards, disappearing from view, nodding fiercely as she did so. I knew she was trying to protect us. She had accepted that her fate was sealed with an assignment to Clearance, whereas Cass and I still had a chance.

But not if we were caught and reported.

A reckoning from a member of Patrol would not be kind. We stood a good chance of an instant reassignment to Clearance ourselves if we were found out at night. But standing out there by herself, Harper was completely vulnerable. Cass and I looked at each other. Her face mirrored mine and we understood that, whatever happened next, we couldn't let Harper take the punishment alone.

I pushed myself up from ground level, stepping out from the alcove and joining Harper on the wall top, hoping that the officer wouldn't notice the trembling legs which betrayed my terror. Cass followed me, as I had known she would, her voice more confident than earlier.

"No. She didn't come up here by herself. In fact she's not alone at all."

Harper spun around, "Why?" Her tone was hurt and I found that I couldn't look her in the eye. "Why couldn't you let me do one last thing for you?"

There had been no tears from her until now. I felt a stab of guilt as I watched them begin to fall. We had caused this pain. Because we had refused to let her take the blame for us, no matter how much she wanted to. But I knew, however hurt she was, that neither of us could have stood by and watched her suffer alone.

I forced myself to meet her gaze, my heart wrenching as I did so. Stepping forwards, I put my arms around her tiny frame. My voice was a whisper in her hair, "Sorry Har, we couldn't let you. In it together, right?"

Her face crumpled. Collapsing against my chest, silent sobs shook her tiny frame. I tried to wrap my arms more tightly around her, desperate to keep my own composure. Cass stood just behind me and laid a hand on Harper's hair awkwardly.

"Uh – sorry to break this up, but..."

For the first time I turned to the Patrol Officer, expecting to see a mocking or angry expression staring back at me. Instead, my gaze was met by a pair of earnest brown eyes which, if I wasn't much mistaken, looked concerned, compassionate even. The guard was tall and slender with close cropped hair the colour of chestnut. He didn't look much older than us.

As his eyes met mine his expression altered quickly, the openness disappearing and being replaced by something else entirely. He appeared more business-like as he stepped towards us.

"Are you from Agric?

I gestured down at my overalls, raising my eyebrows slightly.

He flushed slightly, "Yes. Of course you are. Why are you up here?"

"What she said," Cass nodded towards Harper, "But not alone." Her voice was strong and calm and I was thankful for it, unsure that I could have spoken to him directly and remained composed.

"So the part about Clearance – that's true?"

"For her yes."

"And for you two?"

Not one to waste words, Cass' voice became sharp, "Never mind." She moved away from Harper, taking a deliberate step towards the officer. "What's your plan? What are you going to do?"

He looked thoughtful. "I should radio this in and have you taken before the Director."

He walked forwards, passing Cass slowly and circling around Harper and I. Once he was behind us he stopped. We froze. He was armed. He could claim we attacked him. He could do anything to us at this point and get away with it. I could see the tension in Cass' body and willed her to keep her temper. Her eyes were blazing and she looked like she might leap on the guard at any second and attack him.

His voice came from behind me. "The next Patrol is due up here in ten minutes. If you can get back down off the wall before then and into the fields you should have enough cover to get away."

"What?" Cass' voice was incredulous.

"I said, if you get down–"

"I heard you! You mean you're... you're letting us go?" The calm tone had disappeared in Cass' disbelief.

"Well why not?" He sounded defensive, "What good would it do to..."

He broke off, not finishing his sentence. He was standing so close I could feel the warmth of his body.

"Just go. And do it quickly. If you're found up here and I haven't called it in I'll be in as much trouble as you will." He glanced down at the fields below as though the replacement Patrol could appear at any moment.

"Well, thanks I guess. We will. Go, I mean." Cassidy took hold of Harper's hand and pried her away from me. As she did so, I felt her sway dangerously, the physical exertion and the tears having taken their toll and dissolved any strength she had shown earlier.

"Harper? Harper, we need to leave now. Otherwise-"

But she continued to cry, the tears seemingly unstoppable, rolling constantly down her face. I shook my head at Cassidy, wondering how we would manage this now. Cassidy stepped closer and hooked one of Harper's arms around her shoulders. She motioned for me to do the same. We managed to manoeuvre her into a vaguely comfortable position pointing in the right direction, and started to limp along as fast as we could. She was a dead weight though, and appeared to have completely given up.

"Harper, we have to go. Help us please?"

She mumbled something unintelligible.

"What?"

"Leave."

"We're trying to."

"No. Leave. Leave me. Leave me here."

"What? Don't be ridiculous!"

"I'm done for anyway. Clearance," she hiccoughed, "Clearance tomorrow! What's the difference if I go from the pod or from here – on the wall!"

"She's hysterical. We have to go. The next Patrol will be here soon and I don't think they're all going to be as understanding as this guy."

"You're right – they won't. You need to leave – now." The Patrol officer's voice had begun to sound urgent, "I don't want to, but if they show up now I will have to turn you all in."

He turned and began to make his way back to his post, clearly having finished with helping us. Cassidy and I shuffled faster towards the ladder, making some progress but not enough. Harper sagged against us, moaning quietly, barely moving her legs at all.

"We can make it to the ladder, but how on earth are we ever going to get her down it safely?"

"I don't know Cass, but let's take it one step at a time," I paused to shift Harper's arm more securely around my shoulder, "How much more time do you think we have?"

Cass shrugged, "Not long, perhaps eight minutes if we're lucky."

I stopped and moved awkwardly away from Harper. Taking her by the chin, I forced her to look into my eyes, "Listen. Remember a minute ago when you were prepared to risk everything for us? To give yourself up?"

She nodded.

"Well you have one more chance to help us here. Now. All you have to do is walk. We'll help you. But you have to move, otherwise none of us are going to make it back to Agric. Because we're not leaving you."

Something flashed in her eyes and she managed to straighten up a little. Replacing my arm around her, we started to make more positive progress towards the ladder, but I was still very concerned that we wouldn't be able to make it down. Walking in a straight line on the flat was one thing, descending a twenty-foot ladder was completely different.

We reached the ladder top and both Cassidy and I stared tentatively down into the darkness below. Whoever went first risked having an extremely weak Harper collapsing on top of them. Not a prospect either of us was relishing. Cass spoke first.

"I'll go."

"Nope. She'll drag you off if you're below her. I'm bigger, stronger than you."

"But if she falls," Cassidy eyed Harper's swaying figure doubtfully, "And she might well fall, she's going to take whoever's underneath her out."

At that moment I heard a noise to my right and the Patrol officer was suddenly there again. At first he appeared to be wrestling Harper away from us, and I had a sudden horrific thought that he was going to push her over the side of the wall. I made to shove him away protectively before realising that he was passing a thick coil of rope around her waist.

"What are you–?"

"You go first," he gestured roughly to me, "and try to support her from below. I'll fasten her to me and climb after her." He nodded at Cass, "You come last, and keep a look out."

It only took me a moment to understand his plan. If he supported her from above via the rope then if she fell he could hold her weight while I attempted to get her stable on the rungs of the ladder again. He was stronger than me, but this was still a risky plan. The biggest puzzle was why he would be willing to do this for three strangers, when the next Patrol could appear at any moment. But I wasn't going to stop and ask him why. Cass looked as if she was going to argue, but I shook my head at her, seeing no other choice but to trust him.

Instead, I clambered down the first few rungs of the ladder and prepared to steady Harper's climb. When he moved away from her, the rope seemed to be securely fastened around both her waist and arms, wrapped twice around her body and then fastened to him in the same way. He looked strong, but he was fairly slight and I doubted his ability to support Harper's weight as well as his own. Still, she was skinny, and it was our best chance.

Cass helped Harper on to the ladder and stepped back so

the man could follow her. She managed the first few steps without an issue, and the four of us were soon on the ladder and clambering down one after another. It was slow progress. I didn't want to get too far below Harper, but if I didn't make progress then I held everyone else up. Patrol guy was clearly taking some of Harper's weight already, judging by the grunts of effort he was making. I couldn't see Cass, not daring to lean back and look that far above me. It was hard enough worrying about Harper potentially falling. If I slipped, we would have no chance.

After what seemed like forever, I glanced beneath me to see that we had made it down half of the ladder with no issue. Breathing a sigh of relief, I started to believe that we could do this. Picking up the pace a little, I made it down the next few rungs without checking Harper's progress as carefully as I had been doing. Glancing over my shoulder across the fields, I couldn't see any signs of other Patrol officers approaching. I wondered where Riley was now. Still out, crouching somewhere in the fields, worrying about her reassignment? Or back in her pod, desperately trying to get some sleep ready for tomorrow? I hoped she could manage some rest, she would probably need it.

There was a sudden movement above me and something hit my hand hard. I glanced down to see Harper's foot sliding past my arm. She was slipping. Ignoring the pain lancing through my hand, I wrestled both my arms around both her legs and held on as tightly as I could. Her downward progress stopped abruptly as the rope went taut, and Patrol guy let out a yell. He had managed to hold on, but with most of Harper's weight as well as his own, I knew he couldn't stay on the ladder indefinitely.

Guiding Harper's feet on to a rung level with my own shoulders, I tried to steady her as best I could, but she didn't seem to be taking any of her own weight.

"Har!"

Nothing. Was she unconscious?

"Har! You ok?"

A muffled groan came from above me. I wasn't sure if it was her or Patrol guy. Rubbing the backs of her calves, I tried to massage them into waking up and taking her weight. Another groan from above me, deeper this time, told me that our saviour couldn't hold on for much longer. It also made me think that the first noise had come from Harper, who must be conscious, if exhausted.

"Harper! There's only a few more steps. You don't have to make it much further. Please try – for me?"

Slowly, she shifted both her feet until they were stable and holding at least some of her weight. I released my hold on her legs cautiously, finding that they still held.

"Think she's ok now," I called upwards.

There was no answer. I began to descend the ladder again, my eyes glued to Harper's feet. She was slow, but seemed now to be managing to stumble down without falling, as long as I guided her feet.

We made it to the third rung of the ladder and I jumped down, desperate now to have all four of us safely on the ground. Harper fell backwards from the second rung, taking Patrol guy with her. They landed in a heap at my feet, and Cass quickly followed, glaring at him, suspicious as always despite the help he had just provided. Untangling his limbs from Harper's, he began to untie the knots in the rope. At the same time he massaged his hand against the small of his back, seeming not to notice Cass's hostility. Embarrassed all the same, I moved across quickly to help him, loosening the knot around Harper's waist before passing the rope back with a small nod and speaking to him for the first time.

"She do any serious damage?"

He winced as he removed the rope and as his shirt lifted slightly, I could see a large red welt around his waist. Once I had helped Harper to a comfortable position resting against the wall, I held my hand out to the Patrol Officer. He looked at it for a moment before taking it and easing himself to a standing position. I found myself unable to stop staring at him when I considered what he'd just done for us. He looked at me and then glanced away, clearly uncomfortable. I realised that I was still holding on to his hand and let go immediately.

"Will anyone notice?"

He shrugged, "Maybe. I'll make something up." He glanced down at his watch, "You'd better go now."

I nodded, "Thank you. Really – thank you. We couldn't have managed..."

Nodding briskly, he backed away, coiling the rope. Cass went back to Harper, hoisting her prone figure up and nodding impatiently at me to come and help her.

Realising I was still staring, I shook my head sharply and went to Harper's side. As I did so, I felt Cass freeze. A whistle cut through the air and the corn was suddenly rustling with more than the wind.

"The changeover. Hide!"

He pointed towards an area of the field which would not cross the path of the approaching officer and hoisted the rope over his shoulder.

Quickly, we dragged Harper to the edge of the cornfield

in the direction he had pointed. Crawling several feet into the deep cover of the high stalks, we lay low and still. If we moved, we'd be caught, and the Patrol guy with us. After all he had done, I knew none of us wanted to put him at risk. He wouldn't even have time to get back up the ladder to his post now.

The approaching whistle sounded again, much closer this time. Within a few seconds the footsteps were upon us and we could hear voices.

"Hey Cam! What you doing down here?"

"Thought I heard something."

"Down in the field?"

"Yeah, maybe an Agric or LS sneaking around. You know people go a little crazy after Assessment Day."

"Too right. Find anything?"

"Nope. 'Fraid not. All clear."

"Dammit – thought I might get some action to liven up wall duty. It's so dull." He sighed loudly, "Well I'll keep my eyes open. Been a while since I got to torment any Lower Beck citizens."

The newcomer laughed unkindly, and I heard a noise like he was slapping our Patrol guy on the back hard. I winced for him, imagining the pain he would have to conceal.

"Well don't bother climbing back up then Cam. I'll take it from here."

"Thanks, Donnelly."

He laughed, "Don't mention it. See you at wake up."

The next few moments were filled with the sounds of two sets of footsteps, one ascending the ladder and the other retreating through the corn into the distance. I nudged Cass and pointed to Harper, who had fallen asleep in her arms.

"Give it twenty minutes?"

She nodded. Between Harper needing to rest and the knowledge that the new Patrol Officer would be watching the fields more closely, it was a good idea to be cautious on our return to the pod. Sinking down on to the ground myself, I strained to hear the footsteps of the man called Cam, who had saved us all when he hadn't needed to, but the sound had already faded into the distance.

Chapter Eleven

It took us a long time to get back to the pod, but we made it back while The Beck was still in darkness and collapsed immediately into our cots. Grady was out cold, and anyone else in the pod who was awake had the good grace to pretend they were not. Harper was asleep instantly: Cass and I had been almost carrying her from the fields back to the Agric Compound. For Cass and I, sleep was far more difficult to come by.

As morning light dawned, I realised that I had probably only had a couple of hours sleep at the most. My head ached and my eyes were sore and tired. I was not in good shape for the move to my new Sector. Grady's unnecessary commands ricocheted around the pod like bullets. We knew what to do. Although this wasn't an ordinary day, transfers happened once every six months, and all but the very newest recruits knew what to expect.

We shuffled to the canteen to endure an ordinary breakfast of cool, watery porridge, so unlike the thick, creamy substance we had consumed the previous day. The atmosphere in the room was tense: different than Assessment Day, as not everyone's fate was hanging in the balance, but enough people feeling nervous about their reassignments to affect the general mood. I knew that others were trying to ease the transition for their pod mates, or coping with the idea of saying goodbye. There were few smiles.

After the meal we filed out in silence and went back to our pod. Most of us sat around listlessly, a few trying unsuccessfully to read. Cass, Harper and I lay on our respective cots in silence. Everything we wanted to say had been communicated the night before. We were as ready as we would ever be. All we could do now was wait.

Around an hour later, we all stood again, Harper, Cass and I collecting our bags as we did so. The lines making their way out of the Agric Compound had never seemed so sombre. On our previous visits to the square we had been onlookers, simply attending the Transfer Ceremony to watch others leave and witness the arrival of newcomers to the Agric Compound. This time it was different. Of all of us, only Cass would return to Agric. Even she would return to a different pod, where she would have to prepare to welcome any new recruits. Harper and I would travel into the unknown, alone and clueless as to what lay in wait for us. I drew in a shaky breath and tried to walk steadily as I followed Harper's stumbling form up the path and out of the Agric Compound gates.

In the square we all lined up. Most of the working areas in The Beck were gathered for this particular occasion. All except Clearance citizens, and a few Supers left on duty to keep an eye on things while the Transfer Ceremony took place. The rows of citizens in their different uniforms formed blocks of colour, the lifeline of The Beck laid out like a patchwork quilt, filling the entire square. Our pod always lined up close to the rear and it was sometimes difficult to see, but we could always hear what was said. They made sure of that.

Waiting for all the other Sectors to line up, I didn't dare take hold of Cass and Harper's hands, but I could feel their arms resting against mine on either side. It reminded me of our time on the wall the previous night and I wished that we were back there. This morning, Cassidy's was warm and steady, Harper's cool and shaking almost uncontrollably. Despite her courageous speech of the previous night, she was obviously terrified.

A movement up ahead caught my eye, and at the same time I heard Grady's customary hiss along the line, her charming way of ensuring that we were all paying attention and not disgracing her pod's reputation. Governor Adams himself was making his way onto the podium up ahead, followed closely by Superintendent Carter. They appeared to be deep in conversation, Carter gesturing quickly with her hands, pointing out into the crowd and shaking her head rapidly as she spoke. Adams nodded, before gesturing to a chair to the left of the podium. Looking a little disgruntled, Carter took her seat as Adams approached the microphone.

"Good morning citizens," he began, his voice echoing across the square. Without expecting an answer, he continued, "And so we reach another momentous Transfer Day. I say this, because without these Transfers, our society would not be able to survive. Without constantly checking to ensure that all citizens are performing effectively, we would not be able to grow our crops, tend to our livestock, feed ourselves, investigate new ways to combat the flood waters, and generally continue with our society here in The Beck. We have to make these alterations regularly, to ensure that The Beck is productive and secure. I know that every one of you understands the importance of maintaining strict control over our society here, and following the rules to ensure a fair, equal chance for everyone to thrive under such difficult conditions."

He paused for a moment, and I thought about Harper, and how she was not being given a fair, equal chance of survival by being sent to Clearance. I stiffened at this idea, but immediately felt a cool hand on mine. Harper, again able to read my mind, was making sure she prevented me from any outburst which would jeopardise my own chances of survival. I managed a small, grateful smile before facing the podium again, noticing the daggers that Grady shot in my direction and not wanting to enrage her any more than I already had done.

"So today, as many of you make your way to new Sectors to begin new assignments, I want to thank you all for your patience, for your obedience, for your co-operation. Because without that, I know," he paused again for effect, "I *know*, that we would not be in such good shape."

"And we *are* in good shape. Only today I have been able to grant the Meds Sector permission to birth up to twenty new citizens. That's almost double last year's amount. There have been some interesting breakthroughs in the Dev area which we are hoping will further strengthen the wall and combat the effect of the floodwater when it rises, and an excellent harvest in Agric this season means we may even be able to increase rations. All of this is due to your hard work and commitment to the continuation of The Beck society and its values. So, wherever you go today, go knowing that your community is thriving, and will continue to do so as long as we all work together."

"Another sign of our good shape is the quality and number of new recruits joining us. Today we welcome thirty new citizens. Only Minors yesterday, but today ready to take up the mantle of citizenship and begin training in their assigned Sector."

With a flourish he waved at Carter, who signalled a woman in a Meds uniform at the side of the stage. She led forward a group of young people, all fourteen, I knew, who climbed the steps to the podium and walked across it one by one. All looked nervous and pale. I remembered my own Minors transfer day, when I was brought here from Prep, the training area for all the under-fourteens in The Beck, and brought forwards in a similar way to join the adult citizens of our society. I had been terrified, much as these young people appeared to be. I felt for them.

"I know you will welcome them into our society in the days to come."

Adams waved a hand graciously at the new recruits and backed away from the microphone, motioning for Superintendent Carter to begin the practical side of the proceedings. She approached the microphone quickly and efficiently as ever.

"Can I ask that citizens listen to all instructions before any movement commences please."

Her voice was far less poisonous today. When she spoke in front of Adams she always seemed calm and organised, with no hint of the vicious side that permeated her words and actions when she patrolled the Assessments or visited the different Sectors on Governance business alone.

"First of all, can I ask that citizens who will be moving to Clearance today move towards the West side of the square," she gestured with her hand, "where you will be met by existing Patrol guards who will guide you towards Black Hill in a few minutes. Our newest recruits from Minors, plus those citizens moving from one Sector to another should wait in place while returning citizens leave for their old Sectors. Then you will be given further instructions."

There was a moment of stillness before people started to shuffle. Grady stood forwards and motioned for Harper and myself to step forwards. As we did so, our line began to file away. I was hit by the sudden realisation that this was it and instinctively grabbed Cassidy's hand. She held on to mine and stared at me, her expression tormented and intense. Harper, who was making no attempt to stem the silent tears rolling down her face, also moved towards us, then came to an abrupt halt.

For a moment I wondered why, but a painful stinging sensation on the back of my hand soon clarified the situation. Taking out the thin, reed-like cane Supers were allowed to carry, Grady had swung it viciously at us. Cassidy and I sprang apart, nursing the growing welts on our hands. Having achieved her objective, Grady moved back to the head of the line, smiling in triumph. Cassidy re-joined the Pod 19 line and, as they marched away, turned and mouthed some words at us both. They were silent, but we both understood what she said.

"No giving up."

We nodded at her before she walked away, still cradling her injured hand. We watched the flow of people returning to a normal day in Agric, or LS, or Sustenance, whose lives had only been minimally disrupted by the Transfer Day. As Cass rounded the corner she turned and looked back, the strange, despairing expression still haunting her face. Then she was gone.

The square was beginning to clear now, and most of those left behind looked nervous. Harper motioned towards the West side of the square, where the most frightened group of citizens stood. There were only a few Agric citizens left standing around us. I noticed Miller, the recruit who had cheated on the test, standing to our right, and pushed Harper gently towards her, knowing they had to be going the same way. She looked at me one last time, taking my hand again while there was still enough commotion not to be noticed.

"No giving up, ok?"

"No. No giving up. For you especially."

"Definitely not." She even managed a small smile.

"I'll see you, Har. I promise."

"No you won't. But thanks for the bravado, Quin."

I shook my head to clear the tears, not wanting to break down as she left.

"Go. Go now, or..."

She nodded, understanding. Turning to her right, she nudged Miller, who was standing, frozen to the spot.

"Coming?"

Miller stared at her, uncomprehending. Harper gestured to the Clearance crowd which was growing by the minute. Finally Miller seemed to understand, and together, the two of them started walking across the square, not a lengthy walk, but a terrifying one all the same. I watched her go, battling the tears which threatened to pour down my face as I met my fellow Patrol members for the first time.

Carter's voice boomed again, her lack of feeling helping me somehow to regain control.

"Now, if all the Clearance recruits are ready," she paused as a Patrol Super waved a hand in confirmation, "please begin the walk to Black Hill while I instruct the rest of the transfers."

I found I could not tear my eyes away from the group Harper had joined. Were there always so many Clearance recruits? I realised I had never been here to take notice before. They looked a sorry crowd mostly, and more shuffled than marched out of the square. I lost sight of Miller and Harper in the crowd, but tried to comfort myself with the thought that at least she had a fellow Agric citizen with her.

The square was almost empty now in comparison to earlier. There were perhaps forty people standing around awaiting instructions. I noticed Riley to my left, standing with another Super I didn't know. She nodded at me when I caught her eye. There were perhaps five or six recruits from each Sector waiting to be given instructions as to their transfer. As the last of the Clearance recruits moved off up the path towards Black Hill, Carter spoke again.

"And now for those of you who are left. That should only be citizens moving between Sectors and Minors joining a Sector for the first time, yes?" She paused to check that those of us remaining were still supposed to be there. "Minors, you will all be delivered to your assigned areas by the Patrol Officers to my left," she gestured with her hand.

Nobody moved. Carter pointed again, this time with impatience. I felt for the Minors. It was difficult to be new, and they would never have been outside of Prep before now. Overwhelmed was probably an understatement for them. Slowly, they began to shuffle forwards, the waiting Patrol guards towering over them. With a few sharp orders, the group were rounded up and placed into a line, which marched off in the direction of the Lower Beck.

Carter continued, "Now, those of you going to Meds will

line up at the front. Med Ellis is waiting to escort you to your new pods."

The woman who had escorted the Minors to the ceremony waved from close to the podium. Her turquoise overalls made her easy to spot. Meds had the brightest and most vivid of all the uniforms in The Beck. I liked to think it was because their job, bringing new life to the community, was among the most positive.

"And the rest of you: Sustenance assignments to the West Wall, LS to the East, Rep in the centre. Dev can come to the podium itself and Patrol take the South of the square. Then await further instructions from your assigned Transfer Super."

South of the square was the rear, which meant staying exactly where I was. Feeling very much abandoned by all those familiar to me, I managed a small smile at Riley as she and the other Super made their way towards the front of the square. A few others began to make their way towards me, until we stood, a small rainbow of uniforms, awaiting a Patrol Super to come and instruct us.

I looked at those around me: noticing among the group a pale girl with flame red hair dressed in the tan-coloured Sustenance uniform, a tall, broad shouldered LS boy with a scattering of freckles and, surprisingly, a thin, dark haired boy dressed in the white Dev uniform. Those in the Dev Sector rarely transferred, having to be specially selected for Dev in the first place. I wondered why he was moving to Patrol. Before I had time to assess any of the other recruits, there was a movement from behind us. I turned to see a Patrol Officer towering over the group, an almost mocking look on his face.

"Hope you're ready, 'cause Patrol's not an easy ride. I'm Barnes – one of your Transfer Supers. Let's get moving – sure you're all dying to start training."

He smiled a little wickedly at this statement before turning and setting off towards the far side of the square, not waiting to see if we would follow.

Chapter Twelve

We had been marching for at least thirty minutes before we reached the Patrol Compound. I had always wondered where it was and never been sure. Skirting the side of Black Hill, we walked through a heavily wooded area for some time. The ground underfoot was rough and difficult to navigate, but I was glad of the distraction, not wanting to think about those I had left behind just yet.

The group stumbled on, the only one sure of his footing being Barnes, who seemed now, from my position at the back of the group, to be way ahead. I was close to the rear, and contented myself for now with watching the ground closely for tree roots and staying unnoticed for as long as possible, dreading the Patrol training to come.

I remembered my Agric training vividly. Coming into The Beck community at the age of fourteen had been extremely daunting. Prior to my first Transfer Ceremony, when I was paraded in front of the entire Beck community before being escorted to my assigned Sector and abandoned, as a Minor I had only seen the inside of the Meds Sector. All of my learning and pre-Beck training took place within a small section of The Lower Beck which was purposely fenced off from the rest of the society.

As Minors we were born in a tiny section of the Meds Sector

and cared for by Meds citizens until we were deemed able to function in a training setting, around the age of five. We were then assigned to the more senior Minors Instructors, and allowed access to Prep, a larger section contained within Meds which housed all the equipment required for our training. Genders were kept separate, training mostly focused on physical development and education in the different skill areas contained within The Beck, and there was little or no freedom at all. On my Graduation day, I could remember feeling completely paralysed as I was paraded across the stage with all eyes upon me. It was only Cass, her hand squeezing mine as I stumbled up the podium steps, who saved me from falling on my face.

And then we found ourselves in Agric, woken before dawn each morning, marched to the fields, preparing the soil and sowing and tending, weeding and harvesting in a never-ending cycle. All the time having it drilled into us that failure to complete our assigned duties would result in complete breakdown of The Beck's nutrition system and we would all starve. Eventually, we had managed to become fully functioning Agric citizens. Somehow we had managed to grow in strength, been able to complete more senior duties, and feel proud of the contribution we made to Beck society by feeding everyone.

But I had no idea what Patrol held for me. Patrol protected The Beck. Monitored the activity of all citizens. Watched over the flood waters and guarded the wall. Supervised procedures relating to the laws and justice systems of The Beck alongside Governance. The prospect of all this both fascinated and terrified me all at once. I wanted to see more, to know more, to have a little more freedom to explore our world, but at the same time I was afraid of what I might discover.

It began to grow lighter and I looked up to see that we were exiting the woods. We emerged into a field similar to those in Agric, except for the steep angle it sloped at (I couldn't stop myself making a mental note that few crops could ever be successfully grown here). Beyond the first field lay what I presumed were the Patrol pods. I don't know if I was relieved or disappointed to find that the Patrol dwellings, externally at least, looked exactly the same as those in Agric.

There were more than I had expected. Less than Agric, but enough to suggest there was a significant number of staff in the Patrol Sector. At the moment the pods seemed deserted. I assumed that the majority of the camp were at work or perhaps sleeping. Many Patrol duties continued through the night, which would require sleep during daylight hours to ensure a citizen's ability to perform their role well. On the far side of the field stood several buildings, one I presumed was the canteen, another not unlike the Kennedy Building in the Assessment Sector. A few Patrol staff were entering it as we approached, but none of them seemed to pay any attention to us, their newest recruits.

Barnes had stopped at the far edge of the field and was waiting for us, tapping a foot impatiently. As we reached him, he held up a hand to stop us and put two fingers into his mouth, whistling loudly and visibly startling most of the new recruits.

"This is the Patrol Compound. In front of you are the pods, pretty similar to those you're used to. The wash tents," he gestured around the field at various points, "are also shared in the same way."

My attention was diverted by a single figure who had exited

the large building and was walking in our direction. The figure was female and her approach was rapid and purposeful. She appeared to be carrying a folder or clipboard, which reminded me with a shiver of the previous day's assessments.

Barnes continued to drone on, "The building to your right is the Jefferson Building. Director Reed works there, that's where you get your assigned duties, stuff like that. Behind it is the canteen and the Annexe."

He paused as the woman approached. Up close, she did not look much older than I was, but the badge on her uniform marked her out as a Super and she was clearly in charge. She nodded briefly at Barnes before speaking. He did not seem to mind that she immediately took over the role of induction supervisor.

"Hello. My name is Tyler and I will be your Transfer Super alongside Barnes here. Welcome to Patrol. Let me start by telling you that you were not selected by accident. Your tests have been studied and you are deemed suitable for a Patrol assignment, most importantly meaning that you should be capable of discretion. We live away from the Lower Beck because we know things up here which the Lower Beck don't. We also have certain privileges. Don't think being here will be an easy ride though."

She glanced at the group as she spoke, and I felt like her keen eyes were already assessing my potential.

"There is a lot to learn in a short period of time here. You will be expected to listen attentively and take in everything you can this week, before beginning on-the-job training in seven days' time. There is no substitute for training which actually shows you real life Patrol situations and how you will react to them. Patrol requires a cool head and a calm attitude in a crisis. Our role carries with it a weight of responsibility which you cannot ignore." She paused briefly. "If you do, somebody usually dies."

"And that somebody might be you," Barnes added.

A small snigger ran through the group.

"You think I'm being funny?"

Silence reigned once more. He wasn't joking, that much was clear. The expression on Tyler's face confirmed it. After an awkward silence, she opened the folder and began to speak again.

"It's a lot to take in, I know. For now, we will take you over to the Jefferson Building to pick up your supply allocations and show you the Annexe. That's a kind of a dorm behind the Jefferson Building where you will sleep during your induction week. After that you'll be assigned a permanent pod with other, more experienced, Patrol citizens. You will have thirty minutes to collect your equipment, stow it away and get back here for your first training session. Is that clear?"

Most of us nodded. We knew better than to speak. The Sectors we had come from mostly demanded near-silence and compete obedience. Patrol seemed no different so far.

As Tyler began rifling through the folder, I glanced around. There were ten of us in total, almost a full pod, and we seemed to come from a variety of backgrounds. There were more LS boys than anything else, LS being a Sector which naturally turned out strong men capable of wrestling a variety of farm animals under control, but there were also three Sustenance workers, the boy from Dev and myself. Most of the faces in the group looked increasingly nervous.

Behind us loomed the woods we had just come from. Beyond them lay the Lower Beck Canteen, the Agric Compound, the Assessment buildings and, further away, the wall, but I could see none of them from here. Tyler was right, Patrol was actually quite separate from the rest of The Beck. It made me wonder why they were housed so far away, and what it was they were privy to that the Lower Beck did not know. Tyler's clear voice cut through my thoughts.

"Mason, Davis, Anders, Jackson and Quin. You're Group One. The rest of you are Group Two." She nodded at us. "Group One, you're with me. Let's go."

She set off in the direction of the Jefferson Building without waiting for us. The group around me shuffled awkwardly, those of us assigned to Tyler realising slowly that we needed to follow her. First to leave were the broad, freckled LS boy and another LS who was clearly his friend. They nodded at one another in approval as they jogged to catch up with our newly appointed leader. Next, the boy from Dev moved off, and finally the red-haired girl, who had caught my eye earlier. I noticed her face had fallen at the division of the group, and she shot a pained look at the other Sustenance girls who would remain with Barnes. I felt for her and tried to smile as we set off in pursuit of Tyler. At least there was one other girl in my group, and she might well need a friend as much as I did.

The walk to the building took seconds, and soon we were passing through a set of imposing wooden doors. As we did, we passed another Patrol Super travelling in the other direction. He nodded at Tyler as she passed, and she called back over her shoulder to him, almost playfully.

"New recruits, Donnelly. Try not to scare them."

I jumped at the name and flushed with guilt, recalling the second guard from the previous evening. He smirked as I walked past him, eyeing me in a way I wasn't entirely comfortable with. I felt a stab of fear before remembering that he had no way of knowing that I was one of the citizens who had been out of bed the previous night.

Tyler crossed a hallway and made her way up a set of stairs towards the rear of the building. Like the Lincoln Building, this one was subdivided with makeshift walls creating areas of different sizes for people to work in. The steps were steep and well worn, and led to a floor above which was more open plan and clearly formed the Patrol supply department. There was a counter to one side, and the rest of the space was filled with shelving, all neatly stacked and labelled ready for distribution.

A petite girl sat behind the desk. She looked up expectantly as we approached and greeted Tyler with a smile.

"Hey Ty, gear's all ready over there."

She nodded to a long table towards the back of the room which I hadn't noticed. On it were laid ten piles of equipment ready for collection. I noted the pile of overalls, several pairs by the looks of it; a pair of boots which looked newer than those we had been given in Agric, and a sack filled with various other items. At Tyler's nod we all took a pile and made our way back to the counter.

"You all have new uniforms there. Overalls for heavy work assignments, a uniform for ceremonies and some more protective clothing too. The bag has various other essentials. I'll take you to your dorm now, where you'll need to change into a set of work overalls and then meet me back out in the field where we were earlier. Don't think today's all about settling in – there's training to be done."

She raised an eyebrow at the girl behind the equipment counter, who smiled at her.

"But it's not all bad. After your old pods, you'll soon find that Patrol has its advantages."

With that, Tyler marched back down the stairs, the rest of us trailing behind her as best we could with all our new supplies. Turning sharply at the bottom of the steps, she passed through the lower level of the Jefferson Building, nodding at a few other citizens on the way. Leading us to a door at the far end of the building, she pulled it open and waved her hand towards a small, low building across a courtyard.

"That's the Annexe. New recruits always stay there for their first week here. Should make sure that you all get to know each other before settling in with the rest of Patrol next week. You've got about ten minutes to unpack your stuff and get changed before you're expected for training. Got that?"

Her last comment was accompanied by a stern look, which no one dared to challenge. Taking this as our cue to leave, we began exiting the door one by one. I was last, but just as I was about to leave, Tyler waved a hand to stop me, allowing someone to enter the building from the other direction. I stood back to let the more senior Patrol citizen pass me.

"Hey Tyler, how're the newbies?"

The tone was gentle, teasing almost, and very familiar.

My head jerked up instantly and I found myself staring straight into a familiar pair of brown eyes. Eyes I had last seen at the base of the wall the night before. Our rescuer stopped instantly in his tracks and stared at me, a look of horror on his face.

Seemingly oblivious to any tension, Tyler replied easily, "Oh, you know Cameron, useless, terrified, weak... the usual!" She rolled her eyes at him.

I forced myself to look away, allowing him to recover

himself. I should have been expecting this. I had known he was Patrol. He, on the other hand, had no idea I was being transferred from Agric.

"Anything wrong, Cameron?"

His silence had alerted Tyler to something and now she sounded surprised. A thrill of tension ran through me as I wondered what would happen if anyone found out we had already met. I continued to stare at the floor, gritting my teeth silently. A second later I felt movement and his sleeve brushed against mine as he passed me by. Then he was gone.

"Well, what are you waiting for?" Tyler tutted at me, sounding impatient now.

I hurried through the door and followed the others, who had already disappeared through the door of the Annexe. Glancing back, I was quick enough to catch a glimpse of Tyler hurrying to catch up with Cameron before he went into one of the cubicles and disappeared from view.

Chapter Thirteen

By the time I reached the Annexe and made my way inside, most of the bunks had been taken. Barnes' group had clearly come here before collecting their supplies, and scattered their bags and belongings territorially on the beds. I didn't dare move anything, and instead made my way to the rear of the room where a single top bunk had been left empty. Thankfully, the occupant of the lower bed was the girl from my group, who repeated her smile as I approached. I returned the expression before clambering up to the top bed, not wanting to risk talking to her just yet.

I was still trying to get my breath back. I had almost forgotten about the events of the previous night in all the upheaval of the morning. Seeing Cameron again had startled me. He had helped to conceal our whereabouts the previous night, but who knew how he would react to my permanent presence in the Patrol Compound. He would already have me marked out as a troublemaker, someone who broke the rules. I could only hope that he would have nothing to do with the new recruit training and I could keep away from him.

I glanced down at the rest of my group and realised that they were all dressed in the blue Patrol overalls and ready for training. We only had ten minutes to change, and I had already wasted several of them fretting about Cameron. I didn't like to consider the consequences of being the only one late back to the field for the first session. Quickly, I rifled through the pile of supplies we had been given and located the right items. They were a dark blue colour, but otherwise the same style and shape that the Agric ones had been. I hurried to wriggle out of my green ones, feeling a little uneasy that I would not be wearing them again. I had never loved my work in Agric, but at least its routines and objectives had been familiar. In Agric I could blend in, exist safely, know what to expect. Survival in Patrol was an entirely different matter.

I was half way out of the overalls when I noticed the eyes of the broad LS boy on me. As he realised he had been caught staring, he looked away quickly, his face turning red. It suddenly hit me that I had never experienced a mixed gender pod before. In truth, I had never experienced a mixed gender anything. And where I had changed in and out of my Agric overalls with no thought at all for years in Pod 19, I suddenly felt incredibly self-conscious.

But I was running out of time. Pushing my discomfort to the back of my mind, I turned away from the rest of the room's inhabitants and slid out of the Agric overall top completely, leaving myself covered only by my cotton undershirt. I changed into the blue Patrol top as fast as I could and repeated the procedure for the trousers, feeling slightly ridiculous but knowing I didn't want to be caught with so few clothes on by these people who were still strangers to me. Shuffling down from the bunk, I adjusted the clothes so that they at least looked neat, although they were a little on the large side for me.

I found myself standing at the foot of the ladder as the rest of the recruits began making their way towards the door, almost as one. It was strange how quickly the common uniform had united us. As I started after them, I felt a cool hand on my arm.

"Hey."

I turned to see the girl with the red hair looking at me expectantly.

"Hey yourself."

"How are you finding it so far?" Her voice was just above a whisper, barely audible.

I made a face. "Bearable."

She laughed softly, "That's a good way to describe it,"

"I'm Quin. You?"

"Jackson."

"Well Jackson, shall we get to training?"

She nodded enthusiastically, seeming eager to form a bond with me since she had been divided from her other Sustenance friends. I was grateful for it. There was safety in numbers, and I was sure I would need a female friend here in Patrol. She waited thoughtfully for me to walk ahead of her. In some ways she reminded me of Harper. My stomach lurched as I wondered where my friend was now. Shaking my head, I tried to focus on the task at hand.

"Come on. They'll miss us if we're not there soon."

She followed me without comment and we passed through the door together. As we walked towards the field, the second group of recruits were hurrying back across the courtyard into the Annexe, holding their bundles of supplies. One of the Sustenance girls shot a sympathetic glance at Jackson as she passed. I wondered if Group Two regretted taking the time to go to the Annexe before collecting their equipment. They would have even less time to change than us.

We walked around the side of the Jefferson Building, the two LS boys at the front realising that this path would avoid us navigating the complicated interior of the Patrol Headquarters again before we felt confident enough to do so. As I followed the others, I considered the Patrol citizens I had met so far. Cameron, who had been so kind to us, despite what his Patrol orders told him to do; Barnes, who was in charge of training new recruits, but seemed like he might not have taken the same considerate actions; Donnelly, who had joked with Cameron about actually tormenting Lower Beck citizens and eyed me in an almost predatory way, and finally Tyler, who I wasn't sure what to make of yet. My head ached with the lack of sleep and the strain of being on guard all the time with no idea who to trust.

We reached the field quickly to find it was deserted. Clearly our trainers had better things to do than wait around for us, and since Group Two were not here yet, they were obviously leaving it until the last minute to arrive. The five of us stood waiting awkwardly, unused to Patrol and each other, unaware of the rules and the sanctions which would be given if rules were broken. I looked around at the Jefferson Building, the pods, the fields and training areas surrounding us. Currently, there wasn't a single person in sight.

I risked a glance at the boy from earlier. He was staring at me again. This time, he didn't look away.

"Do you think if we speak to each other we'll get a reckoning?"

"I think we might if we're not careful about it," I said, deliberately angling my body so I was facing away from him.

I heard him move behind me and when I glanced back at him he had copied my idea, facing away from me, staring into the woods through which we had entered the Compound.

"I'm Mason."

"Quin. And this is Jackson," I jerked my head towards her, hoping that from a distance it would not give me away.

Jackson didn't speak.

"Hey Quin. Jackson. My LS buddy over there is Davis. We go way back."

"Hey yourselves."

I saw Davis turn towards me out of the corner of my eye and nodded slowly.

The Dev boy had yet to speak. There was a pause where we waited for him to join in but he did not. I ran through the names Tyler had listed in my head, determined to involve him in some way, if just to make him feel he wasn't alone. Mason, Davis, Anders…

"So that makes you Anders, right?"

I didn't look at him when I spoke, trying not to spook him. I could see him quite clearly standing to my left, looking towards the woods just like Mason was. He did not respond, but I felt rather than saw him react and knew I was right about his name.

"So what do we think of Patrol so far?"

No one replied to Mason's question for a moment. We were silent, all working each other out. A slight wind rippled through the trees. The sky was its usual grey above us. But things were not usual. Patrol was not usual, for any of us. Not yet anyway.

"Think we're all still working things out Mason. Aren't you? We shouldn't say too much, not just yet."

This voice belonged to Davis. I agreed with his sentiments, not wanting to give anything away just yet. For now, exchanging names was enough. Trust was a valuable commodity in The Beck, not to be given away recklessly.

Faint sounds came from the direction of the Jefferson Building, and we turned as one to see the second group hurrying around the side, herded by a frustrated-looking Barnes. At the same time, Tyler came out of the front entrance of the Jefferson Building, her expression as she approached betraying the delight she felt at having her group back first and ready to begin training. Winning seemed so important here.

Tyler reached us just before Barnes and his group, and turned to watch them arrive, smirking slightly at Barnes as he ushered his group into place and faced her.

"Ready everyone?" Tyler cocked an eye at Barnes before continuing. "This afternoon we're going to do some physical training. See what you can do, give you a little idea of the kind of physical shape we expect our recruits to be in. If you thought you were fit in your previous Sectors, think again. Let's go."

She set off running into the woods. At first I thought she would return to the main Beck community, but once in the forest she took a path which led to the right and sloped even more steeply upwards to higher ground. She moved quickly, refusing to give us an easy ride to catch up or even keep abreast of her. Soon, she was far enough ahead to be difficult to follow. Barnes brought up the rear of the group, ensuring that the person in last place knew how slowly they were making him travel, and how much he resented it.

I tried to stay in the middle of the group. Instinct told me that, until I knew where I stood, I needed to avoid being noticed. Those who stood out at this point put themselves in a very risky position. Stand out for negative reasons and I suspected that Patrol would tolerate this even less than the Lower Beck Sectors. Stand out for positive reasons and risk being given a frightening amount of responsibility before having any real concept of what Patrol was all about.

Instead, I jogged in the centre of the group, aware of Jackson running alongside me. Mason and Davis were just ahead to my right. It looked like our group was beginning to bond already, aside from Anders at least. Group Two did not hang together in the same way, splitting into separate groups, including a pair who seemed engaged in furious competition to keep up with Tyler, and three stragglers who were bringing up the rear of the pack: Jackson's two Sustenance friends and a boy who I presumed had come from LS, although it was more difficult to tell now we all wore the same blue uniform. I wondered if the other group had been able to converse yet, exchange names at least, or whether Barnes had stuck so closely with them that this had been impossible.

I turned my attention to the front of the group again, just in time to see Tyler stop and wait for us all to catch up to her. We emerged at the edge of a clearing where the trees thinned out. The path appeared to stop at this point, and I wondered what form our physical training would take. Perhaps we would be asked to run back to Patrol base from here, and be timed to see who made it first. There was certainly no training equipment here. Nothing to lift, and no space for a running track or an assault course like the one in the Assessment Compound. I glanced up at the sky, grateful that the clear weather seemed to be holding.

In fact the clearing contained nothing but hard, bare ground where little grew. Rocks jutted out here and there, making the creation of a smooth track surface impossible. Although the trees in the forest itself were of an impressive height, here they seemed puny and stunted. The only impressive thing about this particular area of the wood was a cliff face which rose, sheer and steep, its outline stark and threatening against the grey skies of The Beck.

"Off you go then," Tyler said, her eyebrows raised.

Ten pairs of eyes stared at her, uncomprehending.

"Off you go."

She nodded towards the base of the cliff. I sensed every eye in the clearing turn towards its base and travel upwards, understanding slowly dawning on each face. Assessing the height, the smooth surface, the limited handholds. Considering the first task Patrol wanted us to undertake.

They didn't want us to run. They wanted us to climb.

Chapter Fourteen

There was a moment of silence while we all considered the undertaking. We were used to climbing during the Physical Assessments, but there were ropes to hold on to, handholds, and the obstacles were manmade. Here there was no support rope, no guidance as to the method we should use, no obvious route upwards. No one seemed willing to go first.

Barnes snorted with laughter before moving to the front of the group.

"Watch and repeat."

He leapt upwards and grasped a section of rock which jutted out a little above the level of his head. At the same time, his feet jammed into crevices which looked too small to hold them. From there he swung himself upwards, the muscles on his upper arms flexing with the effort. For a man so big built, he was extremely agile and climbed with surprising speed, reminding me of Cassidy. Harper had been right. She was a far more suitable candidate for Patrol than I was. I could climb, but she would probably have been the first on the cliff face and half way up it by now.

Barnes was now ten feet above us and still climbing. He glanced down and laughed at us.

"I'd get going – that is if you want to eat tonight."

I started forward at the same time as Mason. We hit the

cliff face together, him emulating Barnes' feet and handholds while I opted for an alternate set of crevices which my own feet would just about rest inside comfortably and for long enough, as long as I kept my climbing speed steady. Grinning at me, the LS boy swung upwards almost effortlessly, his upper body muscles clearly well developed from years of heavy work with livestock. He was looking on this as a race, I realised, and shook my head at him. There was no way I was beating him. I would be happy to simply get to the top without incident or injury. Climbing first was risky and went against my earlier strategy of staying unnoticed, but I knew if I didn't get on with it immediately I would find it difficult to begin at all.

To start with I felt fine, finding the right amount and size of handholds to ensure I made steady progress up the rock face. I heard some of the others below begin the climb and prayed desperately that I didn't lose my grip and fall backwards, taking out both myself and the recruit below. I didn't dare look down. My foot slipped from a particularly small crevice around half way up, and I found myself hanging by my hands. For a terrifying second, I thought I was going to fall. Jamming my foot back into a tiny crevice in the cliff face, I swallowed the pain. I could feel the sweat rolling down my back under the overalls as I regained my balance and continued to ascend.

I was aware of someone gaining on me at one point, coming up too close behind me, and I was about to shout back at them to cool it and back off when I heard their voice.

"Doing well newbie. Not bad at all for a puny little Agric. Glad you're in my group."

It was Tyler, who was climbing at a far faster rate than I was and had soon overtaken me. I appreciated the compliment, but not the off-putting way it was delivered, and wished that she had simply stayed at the foot of the cliff until we were all at the top. Showing off was unnecessary: the majority of us knew we were far inferior in strength to the experienced Patrol citizens. We didn't need to have our noses rubbed in it.

I continued to climb, hand over hand, refusing to glance either up or down. I tried to block everything else out and zone in to nothing but my own body, raising one limb at a time until I had reached the summit of the cliff. There above me were Barnes, Tyler and Mason, who had also managed to get far ahead of me. I was surprised to see Tyler reaching a hand down to help me the final foot, and raised an eyebrow at her quizzically.

"You've done the difficult part," she reassured me, "there's little to be gained by punishing you further. You attacked it, you managed the majority, and you didn't fall and break your neck. That's enough for now."

With that she hauled me up the last foot so suddenly that I found myself collapsed at her feet in a heap. Picking myself up with as much dignity as I could muster, I ignored Mason's triumphant grin and moved to sit with my back against a rock at the top. The view from here was incredible. I had never been so high up before. From here I could easily see the wall, and from there I located the canteen, the assessment buildings, the Agric greenhouses and the LS barns. They looked tiny, insignificant even. I felt a pang of homesickness for my old Sector.

As I waited for the rest to arrive, my gaze strayed back to the wall, and what was beyond it. The floodplains seemed to stretch into infinity. Even from this vantage point I could see nothing but water for miles. In the distance the sky was grey and dense fog clouded the horizon, so I couldn't be sure that there was nothing else out there, but it didn't look very hopeful. My mind returned to the present as I heard the grunts and huffing breath of the remaining recruits heaving themselves to the top of the cliff. I prayed that Jackson could make it, not wanting to lose a potential friend, but she surprised me by being the next to arrive at the top and accepted Mason's helping hand with good grace.

A moment after she had joined me leaning against the rock we heard a cry, followed by a dull thud. Pushing ourselves forwards, we glanced over the edge and looked down, trepidation filling our hearts. I found myself lightheaded as I contemplated the height of the cliff I had ascended without ropes or secure handholds. For a dizzying moment I felt myself tempted to lean further over the edge, but pulled back as I felt Jackson stifle a cry beside me. At the base of the cliff lay the Sustenance girl who had smiled at Jackson earlier, one of the ones who had been bringing up the rear on the way up here from the Patrol Compound. She was sitting up, but was nursing her ankle and groaning loudly.

"She didn't fall far, did she?" Tyler did not sound especially sympathetic.

"Nah. Which one is it?"

"Barnes, they're your group! Don't you even know their names?"

He shrugged, "Not yet. Not worth it if they're not going to last, is it?"

Of the recruits clambering up the cliff face, only three were not at the top yet. Two were half way up and seemed to be managing, although they looked pretty tired. One was Anders, our final group member. The other was Jackson's second Sustenance friend, who looked terrified at her team

116

mate's fall, but was continuing to inch her way up the cliff extremely slowly.

"Oi, you at the bottom! Get going! If you're not up here in the next three minutes we will be leaving. And I'm not sure you'll make it back to the Compound without us to show you the way. Even if you do, failing the first challenge means you won't last long either."

The girl at the base of the cliff stood up. She tested her right foot gingerly, wincing as it touched the floor. It was clearly injured in some way, although how severely it was difficult to tell from this distance. I considered her options. Attempt the wall with a sprained ankle. Stay where she was. Attempt to limp back to the Compound. None of them seemed very appealing. The other new recruits stayed silent, watching and waiting cautiously.

"Fin!"

"What?"

"Fin. That's her name. I've just remembered." Barnes looked proud.

"Well Fin had better get up here quickly, or there'll be no supper for her. Come to think of it, there'll be nothing for her."

I watched, desperately hoping that Fin would be able to gather the strength required to propel her body up the wall. I had no concept of what would happen if she didn't, but I was certain we didn't want to find out. Slowly, she stepped forward, placing her good foot into one of the larger crevices in the rock face and hooking her hands into some of the smaller ones. Managing to step up on to the cliff, she then found herself needing to put the weight on to her other foot, which was clearly painful. She waited a moment and assessed the next handhold she could grab on to once she had placed her weight on to the injured foot for a time. Her plan was clearly to rest on that foot for as short a time as possible, momentarily even, and then place the good foot on to its next stopping point fast so she would cause herself as little pain as possible.

She might manage it. But it all depended on how badly hurt her ankle was. The cliff was steep and had not been easy for someone without an injury. I watched, fascinated and horrified, as she managed to make some progress towards us, grimacing as she did so. Jackson let out a small sigh of relief at her friend's success. She did seem, miraculously, to be managing. I was momentarily distracted as Anders reached the top, and held out a hand to pull him the last few inches. He hesitated before taking hold of my arm and allowing me to help him, looking all the time as if he resented relying on anyone else.

As he scrambled up and over the edge, I heard another scream, and my gaze was once again drawn to the base of the cliff where Fin lay sprawled on her back. She looked totally defeated this time though, her ankle jutting out at a funny angle. I felt rather than heard Jackson's sharp intake of breath beside me.

"Well she isn't going to make it, is she?"

Tyler's question sounded more like a statement of the obvious. She moved to set off across the top of the cliff in a completely different direction. I realised as she did that the remaining Sustenance recruit from Barnes' group had managed to crawl up over the edge of the cliff. She lay there, clearly exhausted, her head buried in her arms as though she couldn't bear to look down at the base of the cliff.

Fin was now the only citizen who had not made it to the top. Glancing back down at her, I felt my insides twist horribly. Her face was white and she looked on the verge of passing out. I silently willed her to try again, knowing that it was useless. Harper had looked like that on a couple of occasions, and when she had, there was no moving her until she had rested and regained some strength.

Barnes peered over the cliff edge. He appeared less willing to leave the site, and I hoped he had a little more humanity and would give Fin a break, another chance. With a sprained ankle, she might have a chance of recovery. If it was broken though, she wouldn't last.

"Barnes, let's get on with this. I'm hungry."

"Think we should see if she can–"

Tyler's tone was matter of fact, "Look Barnes, she tried. She failed. She isn't getting up here, so let's get going."

"But–"

"But nothing. You know the rules. Face it, your group is one down already and there's nothing you can do but deal with it."

Barnes sighed and began to back away from the edge. He motioned to the others to get up and move off, despite the final few recruits to make it over the top still looking pretty shaky. I watched as Jackson and the other Sustenance girl exchanged a look of dread, both of them biting back tears.

"Move it then. There's still a couple of miles hiking before we get any dinner."

"Downhill this time though. We'll go easy on you."

I couldn't believe Tyler and Barnes planned to leave without Fin. The fall had not been her fault and now she was injured, in pain and we were going to abandon her. I spoke before I could stop myself.

"Shouldn't we–"

Tyler's eyes flashed, "What, newbie? Shouldn't we what?"

Everyone stared at me. I felt my face flush, and hesitated before continuing, "Well... try to help her, or something?"

I heard my voice trail off into nothingness. No one else seemed to want to challenge Tyler and Barnes, so I wasn't sure why I felt I should take them on, but I couldn't stand by and do nothing.

"Help her? Jeez, if she can't even make it up the cliff–" Barnes trailed off. "Better to find out now. She'll never make it in Patrol if she's weak."

"But–"

His tone became impatient, "Look, she's my group. I'd help her if I could. But seriously, there's nothing we can do. She's out."

"And speaking of being out, you're risking your own place right now," Tyler chimed in, although her voice warned rather than threatened, "Quin, isn't it?"

I nodded.

"Watch yourself."

Tyler turned away. I stared back down at the foot of the cliff again. Fin was now slumped against one of the trees, ashen-faced and eyes closed.

"They'll send someone to pick her up later. Now come on."

It was an order, and one coming from quite a distance away now. Looking up I realised that Tyler had set off walking and most of the others had followed her. Only Jackson and the other Sustenance girl hung back a little, their faces reflecting their horror. Eventually we heaved ourselves up from the ground and began to walk. I felt a hand squeezing mine gently as we set off. Jackson's face peered into mine, streaked with tears.

"Thank you," she mouthed, "for trying."

I tried to smile, but knew that I failed miserably. My mind was still focused on the girl lying alone, in pain, at the foot of the cliff face. I couldn't help but imagine her to be Harper, or Cass, and understood perfectly how Jackson was feeling. I was glad for now of my position at the rear of the group which, as I walked, hid my own furious tears from the rest.

Chapter Fifteen

We walked in silence for around an hour. No one felt like speaking, even if we had been permitted to. The atmosphere was tense, uncomfortable, Fin's absence keenly felt. Was Patrol going to be even worse than Agric? Although dreading the change, I had expected, hoped, that things might be a little better here. But in Agric, although unsympathetic to those with weakness or injury, the Supers would not have completely abandoned them.

The walk took us along a cliff path for a while, before diverting into a thick wooded area. Here the ground began to slope slightly downwards, and I gathered that we were making our way back to the Patrol Compound by a different route. The only noise was the wind in the trees, and the occasional hiss of Tyler's radio, which she mostly ignored. When we emerged from the trees and were within sight of the Jefferson Building she took it out. Her voice was low and I was a few people behind her, but I caught most of the words and her meaning was clear.

"Control... almost back. Only one down... yes... cliff base. Will need retrieval."

I had to stop myself from challenging her words. Retrieval? She made it sound like Fin was a piece of equipment. But I was already on thin ice as it was. My choice to climb the wall first. My arguing about leaving Fin behind. I couldn't afford to stand out, to be noticed, to become known as the one who was trouble.

The radio crackled in response.

"Which recruit?"

"Fin. Group Two. You'll need a stretcher."

"Right. Take… recruits straight… canteen… ten minutes ago."

"Understood."

Tyler stowed the radio and nodded to Barnes, "Canteen."

"About time. I'm starving."

I exchanged glances with Jackson, whose face still reflected her shock. On her other side, Mason and Davis were communicating silently using some kind of hand gestures, their expressions serious. A communication strategy formed in LS, no doubt. Most of the rest of the group looked utterly defeated, trudging onwards blindly. The incident with Fin had terrified us all.

Within a few minutes we had reached the central field we had first arrived in and headed immediately for the building I had rightly assumed was the canteen. Tyler and Barnes stopped at the door and we marched past them, entering the building where several rows of Patrol Officers were already eating. The room was not silent, like the Lower Beck canteen, but hummed with conversation, which surprised me. Clearly the rules about no communication were relaxed here, at least for meal times. I knew it would be a long time before I felt comfortable talking so openly.

As we marched towards the serving section, the conversations ceased, one by one, until there was a silence in the room. All eyes turned to our group. Clearly Patrol were curious about their new recruits, and I saw several actually counting how many were in our group, perhaps checking which of us had survived the initial challenge. We reached the serving hatches as one and formed a nervous queue behind a few established Patrol citizens. Slowly, the hum returned to the room again as the citizens lost interest in us.

I heaved a sigh of relief. I hated feeling like I was under scrutiny. It made me nervous. Turning my attention to the food on offer, I realised that despite my anger and fear over Fin's fate, I was very hungry. The citizens serving the food to us were not Sustenance staff, but instead wore the blue Patrol Uniform. I found myself surprised that Sustenance staff didn't work up here. Perhaps as Patrol staff we were required to take shifts in the canteen. The girl serving the food looked bored, but attempted a half smile at me, which made me feel a little better. It was stew, no surprise there, but the bowl I received contained almost twice the usual amount I would have received in Agric, and there was a hunk of bread to go with it too. Glancing sideways at Jackson I raised my eyebrows.

I moved away from the serving hatch and crossed to the station to collect a spoon. As I placed it on my tray, Mason caught up with me, keeping his voice low. "Different portion sizes. One of those Patrol advantages?"

He grabbed a spoon and turned away quickly, head down, moving towards the rear of the room where we had been assigned a table.

I followed him slowly, the idea sinking in. Larger portion sizes for Patrol. Perhaps here the work was judged to be more physical, more difficult. I thought of all the mounds of fertiliser I had lugged in wheelbarrows from one side of Agric to the other, of the drainage ditch I had helped to dig only the previous day. Was that work not considered physically challenging? I considered the amount of staff assigned to Agric: the highest population of all the Sectors, as far as I could tell.

Agric was thought of as one of the easiest Sectors, second only to Sustenance. Little skill was required, which was why so many Minors were assigned there at their Transfer Ceremony. But perhaps another reason there were so many Agric citizens was that we were easily replaced, as our job was fairly simple. They didn't need to feed us more than the bare minimum to sustain life. I considered the portion in front of me now, wondering if it would have been enough to sustain Harper better.

Again, I felt fury surge through me, and had to clamp my teeth down over my bottom lip to prevent myself from crying out with the injustice of it all. Instead, I sat down at the table next to Mason and focused on consuming every bit of the meal in front of me. Knowing I had to hide the fury emblazoned on my face, I kept my head bent low over my plate.

Once the meal was over, we were guided back into the Jefferson Building through a side entrance, and gathered together in a larger meeting room. Evening was approaching, and the light in the courtyard outside was fading fast. Tyler and Barnes stayed with us, instructing us to sit down on the low benches provided and wait. Eventually the door to the meeting room opened and a tall man strode into the room. He wore a Patrol Uniform but had on a Director's armband and was clearly important. He was taller than average, broadly built, and rather than the usual buzz-cut, his head was completely bald. He spoke quietly to Tyler and

Barnes before addressing us as a group.

"Good evening and welcome to Patrol. I am Director Reed and I'm in overall charge of the entire Sector. As I am sure you have all gathered, your first week here is about showing us you are strong enough to be a member of Patrol. Many of the jobs we do here are difficult and distressing, so you will need to develop both strong muscles and an iron control over your emotions. Tyler informs me that she has witnessed both physical and emotional weakness today. These must be overcome in order to be a successful Patrol citizen."

He stared around the room, his eyes dark and serious. The words he spoke were harsh, but his tone somewhat softened them and seemed to say that the measures taken here were necessary for The Beck survival. I wanted to believe him, to feel like I understood how difficult it was for him to make the decisions he took daily, but the abandonment of Fin just seemed too cruel.

"Today we lost our first recruit. She fell at the first hurdle, but it is better she find out now that she isn't a suitable candidate for Patrol than later. Let me reassure you that Fin is being brought back here as we speak."

A collective sigh of relief ran around the room. Perhaps they weren't as harsh as they had seemed then. Perhaps Fin would be given a second chance.

"She will stay the night in the Annexe with you, as it is too late to move her tonight, but tomorrow morning she will be transferred."

My heart sank a little, but I still had hope that Fin might be sent back to Sustenance.

"Tomorrow you will begin the second day of your training here and Fin will be taken to Clearance. Let her reassignment be a message to you, of the absolute necessity of keeping up with the programme, of completing each challenge to the best of your ability so that you can be the best Patrol Officer possible. Otherwise—"

He trailed off purposefully and I hated him again. He had a reasonable voice, one which sounded like he was talking sense, giving us a fair chance, but his words told a different story. Do as you're told. Pass the tests, or you're out. I stared down at the floor, horrified at the new world I had entered, which seemed worse than the one I had inhabited before.

"There are advantages to being in Patrol though, and I am sure that you are beginning to discover them. For now I will bid you goodnight. I look forward to meeting you again and witnessing you developing into the kind of Patrol Officers we are immensely proud of here."

He nodded at Tyler and Barnes, turned on his heel, and was out of the door before anyone could react. My eyes were drawn back to the window just to avoid meeting anyone else's gaze before I could gather my emotions and get them under control. There was movement outside in the courtyard, a stretcher being carried by two Patrol Officers who looked to be the strong and healthy type that Reed had just mentioned.

On the stretcher was Fin, looking the complete opposite. I watched, feeling wretched, as they carried her across the back of the building towards the Annexe, her face pale and drawn in the half light. It was only as they passed me by that I registered the second stretcher bearer was Cameron.

Chapter Sixteen

After Reed's pep talk we were ushered out through the building and sent into the Annexe. It was completely dark now, and Tyler advised us to get plenty of sleep, as we would need our rest for tomorrow's training. I couldn't work her out. On the one hand her harsh attitude towards Fin had really bothered me, but she also seemed to genuinely care about getting us through the training and avoiding any more of us being sent to Clearance. I wondered if her own performance was judged on how many recruits she managed to get through the training period.

After she left the Annexe, we got ready for bed in silence. Mason and Davis continued to communicate, signalling occasionally to one another with their hands, but they didn't try and speak to any of the rest of us again. After Fin, we felt vulnerable. We didn't know the rules here yet and we had witnessed the severity of the reckonings dealt out by Patrol. It was vital to work out who we could really trust. Mason was lucky to already have an ally in Davis, and clearly didn't feel as alone as the rest of us. Before he climbed into his bunk however, Mason glanced across at Jackson and I, smiling slightly. He looked exhausted, and the smile was filled with sadness, but I appreciated the attempt to make a connection and perhaps comfort us.

We were all very aware of Fin, who had been left on her bunk before we had returned to the Annexe. She lay there, pale and limp, moaning slightly from time to time. Her bed was close to mine, and as I returned from washing at the small basin at the side of the room, I could see her ankle was badly swollen. Her eyes were closed and she seemed to be trying to ignore the rest of us and block out what was going on around her.

As we all began to settle in our bunks for the night, her groans of pain grew in volume and I wondered why they had placed her back among us. I was torn between a feeling of sympathy and a desperate need to sleep and recover my strength for tomorrow's challenge. It seemed to me that Patrol was risking the successful training of the rest of their recruits by leaving her in the Annexe all night where she would obviously keep us awake. Unless her presence was a warning to further terrify us all.

After changing out of her overalls, Jackson crept closer to Fin's bed and sat with her. She began to whisper in her ear, presumably soothing words aimed at taking her mind off the pain. I tried not to imagine how I would be feeling if the girl in the bed was Harper. I knew I would have wanted to offer comfort too. In contrast, the other Sustenance recruit remained in her bunk, perhaps afraid to risk her own chances. Jackson's face reflected a determination which masked the pain she must have been feeling. She settled herself more comfortably and held her fellow Sustenance colleague's hand, humming a low, sweet melody and smiling slightly whenever Fin opened her eyes. Eventually her moans seemed to ease a little, and I could feel the recruits around me relaxing slightly as the atmosphere in the room became quieter.

After a while of lying there trying to sleep, finding it increasingly difficult to ignore the fact that someone was in an intense amount of pain not two feet from my bed, I took action. Climbing down from my bunk, I edged closer to Jackson. I figured I could risk a quiet conversation without anyone noticing. Crouching by her side, I leaned into her so she knew I was there and wasn't startled. She smiled as she noticed me.

"Know her well?" I kept my voice at a whisper.

She shrugged, "She's younger than me so I didn't know her in Minors. But since she came to Sustenance…" Her voice trailed off.

"You need to get some sleep."

"But she's in pain. I can't let her lie here in agony all night. Alone."

"But you're risking your own chances." I hesitated, "I know it sounds callous, but… if you sit up with her all night you'll be too tired tomorrow to get through training. Who knows what they have planned?"

"I know, but she's in so much pain. She'll probably pass out soon. I'll sleep then."

"You don't want to join her in Clearance though – do you?"

She turned away and I knew I had gone too far. I backed off, shaking my head a little. There was only so much I could do to persuade her to rest. I didn't know why it was so important to me, but she was nice and I didn't want to lose an ally when Patrol was still so new to me. Fin had no chance now, but Jackson had done well today and I found myself wanting to make sure she survived the whole training process now that she was becoming a potential friend.

Not wanting to abandon her, I lay down on the lower bunk

for now, watching as she continued to soothe Fin. I had just begun to drop off to sleep when I heard something. Opening my eyes slightly, I watched as the Annexe door swung open and a figure approached. Jackson was too busy tending to Fin to notice the stranger. I looked for a way to warn her but it was too late. The figure reached Fin's bed and bent down beside her, his back to me.

She jerked back rapidly as she became aware that she was not alone, but the newcomer placed a gentle hand on her arm. I watched out of one eye as he reached into his pocket and brought something out. He showed it to Jackson, whose eyes widened. She began to push his hand away, protesting silently at whatever it contained. He leaned towards her and whispered something I couldn't hear. She stared into his eyes for a long time before nodding slightly and moving further backwards down the bed.

The man, who I could now see was a Patrol Super, helped to support Fin slightly and brought her to a sitting position. As he did so, he turned slightly and I recognised Cameron. He murmured something into Fin's ear and I could see her stiffen slightly for a moment, but then relax and nod. With both eyes wide open now, I witnessed him place whatever was in his hand into Fin's mouth. After that he brought a flask from his pocket and assisted Fin with drinking some of the liquid contained inside it. Then he lowered her back down on to the bed.

He murmured something further into Jackson's ear before backing away and heading out towards the door of the Annexe, his movements stealthy and sure. I was pretty certain that everyone else was asleep now, and as Cameron headed out of the door, something made me follow. I moved through the room quickly, but as I stepped on to the porch of the Annexe, Cameron had already crossed the courtyard and was heading into the Jefferson Building. I knew I had to reach him before he went inside.

"Hey!"

He froze for a moment and then turned slowly, a look of horror crossing his features as he recognised me. He retraced his steps across the courtyard and, grasping my arm so hard it hurt, he guided me around the side of the Annexe.

"What! Ow!"

"Sssh!"

Only when we were hidden out of sight of all other buildings did he let go of me. I rubbed my arm gingerly, shooting an accusing look at him which he returned just as harshly.

"What do you think you're doing? Do you think this is a game?"

"What did you just do to Fin?"

"What?" He looked confused for a moment. "Oh – I gave her a pill – it'll kill the pain, that's all. Only I'm not supposed to…" anger flashed in his chestnut-coloured eyes, "to *waste* it on her. So no one can know I was here."

I took a step backwards, momentarily stunned by the information. He continued.

"Do you know what happens if I'm caught here? With you? If you are caught out of bed? This isn't a joke. They're serious. Fin has no chance now – she'll be off to Clearance in the morning and by the look of her ankle…" He trailed off.

"What?"

"Well let's just say it doesn't look good. And you-following me out here! Shouting at me right outside the Jefferson Building, which is guarded day and night by the way!" He glared at me, "You're taking a huge risk."

"I didn't shout."

"Well it was loud enough. I only hope nobody heard you." He backed away slowly, staring at me as he did, "You're trouble, aren't you?"

I started towards him, my hand held out to stop him leaving. "I just wanted to say—"

"Never mind. Get back to bed. Now. Before anyone sees you."

"But I should've told you last night."

"Told me what?"

"That I was being transferred. To Patrol."

He shook his head, relaxing slightly. "Seems you had enough on your mind with your friend going to Clearance."

"Thank you."

"For what?"

"For this. For helping us last night. For helping Fin." I stammered a little, not knowing how to convey the strength of my feeling, "If I can help you at all…"

He shrugged, "Get back to bed. Don't get caught."

He stared at me for a moment longer. Then he backed away. "Give me a minute. Let me get inside before you come back round."

I nodded slightly, watching him retreating into the darkness. A second later he was gone. Creeping back around the building, I checked that the courtyard was empty before sneaking back on to the porch and through the Annexe door. The room was quiet when I got inside, and I could hear nothing more than the steady breathing of sleepers. When I reached my bunk though, Jackson was still awake. She looked at me quizzically.

"I went to…to see what he did to Fin."

She looked doubtful, "You could have waited in here. I'd have told you that."

I looked across at Fin's bed. She was sleeping now, still white and clammy, but looking more peaceful.

"Did she…?"

"Passed out a couple of minutes after you left. That guy – the Patrol guy – he gave her some kind of pill to help with the pain. I don't think he was supposed to."

"No, he wasn't." I hesitated. "For a moment there I thought that he was giving her something to–"

Jackson cut me off, "Me too. I thought they had decided that sending her to Clearance was a waste of time, and that the pills would…well, you know…"

"Finish her off?"

"Well yes. Like we would find her in the morning and they'd say 'she died of her injuries in the night'."

"But he wasn't."

"No."

We sat in silence for a moment before Jackson spoke again.

"I guess not all Patrol Officers follow the rules."

"No. But that's how it was in Agric. Some citizens were kind… helpful, and others well… weren't. Was Sustenance like that too?"

She nodded.

"At least the pills have stopped the pain for now. We should try and get some sleep. Whatever they have planned for tomorrow isn't going to be easy."

She shook her head, more slowly now. Her eyes were drooping shut as I spoke to her. I realised how late it was and how much we needed to sleep. I needed to take my own advice. Hauling myself to my feet, I clambered up the ladder into the bunk above. I thought I would have trouble sleeping, but within minutes I felt my eyes closing. I drifted into a sleep filled with images of sheer cliff faces, Fin's ankle swollen to ridiculous proportions, and a pair of troubled chestnut eyes.

Chapter Seventeen

When I woke I felt disorientated for several minutes. The Annexe had small, high windows and the room was darker than the pod I was used to, its tarpaulin only muting the daylight. For a moment I thought I had overslept. There were noises around me, but I realised they were soft ones, people waking, stretching, shifting in their bunks as they woke and began to face the day. Rolling on to my side, I peered down at Fin's bed.

It was empty.

"She's gone."

Jackson's face came into view beneath me. She was red eyed and pale.

"Did I sleep through it?"

"We all did. I think they came in the middle of the night. She was gone when I woke up and I've been awake for around an hour I think."

I glanced around the room. No one else seemed to be properly up yet, but Fin's bed was stripped of all blankets and her meagre bag of belongings was gone.

"I'm so sorry."

Jackson shrugged and disappeared into her bunk underneath me.

"Nothing we can do about it now."

She had hidden her face from view, but her voice cracked even as she spoke the words. I found I had no way to comfort her, no words which might help to ease her pain and fear. I slid down from my bed and sat on hers. Her body was turned towards the wall, her back to me. I squeezed her shoulder gently, the only part of her which was accessible to me. My only clue that she didn't reject my comfort was the fact that she didn't shrug my arm away.

A shadow fell across the bed, and for a moment I thought that Cameron might have returned, but when I looked up it was Mason standing there, looking concerned. Silence stretched between us. None of us were used to conversing easily.

"Did you know her well?"

Keeping her back to us, Jackson managed a slight nod.

"I'm sorry."

Slowly, she turned towards us. She was pale and her eyes were red rimmed.

"I just can't believe how fast they– it's terrifying. One tiny slip and… you're out."

"Well we'll just have to make sure not to give them an excuse, won't we?"

There was definitely a little of the rebel in Mason, although his words were clearly meant to comfort. I personally shared Jackson's fear, and privately vowed to try and keep my head down and stay under the radar.

The Annexe door banged open, preventing the conversation from continuing and announcing the arrival of Tyler and Barnes. They strode to the centre of the room, looking far more ready for a second day of training than we were.

"Canteen. Five minutes. Work boots and overalls. As soon

as you've eaten you'll head straight to training."

As they left, the room became a sudden flurry of activity, a mixture of fear and ambition driving us to perform better today. To be more prepared. To be less naïve about the consequences of failure. Mason shot back to his bed, where Davis was waiting. Jackson shoved me away, though not unkindly, so that she could access her kit bag. I climbed back up to my bunk to find the necessary equipment for the day ahead, feeling somewhat comforted that I had made a couple of tentative friendships. I desperately hoped that Jackson's feelings about Fin were not going to hold her back from giving the training her full concentration.

Within minutes we were heading out of the door. This time when we reached the canteen, there were only a few curious glances and no deafening silence as we entered. More keyed into how things worked here now, we grabbed trays and collected our allocated ration. I noted that the porridge supply was also more plentiful than it would have been in Agric, and there was even some fruit to go alongside it. Fruit I knew had been painstakingly tended in the Agric greenhouses, yet was rarely eaten by the Agric citizens themselves. I felt a stab of guilt as I imagined Cass sitting down to her usual meagre ration, but as I swallowed my porridge I realised just how hungry I was. I needed this fuel to get me through the day. I vowed that once I was settled and had managed to build my strength up, I would make it back to Agric and somehow sneak her some extra rations.

After breakfast we were ushered out of the canteen and towards the field. Once the nine of us were there, Tyler motioned to us to follow her, and set off into the woods again. At first I thought she was heading back towards the cliff from the previous day. I felt Jackson stiffen next to me and shared her feeling of dread. None of us wanted to revisit the scene of Fin's downfall just yet. But again we took a different path. I was beginning to think that there were so many paths through the woods that I would never find my way around Patrol. It was so much larger than the area the Agric citizens occupied, and I realised that, with such a narrow frame of reference, anyone brought up in the Lower Beck area would feel lost coming up here to Patrol.

The path meandered through the trees, here and there widening and narrowing. We had to step over several large tree roots and in places the forest was quite dense, but eventually the foliage thinned out and Tyler led us into a large clearing. The cloud cover wasn't as thick as usual today and pale shafts of sunlight pierced through the usual gloom. After the darkness of the woods we came out into the space blinking, and it took my eyes several moments to adjust. When they did, I almost wished that they hadn't.

Standing with Barnes and Tyler was a now familiar face. The three of them stood talking quietly for some minutes before Tyler spoke.

"This is Cameron. He'll be responsible for training you today, instructing you in the use of the first weapons you will be permitted to carry here in Patrol. Cam is one of our weapons experts, aren't you?"

Tyler's voice changed completely when she was in Cameron's presence. She clearly regarded him in a different way than Barnes, who she had no trouble taking charge of. Dragging her gaze away from him, she turned her eyes to us, her voice commanding now. "Come on then, move in. This is only the first of two training sessions today. We need to get started."

The group managed to shuffle into the clearing fully and stood to one side. Cameron was dressed in the same Patrol overalls, but had them pulled down and tied around his waist. He looked warm, even in the regulation vest he was wearing underneath, and I wondered if he had been working in the woods for a while. He had yet to speak, but his face was set, serious and betrayed nothing. Stepping forward, he picked up a sack and tipped it up. With a clatter, a number of metal objects fell from the bag.

Knives. Wooden handled, with slim blades, they looked primitive but were clearly sharp and ready for action. Without speaking, Cameron motioned to us and then to the pile. Mason was the first to step forward and select a weapon. He was swiftly followed by Davis. The rest of us began to move towards the pile, comprehending what we were required to do. Anders surprised me by being the next one to collect a weapon, then Jackson. The other team hastened forward, clearly eager not to be left until last.

I found myself at the rear of the queue for weapons, still wary of Cameron and how he might react to my presence. So far he hadn't even glanced in my direction. Today he was more prepared, I realised. He had expected to see me and been able to react accordingly. Today it was him with the element of surprise on his side, and after last night's conversation I had no idea what to expect.

Realising that the recruit in front of me had moved aside, I bent down to collect a knife, only to find that there weren't any left. Confused, I glanced at the other recruits, all of whom held a weapon in their hands. Looking at Cameron, I thought for a moment I saw a ghost of a grimace shift across his features, but a moment later it was gone. He smiled, a slightly twisted smile, and finally spoke.

"Too bad newbie. You missed out."

I wondered in panic what this might mean for me. Was this a test in itself? A competition to force us to understand the value of speed? If I had missed out on gaining my weapon, what did that mean for me? Glancing at Jackson, I saw that her face was stricken and that she too feared the worst. After what had happened to Fin, was this test one of survival, where the one without a weapon would be hunted, defenceless?

For a moment I daren't speak. Turning to Barnes and Tyler, I tried to gauge their expressions. Barnes was smirking, no doubt thrilled that one of Tyler's team was at risk today. Tyler looked more resolute, for now simply nodding to me and angling her head towards Cameron. She wanted me to listen to him for now and learn from what he was presumably going to teach us all.

Cameron was currently sharpening a knife he had taken from a belt around his waist. He did it slowly and methodically, refusing to rush anything. The tension in the clearing grew with every moment we waited. As far as I knew, this was the first time any of us had held any kind of weapon. Certainly in Agric we had no access to them. Even the Supers only had a cane. They had to use this or their hands or improvise, hence the incident with Grady and the cattle prod.

Davis and Mason looked excited. Anders' face had a kind of calm expression I hadn't seen before. I actually knew very little about Dev. Maybe he had handled weapons. He certainly didn't look uncomfortable holding the knife. Jackson also seemed comfortable, and I realised that in her role in Sustenance she would be used to handling knives.

The others in the group had varying expressions of fear and excitement on their faces. I wondered how mine looked.

Cameron turned towards us and pointed at a thick fallen tree trunk, laid out across the ground at the opposite side of the glade. I hadn't noticed it previously, but upon closer inspection it had a number of marks chiselled into it by some kind of knife or axe. As we studied the log there was a faint whistling sound in the air and a deep 'thunk' which startled us. One of the marks now had a knife lodged firmly in it. Turning back to Cameron, I noted that his hands were now empty. Finally, he spoke again.

"This morning, you will learn to handle a knife. By the end of the session, you need to show me that you can throw it with accuracy and enough force to make the blade stay in that log over there from a range of angles. You will throw on my call only. You will collect your knives on my second call. That's it."

I found him staring at me with a strange expression in his eyes as he finished his speech. Knowing I had to deal with my current defenceless status, I took a deep breath and met his gaze.

"And if we don't have a knife?"

"The purpose of the exercise with collecting your weapons was to demonstrate the need for speed and quick reflexes. If this was a real situation, you would now find yourself without protection of any kind."

"I realise that."

I waited, wondering for a moment whether he would state that I was to become an additional target for the others to practise on. He said nothing. Walking over to the log, he bent down and retrieved his knife, the muscles in his arms flexing with the effort of pulling the weapon from where it was lodged deep in the wood. Turning around, he angled the knife again, this time towards me. Taking aim, he looked as though he was going to throw it directly at me, and watching his previous shot I had no doubt at all that he would hit his mark. Tensing, I planted my feet firmly on the ground and refused to flinch.

The air was still and heavy for a moment as he eyeballed me, a look of anger in his eyes. Then he strode towards me and offered me the knife, handle towards me.

"Use this for now. But it's mine. Look after it."

I reached out and took the weapon from him, the skin of my cool hand brushing against his. He flinched slightly, as though my touch had burned him.

"Ok. Barnes' group first. There are five marks on the log, but of course your group will only need four." His statement was factual and he didn't seem to take any pleasure in Fin's absence. "Line up and aim at one mark each to begin with. Take your time and consider your target. Tyler's group, line up behind them."

We shuffled into place, eager to impress with our second task. I lined up behind another of the boys from LS and waited, Cam's knife clutched in my shaking hand. I wondered how poor my aim would be if I couldn't stop it from trembling.

Motioning to Tyler and Barnes to move back out of range, Cameron spoke again.

"On my first call 'Fire', you will throw your weapons. Do not go and get them until you hear my second call, 'Retrieve'. Got it?"

He glanced around at the group, refusing to meet my gaze again. Checking that everyone was ready and no one was standing in the firing range, he directed his gaze at the tree trunk, waiting to assess our efforts.

"Ok. Fire."

move on."

This time I was first to the box, tucking Cameron's knife away in my belt as I went. I didn't want to fail the speed test a second time. It contained a small, flat bread roll for each of us and an apple. In Agric we had never been provided with any kind of food in the middle of the day, we had always had to last the distance between breakfast and dinner time without sustenance. The unfairness of the system hit me again, as I thought of Cass, and then of Harper. If ration levels were so different between Patrol and Agric, what were they like in Clearance?

Despite my anger, I sat down and ate the roll. It was a little sweet in flavour, although quite hard. I wondered as I went on to eat the apple if it was one which Cass had picked, and then remembered that her Super position probably meant she did little in the way of actual harvesting these days. I was glad of the company when Jackson came and sat beside me. We ate in companionable silence.

The atmosphere around me was almost relaxed. Most of the new recruits were still silent, but Barnes, Tyler and Cameron conversed in low tones, smiling and even laughing at different points. Tyler turned and caught me staring at them. At first her expression was curious, but then an understanding dawned on her and she pushed herself to her feet. For a moment I thought she was coming over to discipline me, but instead she faced the whole group.

I think another thing you all need to understand about [Pat]rol is the permitted level of communication. You are all [use]d to the strict rules about communication in your previous [sec]tors and will no doubt be wondering about the Patrol [citiz]ens' ability to speak fairly freely."

Chapter Eighteen

We spent the entire morning aiming and throwing our knives. To begin with, the majority of us could not make them stick in the wood, let alone hit a target, but by the end of the session most of us were managing to flick the knives with enough force to wedge them into the trunk of the tree somewhere close to our mark.

I actually found myself enjoying the training. The woods were cool but it wasn't raining and Cameron turned out to be a fair and effective instructor. He let us throw the knives with no instruction to begin with, but once it was clear that some of us were struggling, he worked with each recruit in turn, advising quietly about technique, aim, the strength required to make the blade travel the distance and stick in the log. It was clear he did not want anyone to fail his session, and Tyler and Barnes subconsciously echoed his positive behaviour, watching us all closely but not interrupting and even occasionally offering words of encouragement.

I was last in line, having been the one to miss getting a weapon in the first place. Cameron spent a long time with Jackson, who was standing next to me. Despite standing very close by, he was so softly spoken that I couldn't hear a word of what he was saying to her. I noticed that she seemed to like him though, and saw her smiling in a way I had not witnessed since having met her.

Waiting for him to approach me was hell. I had no idea what he would do, and considered every possibility, from him totally humiliating me to refusing to work with me at all. I tried to distract myself, concentrating on delivering the best throws I could and hoping that he wouldn't need to work with me at all if I proved myself to be good enough. I had gone from being a stranger in Agric who he was kind enough to help, to a fellow citizen who stuck her nose into other people's business. Not someone he wanted around.

As I waited for the LS boy in front of me to retrieve his knife, I tried to focus and empty my mind of any worries. I had managed to get Cameron's knife wedged into the wood twice now, but not close enough to the target to make me happy with my progress. Cameron had given no indication of the result of the morning's training, how we might pass or fail it, but so far he had not made any suggestion that recruits would be thrown out. Not yet anyway.

My turn came and I stood still, my mind drilling into the exact spot on the log which I knew I needed to hit. My arm strained, poised ready to throw, when I felt a breath very close against my ear. Startled, I tried not to jump away.

"Close your left eye."

I turned and found myself staring directly into his eyes, inches from his face. Something inside my stomach jolted and I had to fight every instinct to remain still. His expression changed and he broke his eye contact with me, looking instead at the target marked on the tree trunk ahead. With a deep breath, I faced forward and did as he suggested. Only then did I feel him move away slightly.

"Fire."

As the command left his mouth I lanced the knife towards the tree trunk, my left eye tightly closed. I heard the 'thunk' and knew it had held its position, but upon closer inspection I could see that, by taking Cam's advice, I had actually hit my mark. A broad grin spread across my face as I turned to look at him again, but he was already heading back towards the other Supers. My triumph unrecognised, the smile died quickly as it had arrived.

After several hours of practise, Cameron held up his hand for us to stop. The clearing had been quiet, other than the subtle 'thunk' of knives hitting wood, and our shuffling steps as we collected the weapons, but now it fell completely silent. I realised how much respect Cameron commanded. Respect that had been earned in a single morning, simply teaching us fairly. It was a far cry from the type of respect were forced into for leaders like Governor Adams and like Grady, and reminded me more of the way I had felt about Riley.

"You've all worked hard this morning," Cameron said, "and I'm happy to tell you that you'll all be progressing to this afternoon's training. Be aware though, that this was a preliminary session and you will not become proficient with knives until you have practised with them… in more realistic situations. Throwing a knife is not done under pressure. Using a knife on another human being is not the same as throwing it at a tree. Remember that."

He nodded, and motioned to Tyler to take a step forwards, she pointed to a box which had been put on the ground at some point during the training, carried in by Barnes while we had been working on our throws. "Take one each. You have thirty minutes."

She shared a wry grin with her two fellow Supers.

"We were all surprised by it when we arrived. The chatter in the canteen, the conversations between citizens in the pods and during their working day. I know it seems alien, but it's one of the huge advantages to living here. We've told you that there are benefits to being here in Patrol. Well, the ability to talk to other citizens is one of the major advantages of life here."

She stopped, and looked around at us as we took in the information. There were looks of surprise on most faces. We had all realised that citizens of Patrol were able to speak to one another, but were still wary of engaging in speech ourselves. We waited for Tyler to continue.

"So, here it is. While you are out of the Patrol Compound, you can only speak where it is necessary and talk should be kept to a minimum: giving or clarifying orders and so on. But here in the Compound, once you are a fully-fledged citizen, you are free, within reason, to speak to one another. Whilst your training is taking place I would avoid it, but once you pass, well, go for it. Obviously not in meetings or sessions with more senior members of the community. Then, you should only speak when spoken to. And it goes without saying on Assessment days or times when you are in the presence of the Governor or senior Governance members you don't speak. But as long as you understand that, you are not going to receive a reckoning for talking to one another." She glanced around to see how we had taken the news before continuing, "Ok, five more minutes and then we need to hike out to the upper fields."

She sat back down and resumed her quiet conversation with Cameron. I felt a small bubble of excitement rise up in my chest. The thought of being able to speak to those around me without hiding it, with no fear of reprisal, was wonderful. But it was also terrifying. I had been so used to having to limit my conversations to only those which were absolutely necessary that I wasn't sure what I would talk about when I had all the words in the world available to me and little limit on how I used them. Would I have enough to say?

I comforted myself with the thought that I wouldn't be needing to speak very much until I had passed the training. First things first. I wondered what was contained in the upper fields and what our afternoon training would require of us. Coming from Agric, I was happy with fields, well used to them, but what we would do in them was another matter.

The food eaten and flasks of water passed around for us all to drink, we stood and stretched our legs as Barnes got to his feet.

"Pack up the box." He nodded to Jackson, who obliged. "Cam, you alright to take it back to base?"

Cameron nodded.

"Ok. Let's go."

He set off into the woods again at quite a pace. He was so competitive, always trying to prove something, even in between training sessions. I wondered whether he was trying to prepare us for a tough life in Patrol, or was perhaps simply someone who got off on making others uncomfortable. Either way, I wasn't sure I liked Barnes.

"I'll catch you up," Tyler called to him as he exited the clearing.

I ended up close to the rear of the group, marching quietly but not unhappily in front of Jackson and behind Davis. He didn't seem at all tired, his movements were strong and powerful, but watching him I realised that I also felt quite refreshed. The food and rest had clearly done us all some good physically, but also mentally. I couldn't quite believe how revived I felt from the consumption of the bread and fruit. As I picked up the pace a little, I felt something banging against my side.

The knife.

With a groan I realised that I still had the weapon tucked into my belt. Not only had I removed it from the equipment bag and the training area, I had also taken the knife belonging to the instructor himself. Heat flooded my body as I realised that I would have to admit my mistake and fix it. The thought of returning to Cameron with the knife sent a shudder through me. One of dread, but also, strangely, excitement. I called ahead.

"Barnes! Barnes?"

I could only just see him at the front of the line, disappearing into a thick copse of trees. He heard me though, and stopped immediately. The LS boy behind him almost collided with him. Turning quickly, he moved his accusing eyes down the line, trying to work out who had dared to stop him.

Taking a deep breath I stepped out of line and held the knife aloft.

"Sorry. So sorry. I forgot to return this."

Barnes glared at me for a moment, then broke into a strange smile, "Well you'd better take it back, hadn't you?"

I turned, ready to head back in the direction we had come from, hardly believing the lack of chastisement. At the last moment I glanced back at Barnes who was still watching me. Finally, it dawned on me why he was smiling.

"Will you wait?"

He shook his head, "Nope. No time. If you're lucky you can catch us up, or maybe Tyler will still be there."

He set off at the same rapid pace, this time not glancing back. Jackson widened her eyes at me, clearly concerned, but there was little she could do. With a small shrug and a helpless look, she too set off after the rest of the group. I was left with no option but to continue back to the clearing.

I considered the route back and the length of time we had been walking. It was probably less than five minutes back to the training ground. If I ran, I might make it in less. Trying not to think about how I would possibly find them again when I had no idea where they were going, I began to sprint in the opposite direction.

Luckily the path we had taken had so far been clear and fairly straight. I found the entrance leading into the clearing quite quickly and slowed down to consider how I could best approach Cameron and Tyler. I had not passed her, so assumed she was still here. I was hoping, given the fairly friendly way she had treated us all this morning, that she would agree to guide me back to the others. I didn't have another plan if she refused.

The space appeared empty as I approached, yet the bag of knives and empty box of food still lay on the ground. Puzzled as to why they were not there, and unable to hear voices, I stopped before I entered the clearing and looked around. A slight rustling put me on edge, and I ducked behind a tree. Then I spotted them. They were partially hidden in a thick copse of trees. They stood strangely close together, and for a moment I was confused, unable to work out where Cameron ended and Tyler began.

Then I realised that they were somehow wrapped around

Chapter Eighteen

We spent the entire morning aiming and throwing our knives. To begin with, the majority of us could not make them stick in the wood, let alone hit a target, but by the end of the session most of us were managing to flick the knives with enough force to wedge them into the trunk of the tree somewhere close to our mark.

I actually found myself enjoying the training. The woods were cool but it wasn't raining and Cameron turned out to be a fair and effective instructor. He let us throw the knives with no instruction to begin with, but once it was clear that some of us were struggling, he worked with each recruit in turn, advising quietly about technique, aim, the strength required to make the blade travel the distance and stick in the log. It was clear he did not want anyone to fail his session, and Tyler and Barnes subconsciously echoed his positive behaviour, watching us all closely but not interrupting and even occasionally offering words of encouragement.

I was last in line, having been the one to miss getting a weapon in the first place. Cameron spent a long time with Jackson, who was standing next to me. Despite standing very close by, he was so softly spoken that I couldn't hear a word of what he was saying to her. I noticed that she seemed to like him though, and saw her smiling in a way I had not witnessed since having met her.

Waiting for him to approach me was hell. I had no idea what he would do, and considered every possibility, from him totally humiliating me to refusing to work with me at all. I tried to distract myself, concentrating on delivering the best throws I could and hoping that he wouldn't need to work with me at all if I proved myself to be good enough. I had gone from being a stranger in Agric who he was kind enough to help, to a fellow citizen who stuck her nose into other people's business. Not someone he wanted around.

As I waited for the LS boy in front of me to retrieve his knife, I tried to focus and empty my mind of any worries. I had managed to get Cameron's knife wedged into the wood twice now, but not close enough to the target to make me happy with my progress. Cameron had given no indication of the result of the morning's training, how we might pass or fail it, but so far he had not made any suggestion that recruits would be thrown out. Not yet anyway.

My turn came and I stood still, my mind drilling into the exact spot on the log which I knew I needed to hit. My arm strained, poised ready to throw, when I felt a breath very close against my ear. Startled, I tried not to jump away.

"Close your left eye."

I turned and found myself staring directly into his eyes, inches from his face. Something inside my stomach jolted and I had to fight every instinct to remain still. His expression changed and he broke his eye contact with me, looking instead at the target marked on the tree trunk ahead. With a deep breath, I faced forward and did as he suggested. Only then did I feel him move away slightly.

"Fire."

As the command left his mouth I lanced the knife towards the tree trunk, my left eye tightly closed. I heard the 'thunk' and knew it had held its position, but upon closer inspection I could see that, by taking Cam's advice, I had actually hit my mark. A broad grin spread across my face as I turned to look at him again, but he was already heading back towards the other Supers. My triumph unrecognised, the smile died as quickly as it had arrived.

After several hours of practise, Cameron held up his hand for us to stop. The clearing had been quiet, other than the subtle 'thunk' of knives hitting wood, and our shuffling foot-steps as we collected the weapons, but now it fell completely silent. I realised how much respect Cameron commanded. Respect that had been earned in a single morning, simply by teaching us fairly. It was a far cry from the type of respect we were forced into for leaders like Governor Adams and Supers like Grady, and reminded me more of the way I had always felt about Riley.

"You've all worked hard this morning," Cameron began, "and I'm happy to tell you that you'll all be progressing to this afternoon's training. Be aware though, that this is only a preliminary session and you will not become experts with knives until you have practised with them… used them in realistic situations. Throwing a knife is not as easy under pressure. Using a knife on another human being is not as easy as throwing it at a tree. Remember that."

He nodded, and motioned to Tyler to take over. Stepping forwards, she pointed to a box which had appeared on the ground at some point during the training, perhaps collected by Barnes while we had been working on our knife skills.

"Take one each. You have thirty minutes to rest before we

move on."

This time I was first to the box, tucking Cameron's knife away in my belt as I went. I didn't want to fail the speed test a second time. It contained a small, flat bread roll for each of us and an apple. In Agric we had never been provided with any kind of food in the middle of the day, we had always had to last the distance between breakfast and dinner time without sustenance. The unfairness of the system hit me again, as I thought of Cass, and then of Harper. If ration levels were so different between Patrol and Agric, what were they like in Clearance?

Despite my anger, I sat down and ate the roll. It was a little sweet in flavour, although quite hard. I wondered as I went on to eat the apple if it was one which Cass had picked, and then remembered that her Super position probably meant she did little in the way of actual harvesting these days. I was glad of the company when Jackson came and sat beside me. We ate in companionable silence.

The atmosphere around me was almost relaxed. Most of the new recruits were still silent, but Barnes, Tyler and Cameron conversed in low tones, smiling and even laughing at different points. Tyler turned and caught me staring at them. At first her expression was curious, but then an understanding dawned on her and she pushed herself to her feet. For a moment I thought she was coming over to discipline me, but instead she faced the whole group.

"I think another thing you all need to understand about Patrol is the permitted level of communication. You are all used to the strict rules about communication in your previous Sectors and will no doubt be wondering about the Patrol citizens' ability to speak fairly freely."

She shared a wry grin with her two fellow Supers.

"We were all surprised by it when we arrived. The chatter in the canteen, the conversations between citizens in the pods and during their working day. I know it seems alien, but it's one of the huge advantages to living here. We've told you that there are benefits to being here in Patrol. Well, the ability to talk to other citizens is one of the major advantages of life here."

She stopped, and looked around at us as we took in the information. There were looks of surprise on most faces. We had all realised that citizens of Patrol were able to speak to one another, but were still wary of engaging in speech ourselves. We waited for Tyler to continue.

"So, here it is. While you are out of the Patrol Compound, you can only speak where it is necessary and talk should be kept to a minimum: giving or clarifying orders and so on. But here in the Compound, once you are a fully-fledged citizen, you are free, within reason, to speak to one another. Whilst your training is taking place I would avoid it, but once you pass, well, go for it. Obviously not in meetings or sessions with more senior members of the community. Then, you should only speak when spoken to. And it goes without saying on Assessment days or times when you are in the presence of the Governor or senior Governance members you don't speak. But as long as you understand that, you are not going to receive a reckoning for talking to one another." She glanced around to see how we had taken the news before continuing, "Ok, five more minutes and then we need to hike out to the upper fields."

She sat back down and resumed her quiet conversation with Cameron. I felt a small bubble of excitement rise up in my

chest. The thought of being able to speak to those around me without hiding it, with no fear of reprisal, was wonderful. But it was also terrifying. I had been so used to having to limit my conversations to only those which were absolutely necessary that I wasn't sure what I would talk about when I had all the words in the world available to me and little limit on how I used them. Would I have enough to say?

I comforted myself with the thought that I wouldn't be needing to speak very much until I had passed the training. First things first. I wondered what was contained in the upper fields and what our afternoon training would require of us. Coming from Agric, I was happy with fields, well used to them, but what we would do in them was another matter.

The food eaten and flasks of water passed around for us all to drink, we stood and stretched our legs as Barnes got to his feet.

"Pack up the box." He nodded to Jackson, who obliged. "Cam, you alright to take it back to base?"

Cameron nodded.

"Ok. Let's go."

He set off into the woods again at quite a pace. He was so competitive, always trying to prove something, even in between training sessions. I wondered whether he was trying to prepare us for a tough life in Patrol, or was perhaps simply someone who got off on making others uncomfortable. Either way, I wasn't sure I liked Barnes.

"I'll catch you up," Tyler called to him as he exited the clearing.

I ended up close to the rear of the group, marching quietly but not unhappily in front of Jackson and behind Davis. He didn't seem at all tired, his movements were strong and

powerful, but watching him I realised that I also felt quite refreshed. The food and rest had clearly done us all some good physically, but also mentally. I couldn't quite believe how revived I felt from the consumption of the bread and fruit. As I picked up the pace a little, I felt something banging against my side.

The knife.

With a groan I realised that I still had the weapon tucked into my belt. Not only had I removed it from the equipment bag and the training area, I had also taken the knife belonging to the instructor himself. Heat flooded my body as I realised that I would have to admit my mistake and fix it. The thought of returning to Cameron with the knife sent a shudder through me. One of dread, but also, strangely, excitement. I called ahead.

"Barnes! Barnes?"

I could only just see him at the front of the line, disappearing into a thick copse of trees. He heard me though, and stopped immediately. The LS boy behind him almost collided with him. Turning quickly, he moved his accusing eyes down the line, trying to work out who had dared to stop him.

Taking a deep breath I stepped out of line and held the knife aloft.

"Sorry. So sorry. I forgot to return this."

Barnes glared at me for a moment, then broke into a strange smile, "Well you'd better take it back, hadn't you?"

I turned, ready to head back in the direction we had come from, hardly believing the lack of chastisement. At the last moment I glanced back at Barnes who was still watching me. Finally, it dawned on me why he was smiling.

"Will you wait?"

He shook his head, "Nope. No time. If you're lucky you can catch us up, or maybe Tyler will still be there."

He set off at the same rapid pace, this time not glancing back. Jackson widened her eyes at me, clearly concerned, but there was little she could do. With a small shrug and a helpless look, she too set off after the rest of the group. I was left with no option but to continue back to the clearing.

I considered the route back and the length of time we had been walking. It was probably less than five minutes back to the training ground. If I ran, I might make it in less. Trying not to think about how I would possibly find them again when I had no idea where they were going, I began to sprint in the opposite direction.

Luckily the path we had taken had so far been clear and fairly straight. I found the entrance leading into the clearing quite quickly and slowed down to consider how I could best approach Cameron and Tyler. I had not passed her, so assumed she was still here. I was hoping, given the fairly friendly way she had treated us all this morning, that she would agree to guide me back to the others. I didn't have another plan if she refused.

The space appeared empty as I approached, yet the bag of knives and empty box of food still lay on the ground. Puzzled as to why they were not there, and unable to hear voices, I stopped before I entered the clearing and looked around. A slight rustling put me on edge, and I ducked behind a tree. Then I spotted them. They were partially hidden in a thick copse of trees. They stood strangely close together, and for a moment I was confused, unable to work out where Cameron ended and Tyler began.

Then I realised that they were somehow wrapped around

one another. Tyler's body was pushed up against Cameron and her arms were wound around his neck. I wondered if she was upset about something, remembering nights where I had put my arms around Harper to comfort her when she was sad. But this situation seemed very different. It didn't feel comforting. There was something else going on, but I couldn't work out what. And then my eyes travelled upwards to Tyler's face, widening as she leaned forwards and did something very strange. Tilting her head upwards, she leaned towards Cameron and placed her lips very gently against his.

Chapter Nineteen

I looked away, heat flooding my face. The moment was private, and despite my lack of understanding of what was going on between Tyler and Cameron, I knew instinctively that they would not appreciate being witnessed. Still, my eyes were drawn back to the couple: their bodies so closely entwined; the unfamiliar movement of their lips mesmerising.

As I stood there trying to decide what to do, Cameron stepped back, gently untangling Tyler's arms from around his neck. He spoke quietly in her ear for a moment. Then, abruptly, she turned away and I caught a glimpse of her face, hurt and tearful, the most vulnerable I had seen her.

Moving backwards quietly, I crept further up the path and decided to make a noisy entrance. Though they still might not appreciate being interrupted, at least it would startle them into realising I was there and give them time to prepare themselves. Giving myself enough of a run up, I raced the rest of the way towards the clearing, pounding my feet as loudly as I could on the forest floor and even calling out as I reached the opening in the trees.

"Hey, anyone here? Tyler?"

I was unused to the volume of my voice being above whisper-level, and cringed inwardly at how much noise I was making. It was the lesser of two evils though. I was certain that their annoyance at my clumsy entrance would be less frightening than their fury if they realised I had witnessed what had just happened.

Cameron emerged from the gap in the trees first, the all too familiar anger clouding his features.

"You again? Why are you back?"

His eyes travelled to my hand which held up the knife, words failing me after the shame of my initially noisy arrival. Shaking his head, he strode towards me and took it, swiftly enough to demonstrate his annoyance, but still being careful not to slice into one of our hands. I found myself unable to tear my gaze from Cameron's for several moments before Tyler appeared. Her masked expression displayed nothing of the pain I had witnessed a moment ago. That was now firmly under control. She did not seem as angry as Cameron, but was still unhappy to see me.

"Really Quin, you need to be very careful. First you miss getting a weapon and now you've been separated from the rest of the recruits. It's only the second day! Look - you're in my group- I don't want to see you fail, but you have to start improving, or we're going to lose you."

My face flamed again. I had no idea what I could say to repair the situation and was only glad that Tyler didn't know what I had witnessed between her and Cameron which, from my viewpoint, had looked like some kind of rejection.

"How are you planning to find the others now? If you don't get to training, you can't pass. You know there are no second chances?"

"I know."

Until now she had not glanced at Cameron. Now as she did, there wasn't even a flicker of the emotion she had displayed earlier. I admired her iron control.

"I'll try and get her caught up. See you back at base, Cam."

Without waiting for a response, she jogged off in the direction I had come from. For a moment I stood rooted to the spot, unable to follow. My eyes moved to Cameron who was watching Tyler's exit. The fury was gone from his face and for a moment he looked regretful. Then he looked back at me and his anger returned.

"What?"

I stared mutely at him, wondering what he was thinking.

He almost spat the words at me, "What are you waiting for? Follow her."

I couldn't move. He sighed and looked down at the ground.

"Piece of advice? You've put yourself at risk twice this morning. A different Super might have already gotten rid of you. Your behaviour from the moment I met you has been reckless. You need to be careful. Get after Tyler now, and I mean now. And when you get to that next training session, focus. You have no idea what will happen to you if you fail."

Shaking his head, he turned to pick up the box from the ground as Tyler's voice bellowed from within the woods.

"Quin!"

She hadn't reappeared, but was clearly losing patience now she had noticed that I wasn't following. With a final glance at Cameron, who refused to meet my gaze, I turned tail and raced back in the direction I had come, hoping desperately that we would reach the next session before it was too late.

I caught Tyler with some difficulty. She was certainly a fast runner and her frustration seemed to be spurring her on. When I finally reached her, I realised how my weeks of night time preparation and training with Harper and Cassidy had paid off. I really was stronger, fitter than I had previously been. That must have played a part in my selection for Patrol. Clearly only the strongest citizens were eligible for consideration.

I had begun to work out how the different levels of The Beck worked. The treatment of individuals in the different areas was vastly different. Clearly the majority of us started out in one of the Lower Beck Sectors, which were considered less important. If we made it through in that area we would be considered for something better. But Sectors in the Lower Beck seemed to weed out the weak: if you couldn't survive on basic rations and cope with the level of work and amount of rest permitted in the Lower Beck, then you were removed, banished to Clearance. But if you proved you could survive in Agric, Rep, Sustenance or LS, you could be promoted to a better area, where life was more rewarding.

But then I thought about Harper, and all those citizens I had seen sent away over the last three years, simply for being weaker than others, for falling ill or becoming injured. Not through laziness or lack of work ethic. It wasn't fair. It seemed to me that the weakest of us should be receiving the better share of rations, for that was the only way they would become strong again. And how could those who ran The Beck believe that the provision of food was of lower importance? Surely the cultivation of crops, the rearing and care of livestock, the preparation of the very sustenance which allowed us to stay alive was more vital to Beck survival than anything else. I wondered if others felt like I did. Harper certainly would have agreed with me.

Tyler paid me no attention at all. She showed neither surprise nor admiration that I was managing to keep up with her. She barely even glanced at me as we ran, just kept pushing herself farther and faster, as though it might allow her to forget what had just happened. Her face did not betray any emotion, but the focus and speed with which she ran demonstrated an almost demonic need to block out any other thoughts.

I considered the scene I had witnessed in the woods. I wasn't sure what had happened. Only that one moment Tyler's mouth was moving against Cameron's and the next it was not. I was certain of only one thing: Tyler had been the one to move towards Cameron, and he had been the one to move away. For a moment they had seemed to be locked together in a shared emotion I didn't quite understand, but when Cameron had stepped back it was clear that he did not want to continue the embrace.

Tyler had acted differently around Cameron every time she had been in his presence. She talked to Barnes like an equal, sometimes even inferior, citizen. She clearly felt at ease with him, and I had seen her give him orders, converse with him comfortably and even mock him. With Cameron she was different. She was quieter, almost nervous around him, wanting to impress him. I understood the feeling, although I had so far attributed my own reaction to Cameron to my concerns about my original meeting with him on the wall, and my fears that he was aware of potentially damaging information about me.

Now I questioned the feeling. I wondered what it would be like to press my own lips and body against his. I had never seen anything like it before. Contact between citizens in the Lower Beck was so restricted. Considering that talking was forbidden, the thought of touching another citizen that way was unthinkable. But I found my mind kept wandering back to the idea as I raced along next to Tyler.

We had been running for around fifteen minutes when the trees thinned out and we emerged into another large field filled with strangely shaped objects. I hardly had time to notice them before my attention was drawn to the noise being made by the group at the opposite end of the field. Led by Barnes, my fellow recruits were running laps around the area, and looked like they had been doing so for some time. I watched as Jackson sprinted past, her arms pumping, her legs rotating slowly but surely as she ran. A look of relief crossed her face as she noticed me. Behind her came Mason, a broad smile on his face, and then Anders, who appeared to be an excellent runner, looking less tired than anyone else on the field, his slender form perfectly streamlined for speed.

"Get on with it then," Tyler's voice cut across my thoughts, "Don't think you're escaping the pre-training run."

I knew better than to ask for special treatment. I could have claimed that I had already been running through the woods with her, but knew that would earn me no points and probably gain me even more laps of the field. Waiting until Davies had run past, a gentle smile crossing his face as he noticed my return, I moved out into the centre of the track and followed the others. Digging deep and remembering Harper's struggle, I found some strength to continue the run.

The first lap was agony, but once I had completed it I somehow zoned out and got into a rhythm which allowed me to continue. As I ran, I considered the strange shapes which filled the field more closely. They were large, flat structures, each one made up of several metallic looking panels. They all sat at an angle to the ground and some of them caught the light as I passed them, reflecting it back at me and creating a shimmering effect. There were at least twenty of the large structures in the field, spaced evenly apart, and looking rather eerie and alien. I wondered what their purpose was as I counted each recruit finishing their own run and dropping to the ground to rest.

I feared that Tyler or Barnes would make me complete more laps once the others had finished, but when they called a halt and I continued running, Tyler motioned for me to join the rest of the group. Somehow she had taken pity on me and allowed me to stop. I felt that perhaps I had earned a little respect for my lack of complaint earlier.

I could see no other Supers, so presumed that Tyler and Barnes were going to deliver the afternoon's training themselves. Tyler stepped forward to speak, looking around the group as she did so.

"So, you made it through this morning's training. You can handle a knife. But so far no one has explained to you why you might need to use one."

She paused before continuing to make sure we were all listening.

"You will need to use them in your Patrol assignments if you come across any kind of enemy. A lot of Patrol assignments, especially those you will complete when you are a new member, involve guarding The Beck's assets. One of its main assets is its power supply."

She motioned behind her to the alien structures.

"These are solar panels. They are one of the ways we produce electricity for use in The Beck. Without them we would not have light, or power to run the various pieces of equipment that we need. They need a constant guard because, if they were to fail, a major provider of The Beck's power supply would disappear. And without power, we would quickly find ourselves in chaos. Our other major power source comes from our Hydro Plant. Water is an obvious way to generate our electricity and take advantage," she paused and smiled wryly, "the only advantage as far as I can see, of the volume of water we have surrounding us. We will take you to look at it tomorrow. It also requires guarding round the clock. Our power supply is essential and protecting it from harm is our primary concern here in Patrol."

Barnes took over, "So this afternoon we'll be training here at the Solar Plant. You need to know how to clean the panels and check that they're operational, as well as how to protect them from harm. It's a vital resource, so-"

He stopped and was suddenly staring over my shoulder at someone behind me, a look of disgust crossing his face. Turning around I could see Mason had raised his hand to speak.

"Yes?"

"You said to protect the power supply from harm. Do you mean breakdown?"

"What?"

"Do you mean it's essential to make sure that they don't break down? Like we need to notice if they need repairing?"

Barnes looked uncertainly at Tyler, "Well yes, obviously."

"But any citizen could do that. Why does it require us being the fittest and strongest? You're talking as though we have to defend the plant from attack."

It was Tyler who replied, "Just accept that it's important that we are at the peak of physical fitness and can fight where necessary. Don't ask questions. The Beck has enemies who would attack us and see us fail in a heartbeat."

"But–"

Tyler's expression darkened and a note of warning entered her tone, "Be quiet Mason. Stop asking questions."

Mason's expression darkened but he fell silent. The relaxed air which had surrounded the group earlier disappeared and I found myself wondering how much more we didn't know about the place we had spent our whole lives.

Chapter Twenty

The remainder of the afternoon was dull, and consisted of a lengthy session where we learned about maintenance of the solar panels, plus being drilled on the rules we were to follow when on duty guarding them. There were ten fields of solar panels in total, all up here in the hillier regions of The Beck. I couldn't believe that I had lived here all my life and not known about them. It seemed that their clever positioning and the narrow lives of the Lower Beck citizens meant that it was a fairly simple task to conceal their existence from the general population.

What I was more concerned about was my growing realisation that our entire lives in The Beck had been extremely limited. Those in higher positions had always taught the doctrines of teamwork and hardship going hand in hand to keep The Beck running safely and ensure the survival of our society. Yet what they kept hidden from us clearly demonstrated that some citizens were valued more than others, and treated accordingly. All the Agric citizens slaving in the Lower Beck fields knew that their work was essential to keep The Beck community from starving, but they endured minimal rations and harsh conditions with little complaint because they believed that everyone was the same.

We all worked under the constant threat that life in The

Beck was fragile, believing that one storm or poor harvest could ruin us and result in the death of the entire society. This kept the majority of us obedient, and following the rules without question. Yet here I was in Patrol, already receiving better rations, and privileges like the ability to communicate with others without fear of reprisal. I felt ashamed that I had accepted that without question too. I also wondered what the lives of those above Patrol were like: those in Governance, at the highest end of the spectrum.

And the mysterious threat that Mason had tried to clarify earlier. What was it? Why were Patrol citizens required to fight with weapons to prevent our power supplies being taken over or destroyed? Was it citizens within The Beck who wished to cause havoc, or an unknown external force? I shuddered at the thought of something outside of our society trying to come in and take over. And the thought of trying to fight off an unknown enemy using one of the knives we had trained with this morning was terrifying.

Since Tyler had reprimanded Mason we had all been extremely quiet, listening to Barnes as he took us on a tour, showed us the equipment shed, demonstrated the methods we needed to use to clean the panels and listed the number of guards required at any one time on the Solar Fields. Jackson and I had exchanged concerned glances several times, and I could tell Mason was inwardly fuming every time I passed him. At one point he looked like he would tackle Barnes on the subject for a second time, but Davis quickly put a cautionary hand on his arm, and he appeared to bite his lip for the time being.

Eventually Tyler held up a hand for us to stop, and we gathered around her.

"Time to head back now. Watch your step, it's getting dark. We're going to move fast, so keep up."

And like a wild cat, she streaked out of the fields towards the woods, setting an even faster pace than earlier. The majority of the recruits fell in line behind her, resigned to the fact that they had to keep pace if they didn't want to risk getting lost and missing a meal back at base. Barnes fell in somewhere around the middle, not bothering to see if the rest of us were still with them. Close to the rear were myself and Jackson, who ran next to each other in companionable silence, too exhausted to attempt conversation. Mason and Davis followed at the very back, gesturing to one another furiously. Mason seemed angry still, and it was clear that Davis was trying to calm him.

We reached camp and headed straight for the canteen, our route now familiar. It was almost empty of citizens and we seemed to be among the last, which meant that our rations were more like those I was used to in Agric. Clearly arriving for meals early meant getting the lion's share of the food. We ate in silence, even Mason and Davis lost in their thoughts, their hands idle apart from using their forks to place the food in their mouths. I wondered where Cameron was, and whether he had already eaten, as well as what was in store for us the following day. My body was completely drained of energy, yet I couldn't stop my mind from racing.

We returned to the Annexe as soon as the meal was finished and most recruits clambered into bed immediately. Jackson smiled at me and squeezed my hand as I began to climb the ladder to my bunk, determined not to have a second disturbed night.

"I'm glad you caught us earlier. I spent an hour feeling sick at the thought of you lost in the woods."

I managed a small grin, "Can't get rid of me that easily."

I continued up the ladder and hoisted myself on to the bed. Removing my overalls took seconds. I no longer felt self-conscious about undressing in front of the rest of the recruits. Firstly, the vest underneath pretty much covered me, and secondly, everyone was so tired that no one was even bothering to glance in my direction. As my eyes travelled around the room I noticed that Mason's bed was, as yet, empty and wondered where he was. Davis was lying still with his eyes closed, but something told me he wasn't asleep. If anything, he looked troubled, and I wondered if he and Mason had argued. They seemed as close as Harper, Cass and I, and I had imagined that this would help them through the first few days in a new Sector, but perhaps it had caused a rift between them instead.

Settling down to sleep, I thought about the tentative friend-ship I had begun with Jackson. She reminded me a little of Harper, and while I was glad to have found someone to share a smile with and support, I couldn't help but wonder where Harper was now. How big was Clearance? How many people lived there? I imagined her sitting at a workbench sewing overalls, with Miller on one side and Fin on the other. Somehow the picture seemed wrong. After discovering there was so much I didn't know about The Beck today, I wondered just how bad Clearance could be.

And then there was Cass, who was more like Mason than Jackson. Back in Agric I could at least imagine her, working on the same tasks we had fulfilled for the last three years, taking charge of a group of citizens and turning them into a productive team. I was certain that she would have embraced her Super role with relish. I hoped that it was enough to ensure that she wasn't too lonely without us. Making up my mind that I would sneak out one night soon and go down to Agric to see her, I felt a little better. With this decision made, I settled down to get some much-needed sleep.

It seemed like only moments later I was woken by the door to the Annexe banging open. Lurching into an upright position, I glanced around. It was still dark, surely too early to be getting up, even with the crazy shifts here in Patrol. Barnes stood in the doorway, glaring around at us all.

"Up!" he shouted, "Up, and get out here. Now!"

There was a moment of stunned silence before the majority of the recruits began to pull on overalls.

"Leave them!"

Barnes' tone left no room for argument. As one, we shuffled out of beds and headed out through the door in vests and shorts. Glancing around, I wondered if everyone else felt as uncomfortable as I did. The rain had set in for the night and I shivered as the cold droplets began to soak my flimsy garments. For a moment I wondered if it was some kind of insane night-training, but when I reached the door I could see why we were being brought out. To bear witness.

In the centre of the courtyard was Director Reed, and at his feet lay a figure. The yard was dark and it was difficult to make out who the figure might be, but the citizen, dressed in Patrol overalls, was clearly unconscious. Around the yard stood several other senior Patrol citizens, Tyler, and Cameron, and I recognised Donnelly with a sinking heart.

"Tonight," Reed's voice was quiet and menacing, "One of you has put the entire programme at risk by attempting to sneak back to his old Sector."

I stared at the figure in horror, remembering Mason's empty

bed. Looking around at the recruits standing shell shocked on the porch of the Annexe, I knew he would not be there. I noticed Davis standing just behind me, his face starkly white in the darkness. I thought about my own vow to sneak down to Agric to see Cass and shuddered inwardly, knowing it could just as easily have been me lying there on the ground.

Reed continued, "Up until now, Mason here has shown real promise as a Patrol recruit. But tonight he put that in jeopardy. Until you are declared fully fledged Patrol citizens, you are to remain within the confines of the Upper Beck, at and around Patrol base. Once you have been given all of your training you will be asked to take the Patrol pledge, which makes it very clear that the privileged information you are given as a citizen of Patrol is not to be revealed to those working in the Lower Beck. Our society is fragile. Our society is strict, but it is run the way it is to ensure our survival, and for this purpose, some secrecy is necessary to protect the Lower Beck citizens."

He paused, and I glanced around at the bewildered and terrified faces.

"Luckily, Mason was caught by an experienced Patrol citizen before he made it back to the LS Compound." Reed motioned to Donnelly, who smirked, "If not, he would have found himself in Clearance immediately. As it is, he will receive a fitting punishment for this misdemeanour now and be able to return to training tomorrow. He will not, however, be given any second chances."

Reed stepped back and held a hand out towards Donnelly, who handed something to him. Donnelly stepped forwards and hoisted Mason up off the floor. His face streamed with blood from a nasty-looking cut on his forehead. I wondered how he had got it. Donnelly dragged Mason over to a large boulder which lay at the side of the courtyard, as if placed there on purpose. Pushing Mason's body down across the rock, he picked up a bucket from beside it and threw its contents over Masons' head. Water cascaded over him as he came to, spluttering and choking, struggling to breathe under the sudden flow of water.

He tried to protest, but Donnelly knelt hard on his back and nodded to Cameron, who came forwards, head lowered, and bound Mason's hands.

Reed continued, "Mason, you let us down by trying to go back to LS. Take the punishment and get back to training tomorrow and you will still stand a chance of succeeding here in Patrol."

Mason stiffened, as though he wanted to argue, but seemed to think better of it and slumped over the rock instead. My eyes filled with tears, mingling with the increasing downpour. I watched Reed move forwards and realised what Donnelly had handed him. He raised his arm above his head and a whip sliced through the air, viciously biting into Mason's skin as it came down across his back. He made no sound on the first stroke and I wondered if he had passed out again, but as the second one hit home in the same spot, he cried out.

I had been aware of similar punishments being given out in Agric, but they had never been done so publicly. Something about the way that Mason's humiliation was being witnessed by so many of us made the punishment seem harsher and more unfair. But I knew that if any of us tried to move from our spot on the porch we would be noticed and punished too. This was meant as a lesson. To teach us not to follow in Mason's footsteps.

There was a movement beside me and I felt, rather than saw, Davis start forwards. Grasping his arm, I stared into his face, desperate to get across the message that he could not help Mason now. He looked into my eyes, his expression wild and desperate. I completely understood his need to run to his friend's aid, but at the same time I knew I had to stop him, to prevent him from landing himself in the same situation. If Mason was to stay in Patrol, he would need all the friends he could muster. He stopped and looked back at me, seeming to understand.

I glanced around. It didn't look like anyone had noticed, their eyes transfixed by the spectacle of Mason sprawled across the rock. Shuffling myself closer to Davis, I took his hand in mine quietly, stroking my thumb across the back of it to try and calm him. Finally Davis took a deep breath and stepped back as his friend's screams echoed round the courtyard.

Chapter Twenty-One

The sound of the whip cutting through the night air seemed to go on forever, but eventually Reed's arm stilled and he dropped the weapon abruptly, as though he was exhausted. He moved into the centre of the courtyard and looked hard at each of us in turn, nodding as though he felt his message was clear. Then he turned on his heel and strode into the Jefferson Building, closely followed by Donnelly. Tyler stepped out from where she had been standing underneath the trees at the far side of the yard and walked slowly into its centre.

"Get back to bed, all of you."

Her words were spoken softly. She looked pale, and I wondered if she had been as sickened by what had just taken place as I had, but couldn't say so. It seemed that survival in Patrol was all about playing by the rules, even when you didn't agree with them. She nodded abruptly to Barnes, who had been standing close to the boulder the whole time, a fascinated expression on his face. He quickly collected the whip from where Reed had cast it to the ground and the two of them set off in the direction of the pods.

I watched as Cameron, the only Super left, began to untie Mason. He seemed to be doing it gently, and spoke quietly into his ear as he did so, but I found I couldn't watch. How could he willingly participate in the atrocity which had just taken place? I turned my attention to Davis instead. He stood at my side, shaking with anger and resentment. His hand was still clamped so tightly around mine that it hurt. He seemed to have forgotten he was holding it.

As the other recruits began to drift back inside, Jackson appeared next to us and nodded over at Mason.

"He'll need some help. Unless they're coming back to take him somewhere else."

"They won't be. They left Fin here that first night and she was in a similar state."

Cameron had helped Mason to his feet and was beginning to escort him across to the Annexe. Their progress was slow. When they reached us, Mason looked up at Davis and shook his head, mumbling something incoherently. Davis stiffened, but I held on to his hand, preventing him from turning it into a fist and swinging it at Cameron. He turned and looked at me, his eyes dark and resentful.

"Come on," I coaxed, "he needs you."

I took both Davis' hands in mine, squeezing them gently.

"Save it for now. Help him."

When I looked up, Cameron was standing inches away still holding Mason up. He was eyeing us with a strange expression on his face. Jackson stepped forwards and looped Mason's free arm around her neck. I gave Davis a little push forwards, and he supported Mason's other arm, refusing to look Cameron in the eye. Moving back across the porch of the Annexe, the awkward trio reached the door and stopped, unable to go any further. I hurried to pull the door open for them and they managed to shuffle through, Mason wincing with the pain. Purposefully keeping my back to Cameron, I made to follow the others, but felt him standing close behind me.

I didn't want to turn around and look at him, but knew that I had to. When I did, he stared at me for a moment before backing away slowly. When he reached the far edge of the porch, he motioned with a hand for me to follow him. Reluctantly I stepped outside and closed the door, refusing to move any closer, my anger barely contained.

"What? Last night you couldn't wait to get away. Now you want to talk?"

When he spoke, his voice was soft and low, "Don't look at me like that."

"Like what?"

"Accusingly. Like I've done something terrible."

"Haven't you though?"

"What?"

"Done something terrible," I felt my voice cracking slightly as I spoke, disappointment evident in my tone. I tried desperately to control it, "How could you tie him up? Participate in that…that…"

"If I hadn't, someone else would have."

"Yes, but why you? Why did you have to involve yourself?"

He grimaced, "You sound disappointed in me."

I sighed, "Look, when we met you on the wall that night I thought we were finished, but you helped us all… you saved us. But just then…"

"I know. But it's different when they're watching. I didn't…" Now it was his turn to falter, "Do you think I wanted to?"

I shook my head and turned away, not knowing what to think.

"Look, you've a lot to learn. You've no idea what The Beck is really like."

I spun back to face him, "Then tell me. Don't make grand

173

statements about everything I don't know. Fill me in! Then maybe I'd understand."

"I can't. You'll know soon enough anyway. And then you'll understand that we have to do things we hate just to survive here. You can't be sentimental."

"Then why call me out here then? Why do you care what I think?"

He sighed, running a frustrated hand across his closely shaven head, "I don't know. I just do. I've tried not to, believe me." He gave a wry smile. "I just know I don't want you to think badly of me."

"That doesn't make any sense."

"Tell me about it."

The door behind me creaked open and I heard Jackson's soft voice, "Everything alright Quin?"

I said nothing.

"Quin?"

Cameron stepped around me and addressed her, "Take these for Mason." He dug into his pocket and took out more of the white pills he had given to Fin and a small white tub. "One tonight, one tomorrow morning, right?"

I felt, rather than saw, her nodding.

"Tell him to take this and sleep. And spread some of this on his wounds in the morning—stop any infection. Tomorrow we'll try and go easy on him, though we can't make it look like that's what we're doing, understand? It needs to look like he's survived the disciplining on his own."

"Yes. I'll tell him. Thank you, Cameron."

I heard the door close behind her. She didn't sound angry with him. I wondered why not. I turned, intending to go around Cameron and through the door, leaving him alone, but

...od up and whispered something to Davis, who
...nd left the Annexe immediately. All the recruits
...ke now, and most had started to dress themselves,
...e for the day's training. Everyone had half an eye on
...ough, as if trying to gauge whether or not he would

...moments later Davis returned with a bowl in his
...which he filled with water from the small sink in the
... He passed it to Jackson, who placed it on the floor
...earing off a strip from the front of Mason's blood-
...vest, which was cleaner than the back. Dipping it
...e bowl, she motioned for him to turn his back to her
...gan bathing his wounds. There were several gasps as
...t of the Annexe witnessed the angry red welts which
...ed his back.

...son sat and patiently washed each of the wounds in turn.
...moaned slightly, but realised how necessary it was to
...his wounds, so acquiesced with little protest. I thought
...wounds I had previously seen back in Agric, where
...ns had suffered injuries which had not been properly
...d to. I had seen some become infected, oozing dark
...or yellow pus, angry red coloured flesh surrounding
...Those citizens had disappeared off to Clearance very
...kly. I mentally thanked Cameron for the antiseptic he
...also provided.

...ost of the recruits had turned away from Mason now out
...espect, or simply sickened by the appalling sight of his
...nds. I was unable to tear my eyes away, fascinated by the
...tleness with which Jackson tended to them. I wondered
...would have been able to offer him the same care. I liked
...son, had begun to consider him a friend, but I wasn't good

CHAPTER TWENTY-ONE

I found him blocking my way, his expression unfathomable again.

"Don't be angry with me."

I shrugged. He reached out towards me and for a moment I had no idea what he was going to do. I froze, unable to speak, while his fingers brushed away some of the droplets of water on my cheek, then rested against the side of my face.

"Don't judge me yet."

I shook my head and he took his hand away. My cheek burned. A moment later, he ducked around me and was gone.

It took me a while to make my feet move back into the Annexe. When I did, things were quiet again. Mason was installed on Davis' lower bunk and looked as though he had passed out. Above him, Davis' eyes were open and he lay quietly, as though still trying to take in what had just happened. He sat up and I reached out, squeezing his hand as I passed.

"Thank you, Quin. For stopping me," he hesitated, "you were right."

I managed a small smile, "No worries. You'll repay the favour."

He nodded before turning over and facing the other way.

Jackson was still awake, although she too lay still in her bed. She handed me a towel as I reached our shared bunk. I smiled gratefully, beginning to dry myself off as she spoke.

"I gave him the pill. Think it'll help with the pain. At least he'll sleep."

I nodded.

"What was going on out there? With Cameron I mean?"

"Nothing." I knew my reply was too quick, but she let it go.

"Sleep well then. Tomorrow'll be a whole new challenge."

"Cameron said they'd go easy on Mason where they could."

"Good. I do think they're mostly on our side."

"Aren't you angry with Cameron?   For what he did to Mason?"

She looked at me, surprised, "No. It seems to me he was the only one to show Mason any care, afterwards at least."

"Really?"

"Well, yes. He gave us the painkillers. It's not the first time he's done it. Shows a lot of courage… kindness."

"But he helped to bind Mason's hands."

"And if he hadn't, someone else would've done. He'd have landed himself in a whole lot of trouble for refusing."

"But I…"

"Let it go, Quin." She looked exhausted. "Why do you care so much anyway? Go to sleep."

She turned away. I clambered up to my bunk, frustrated. I didn't know why I cared. Touching my fingers to the spot on my cheek where Cameron's fingers had been, I resigned myself to another disturbed night. I was still seething with frustration but, despite this, exhaustion took over and I was asleep within minutes.

Chapter Tw

When I woke the next morning n
running the previous day, and I was
in the middle of the night. Most of
suffering from a similar malaise. M
different condition altogether. The
his face had reduced somewhat, but
stained crimson and he could barely

He moaned loudly as he sat up an
his vest. I could see him biting his lip
noise. He was clearly determined to c
his courage. After several unsuccess
loudly, his face scarlet with the effort.
go to his aid, but as the thought crossed
arrive at his side. Sitting shyly beside hin
to remove the vest. He winced, but didn

The bleeding had bound the clothing to
night and its removal was clearly painfu
began to tear the vest away. She was
could see his bare torso, and she did a g
demonstrating her horror at the sight. I
in her eyes, but she maintained a calm e
something quietly in Mason's ear. He a
weak grin at her comment and nodded his

She st
turned a
were aw
to prepar
Mason t
make it.

A few
hands,
Annexe
before
stained
into th
and be
the res
dissec

Jack
Masor
clean
about
citize
tend
greer
them
quic
had

M
of r
wou
gen
if I
Ma

with blood and didn't feel that I could have been as tender as Jackson was.

Mason looked almost peaceful by the time she had finished applying the ointment. As she stooped to clear the bowl away, he turned around to face her. When she sat back up again, a look passed between them which I couldn't interpret. He reached a hand out to her and she stood up suddenly, slopping some of the water out of the bowl. It seeped into the wooden floor below and she hurriedly mopped it up with the remaining strips of Mason's vest. She pressed something into his hand before hurrying red-faced towards the door. He understood, swallowing the painkiller she had given him quickly, but stared after her with a confused expression on his face.

When she returned, she went quickly to her bed, collected a vest of her own and tore it in half. Returning to Mason's bed, she motioned for him to stand. He obeyed slowly, breathing heavily as if to try and cope with the pain he clearly felt. Even slightly hunched over, he was much taller than her. She passed the torn vest around his chest several times, until she had covered the majority of his wounds. Once done, she secured it by tucking it tightly into itself. Then she reached for Mason's clean vest and helped him to get it over his head.

After she had pulled it over his torso, they stood for a moment too long, closer to each other than they should have been. Something about them reminded me of Tyler and Cameron in the forest the day before. Jackson did not meet Mason's gaze, instead keeping her eyes fixed on his chest. He seemed about to say something to her, but she moved backwards abruptly and rushed away to her own bed. There, she busied herself getting changed with her back to the entire room. Mason sat back down on his bed heavily, a hand on his head as though he felt dizzy.

A few minutes later, Tyler arrived. I felt like she had come in later than the previous day and wondered if that was part of the 'taking it easy' on Mason. I appreciated it anyway. She looked around the room, her eyes settling on Mason who was still seated and pale, but at least dressed and looking alive. A look of relief crossed her features before she quickly stifled it. Then she was all business.

"Today will involve a visit to the source of our second power supply: the Hydro Plant. As you know, this is located in the Lower Beck. It will involve us travelling through many of the Sectors you came from. Clearly after last night," she glanced at Mason again, "you understand the necessity of keeping yourselves separate from your old Sectors. I shouldn't have to remind you of the consequences of speaking to those citizens and conveying any information which you have been made privy to since you began your training here."

Barnes now marched through the door noisily, looking as tired as I felt.

"Where were you?" he demanded, "Why didn't you wait?"

She shot a look at him, "Because you didn't look like you wanted to wake up."

He sneered back at her before scanning the room, his eyes coming to rest on Mason.

"Survived the night then? Good luck with training today." He grimaced slightly, giving an exaggerated wince, "Your back must burn so badly."

So much for taking it easy on him. It seemed that the promise only applied to Tyler and Cameron. Barnes was a different matter altogether. I wondered how Mason would fare with such a lengthy journey in front of him, but then felt glad that he wasn't required to run or climb. The solar panels training had been dull, but not hugely taxing. Hopefully the Hydro Plant session would be much the same.

Tyler's voice cut across my thoughts again, "Everyone in the canteen for breakfast in five please. We'll get going to the Hydro Plant soon afterwards.

The meal passed without incident and we were soon gathered in the field where we had first entered the Patrol Compound. The air was unusually humid and despite a weak sunlight filtering through the woods into the field, there were larger than usual grey clouds gathering on the horizon. Barnes still looked a little wild and I wondered what had caused his pale features and sweaty appearance. Perhaps he was ill.

Just as we were about to set off, a voice called him from the Jefferson Building. Barnes put up his hand to halt us and turned to see who had stopped him. I knew from the voice who it was instantly, and did not turn. I had no wish to see Cameron this morning, no idea how to behave around him after the previous night.

"Barnes, wait!"

It took him a moment to reach us and he didn't even look at me. He exchanged a few quiet words with Barnes, who looked surprised, and then frustrated. He stepped back, looking like he wanted to argue. Tyler joined the discussion, and a few minutes later Barnes shook his head, then turned and began jogging in the direction of the Jefferson Building. Cameron grinned at Tyler and they set off down the hill at the front of our group.

Clearly they had realised there would be no taking it easy for Mason if Barnes was anywhere near the day's training.

Somehow, they had engineered a swap where Cameron was able to replace him and therefore make sure that Mason got through the day. I was torn: insanely grateful for Mason's sake, yet distressed that I would have to spend so much time in Cameron's company today.

The journey through the wood was fairly pleasant. Tyler and Cameron took it easy, marching at an easy pace for Mason's sake. He was managing to keep up, although the expression on his face betrayed him, he was clearly fighting considerable pain.

I began to think about where we were headed. If we were going through the Lower Beck, was there any chance of me seeing anyone I knew? I wondered if we might pass by the fields where Cass was working, or spot her on the way to the canteen. I wondered what my reaction would be. Could I pass her by without a word?

But when we reached the Lower Beck and ran through the square it was deserted, aside from the Patrol citizens on guard there. I noticed Cameron picking up the pace and realised it was to demonstrate that no one was taking it easy on Mason. Clearly we couldn't trust all members of Patrol to show the same compassion to an injured recruit. We nodded at the two men guards as we passed by, and headed towards Agric.

There were lots of citizens in the fields, most bending over the crops, busy with the harvest. It was a key time for us and I knew exactly what each team would be doing. With the clouds thickening on the horizon, the battle would be on to get as much of the crop as possible securely in the barns before rain hit The Beck. I did see a few faces I recognised as we passed, but there was no sign of either my old pod or Cass's new one. Most of the Agric citizens kept their heads down, focusing on their work, either because they were busy or scared. A few curious faces glanced up at us as we marched past, brave souls who didn't mind risking a sharp word from their Super if they were caught.

I knew that Cass and I fell into the latter category. We had never been able to resist staring at the passing members of other Sectors. I had always felt as though there were more to know, more to understand. That things were not as they seemed. And I had been right. Harper, on the other hand, was always quite happy to continue with her work, finding tending to the crops soothing and absorbing, rather than dull, as Cass and I did.

Before I could search the greenhouse entrances and look over at the far fields, we had travelled through the Agric Compound and reached the Hydro Plant on the other side. Situated at the side of the powerful river which ran down the hillside The Beck was built on, it was housed within a walled compound. As Agric citizens we had been aware of its existence and relied on the waters of the river to feed our crops, but we had never been allowed access to the plant itself. We knew that the river ran through the centre of it, and that it was staffed by Patrol citizens, but other than that were ignorant to the way it was run and the exact machinery contained within it.

Cameron stopped at the gated entrance to the plant and nodded at the Patrol guard on duty. Then he glanced along our line, as if to make sure that we had all kept up. His gaze lingered on Mason for a moment and he seemed satisfied and pleased that he had managed to cope with the journey despite his injuries.

"This is the entrance to the Hydro Plant. Well-guarded, to

protect from intruders. The Beck's engineers designed and created it very early on in our existence," Cameron began, once we had gathered around him. "It is far smaller than many of the Hydro Plants created in the past, but it serves as an effective way to create electricity for The Beck society. And one thing we are never short of here," he stopped, smiling ruefully, "is water."

Tyler stepped forward and took over, "It harnesses the considerable force of water provided by the river's constant flow down the hillside and uses turbines to convert the water's kinetic energy into mechanical energy. A generator then converts this into useable electrical energy to serve the areas of The Beck which require it most."

I wondered which areas these were, and where all the energy was put to use. Certainly in Agric we didn't get to see a lot of it: the work there was mostly manual and there were no machines powered by the energy to assist us in the sometimes exhausting tasks we had to complete. Only the greenhouses occasionally made use of the power provided by the plant. Perhaps power, like food rations, was distributed unevenly throughout The Beck.

Cameron continued, "The Hydro Plant is mostly staffed by Patrol, with occasional visits from a few of the Dev department engineers who check it over and ensure it is running properly. No other citizens are permitted here and restrictions are in place to make sure that only those who are supposed to be here are allowed to enter. This morning you will be shown the various tasks entailed in a Patrol shift down here."

The duty guard swung the gate open and Cameron beckoned for us to follow him, glancing upwards at the darkening

I found him blocking my way, his expression unfathomable again.

"Don't be angry with me."

I shrugged. He reached out towards me and for a moment I had no idea what he was going to do. I froze, unable to speak, while his fingers brushed away some of the droplets of water on my cheek, then rested against the side of my face.

"Don't judge me yet."

I shook my head and he took his hand away. My cheek burned. A moment later, he ducked around me and was gone.

It took me a while to make my feet move back into the Annexe. When I did, things were quiet again. Mason was installed on Davis' lower bunk and looked as though he had passed out. Above him, Davis' eyes were open and he lay quietly, as though still trying to take in what had just happened. He sat up and I reached out, squeezing his hand as I passed.

"Thank you, Quin. For stopping me," he hesitated, "you were right."

I managed a small smile, "No worries. You'll repay the favour."

He nodded before turning over and facing the other way.

Jackson was still awake, although she too lay still in her bed. She handed me a towel as I reached our shared bunk. I smiled gratefully, beginning to dry myself off as she spoke.

"I gave him the pill. Think it'll help with the pain. At least he'll sleep."

I nodded.

"What was going on out there? With Cameron I mean?"

"Nothing." I knew my reply was too quick, but she let it go.

"Sleep well then. Tomorrow'll be a whole new challenge."

"Cameron said they'd go easy on Mason where they could."

"Good. I do think they're mostly on our side."

"Aren't you angry with Cameron? For what he did to Mason?"

She looked at me, surprised, "No. It seems to me he was the only one to show Mason any care, afterwards at least."

"Really?"

"Well, yes. He gave us the painkillers. It's not the first time he's done it. Shows a lot of courage… kindness."

"But he helped to bind Mason's hands."

"And if he hadn't, someone else would've done. He'd have landed himself in a whole lot of trouble for refusing."

"But I…"

"Let it go, Quin." She looked exhausted. "Why do you care so much anyway? Go to sleep."

She turned away. I clambered up to my bunk, frustrated. I didn't know why I cared. Touching my fingers to the spot on my cheek where Cameron's fingers had been, I resigned myself to another disturbed night. I was still seething with frustration but, despite this, exhaustion took over and I was asleep within minutes.

Chapter Twenty-Two

When I woke the next morning my body ached from all the running the previous day, and I was exhausted from the drama in the middle of the night. Most of the recruits seemed to be suffering from a similar malaise. Mason, however, was in a different condition altogether. The swelling from the cut on his face had reduced somewhat, but the back of his vest was stained crimson and he could barely move.

He moaned loudly as he sat up and attempted to change his vest. I could see him biting his lip to prevent any further noise. He was clearly determined to carry on, and I admired his courage. After several unsuccessful attempts, he swore loudly, his face scarlet with the effort. I wondered if I should go to his aid, but as the thought crossed my mind I saw Jackson arrive at his side. Sitting shyly beside him, she carefully started to remove the vest. He winced, but didn't cry out.

The bleeding had bound the clothing to his back through the night and its removal was clearly painful. Jackson eventually began to tear the vest away. She was the only one who could see his bare torso, and she did a good job of avoiding demonstrating her horror at the sight. I could see the shock in her eyes, but she maintained a calm expression and said something quietly in Mason's ear. He actually managed a weak grin at her comment and nodded his head.

She stood up and whispered something to Davis, who turned and left the Annexe immediately. All the recruits were awake now, and most had started to dress themselves, to prepare for the day's training. Everyone had half an eye on Mason though, as if trying to gauge whether or not he would make it.

A few moments later Davis returned with a bowl in his hands, which he filled with water from the small sink in the Annexe. He passed it to Jackson, who placed it on the floor before tearing off a strip from the front of Mason's blood-stained vest, which was cleaner than the back. Dipping it into the bowl, she motioned for him to turn his back to her and began bathing his wounds. There were several gasps as the rest of the Annexe witnessed the angry red welts which dissected his back.

Jackson sat and patiently washed each of the wounds in turn. Mason moaned slightly, but realised how necessary it was to clean his wounds, so acquiesced with little protest. I thought about wounds I had previously seen back in Agric, where citizens had suffered injuries which had not been properly tended to. I had seen some become infected, oozing dark green or yellow pus, angry red coloured flesh surrounding them. Those citizens had disappeared off to Clearance very quickly. I mentally thanked Cameron for the antiseptic he had also provided.

Most of the recruits had turned away from Mason now out of respect, or simply sickened by the appalling sight of his wounds. I was unable to tear my eyes away, fascinated by the gentleness with which Jackson tended to them. I wondered if I would have been able to offer him the same care. I liked Mason, had begun to consider him a friend, but I wasn't good

with blood and didn't feel that I could have been as tender as Jackson was.

Mason looked almost peaceful by the time she had finished applying the ointment. As she stooped to clear the bowl away, he turned around to face her. When she sat back up again, a look passed between them which I couldn't interpret. He reached a hand out to her and she stood up suddenly, slopping some of the water out of the bowl. It seeped into the wooden floor below and she hurriedly mopped it up with the remaining strips of Mason's vest. She pressed something into his hand before hurrying red-faced towards the door. He understood, swallowing the painkiller she had given him quickly, but stared after her with a confused expression on his face.

When she returned, she went quickly to her bed, collected a vest of her own and tore it in half. Returning to Mason's bed, she motioned for him to stand. He obeyed slowly, breathing heavily as if to try and cope with the pain he clearly felt. Even slightly hunched over, he was much taller than her. She passed the torn vest around his chest several times, until she had covered the majority of his wounds. Once done, she secured it by tucking it tightly into itself. Then she reached for Mason's clean vest and helped him to get it over his head.

After she had pulled it over his torso, they stood for a moment too long, closer to each other than they should have been. Something about them reminded me of Tyler and Cameron in the forest the day before. Jackson did not meet Mason's gaze, instead keeping her eyes fixed on his chest. He seemed about to say something to her, but she moved backwards abruptly and rushed away to her own bed. There, she busied herself getting changed with her back to the entire

room. Mason sat back down on his bed heavily, a hand on his head as though he felt dizzy.

A few minutes later, Tyler arrived. I felt like she had come in later than the previous day and wondered if that was part of the 'taking it easy' on Mason. I appreciated it anyway. She looked around the room, her eyes settling on Mason who was still seated and pale, but at least dressed and looking alive. A look of relief crossed her features before she quickly stifled it. Then she was all business.

"Today will involve a visit to the source of our second power supply: the Hydro Plant. As you know, this is located in the Lower Beck. It will involve us travelling through many of the Sectors you came from. Clearly after last night," she glanced at Mason again, "you understand the necessity of keeping yourselves separate from your old Sectors. I shouldn't have to remind you of the consequences of speaking to those citizens and conveying any information which you have been made privy to since you began your training here."

Barnes now marched through the door noisily, looking as tired as I felt.

"Where were you?" he demanded, "Why didn't you wait?"

She shot a look at him, "Because you didn't look like you wanted to wake up."

He sneered back at her before scanning the room, his eyes coming to rest on Mason.

"Survived the night then? Good luck with training today." He grimaced slightly, giving an exaggerated wince, "Your back must burn so badly."

So much for taking it easy on him. It seemed that the promise only applied to Tyler and Cameron. Barnes was a different matter altogether. I wondered how Mason would

fare with such a lengthy journey in front of him, but then felt glad that he wasn't required to run or climb. The solar panels training had been dull, but not hugely taxing. Hopefully the Hydro Plant session would be much the same.

Tyler's voice cut across my thoughts again, "Everyone in the canteen for breakfast in five please. We'll get going to the Hydro Plant soon afterwards.

The meal passed without incident and we were soon gathered in the field where we had first entered the Patrol Compound. The air was unusually humid and despite a weak sunlight filtering through the woods into the field, there were larger than usual grey clouds gathering on the horizon. Barnes still looked a little wild and I wondered what had caused his pale features and sweaty appearance. Perhaps he was ill.

Just as we were about to set off, a voice called him from the Jefferson Building. Barnes put up his hand to halt us and turned to see who had stopped him. I knew from the voice who it was instantly, and did not turn. I had no wish to see Cameron this morning, no idea how to behave around him after the previous night.

"Barnes, wait!"

It took him a moment to reach us and he didn't even look at me. He exchanged a few quiet words with Barnes, who looked surprised, and then frustrated. He stepped back, looking like he wanted to argue. Tyler joined the discussion, and a few minutes later Barnes shook his head, then turned and began jogging in the direction of the Jefferson Building. Cameron grinned at Tyler and they set off down the hill at the front of our group.

Clearly they had realised there would be no taking it easy for Mason if Barnes was anywhere near the day's training.

Somehow, they had engineered a swap where Cameron was able to replace him and therefore make sure that Mason got through the day. I was torn: insanely grateful for Mason's sake, yet distressed that I would have to spend so much time in Cameron's company today.

The journey through the wood was fairly pleasant. Tyler and Cameron took it easy, marching at an easy pace for Mason's sake. He was managing to keep up, although the expression on his face betrayed him, he was clearly fighting considerable pain.

I began to think about where we were headed. If we were going through the Lower Beck, was there any chance of me seeing anyone I knew? I wondered if we might pass by the fields where Cass was working, or spot her on the way to the canteen. I wondered what my reaction would be. Could I pass her by without a word?

But when we reached the Lower Beck and ran through the square it was deserted, aside from the Patrol citizens on guard there. I noticed Cameron picking up the pace and realised it was to demonstrate that no one was taking it easy on Mason. Clearly we couldn't trust all members of Patrol to show the same compassion to an injured recruit. We nodded at the two men guards as we passed by, and headed towards Agric.

There were lots of citizens in the fields, most bending over the crops, busy with the harvest. It was a key time for us and I knew exactly what each team would be doing. With the clouds thickening on the horizon, the battle would be on to get as much of the crop as possible securely in the barns before rain hit The Beck. I did see a few faces I recognised as we passed, but there was no sign of either my old pod or Cass's new one. Most of the Agric citizens kept their heads down, focusing

on their work, either because they were busy or scared. A few curious faces glanced up at us as we marched past, brave souls who didn't mind risking a sharp word from their Super if they were caught.

I knew that Cass and I fell into the latter category. We had never been able to resist staring at the passing members of other Sectors. I had always felt as though there were more to know, more to understand. That things were not as they seemed. And I had been right. Harper, on the other hand, was always quite happy to continue with her work, finding tending to the crops soothing and absorbing, rather than dull, as Cass and I did.

Before I could search the greenhouse entrances and look over at the far fields, we had travelled through the Agric Compound and reached the Hydro Plant on the other side. Situated at the side of the powerful river which ran down the hillside The Beck was built on, it was housed within a walled compound. As Agric citizens we had been aware of its existence and relied on the waters of the river to feed our crops, but we had never been allowed access to the plant itself. We knew that the river ran through the centre of it, and that it was staffed by Patrol citizens, but other than that were ignorant to the way it was run and the exact machinery contained within it.

Cameron stopped at the gated entrance to the plant and nodded at the Patrol guard on duty. Then he glanced along our line, as if to make sure that we had all kept up. His gaze lingered on Mason for a moment and he seemed satisfied and pleased that he had managed to cope with the journey despite his injuries.

"This is the entrance to the Hydro Plant. Well-guarded, to

protect from intruders. The Beck's engineers designed and created it very early on in our existence," Cameron began, once we had gathered around him. "It is far smaller than many of the Hydro Plants created in the past, but it serves as an effective way to create electricity for The Beck society. And one thing we are never short of here," he stopped, smiling ruefully, "is water."

Tyler stepped forward and took over, "It harnesses the considerable force of water provided by the river's constant flow down the hillside and uses turbines to convert the water's kinetic energy into mechanical energy. A generator then converts this into useable electrical energy to serve the areas of The Beck which require it most."

I wondered which areas these were, and where all the energy was put to use. Certainly in Agric we didn't get to see a lot of it: the work there was mostly manual and there were no machines powered by the energy to assist us in the sometimes exhausting tasks we had to complete. Only the greenhouses occasionally made use of the power provided by the plant. Perhaps power, like food rations, was distributed unevenly throughout The Beck.

Cameron continued, "The Hydro Plant is mostly staffed by Patrol, with occasional visits from a few of the Dev department engineers who check it over and ensure it is running properly. No other citizens are permitted here and restrictions are in place to make sure that only those who are supposed to be here are allowed to enter. This morning you will be shown the various tasks entailed in a Patrol shift down here."

The duty guard swung the gate open and Cameron beckoned for us to follow him, glancing upwards at the darkening

sky before he moved through the gateway. I wondered again at the heightened security levels here. What threatened the power plant so much that it required a round-the-clock guard and a locked entrance? For the second time in two days, I shuddered to think about the threat which might lie outside of The Beck, the place that I had always felt fairly safe in.

Chapter Twenty-Three

The Hydro Plant was smaller than I had anticipated. Once we were through the gate, Cameron ushered us into an area only a little larger than the Annexe. The walls formed a kind of open courtyard, with the river rushing powerfully through the centre. At two sides of the square, the walls had been built over the river, forming narrow bridges where the river could enter and exit the space. The walls enclosed the plant and protected it from view, or attack. A smaller, wooden bridge had been constructed across the river in the centre of the courtyard, so that the officers on duty could easily pass back and forth across the river to access the equipment on both sides of the plant.

The powerful flow of the falling water was mesmerising and I found I couldn't easily tear my eyes away from it. The noise was almost deafening in volume though, echoing off the walls around us and amplified in the enclosed area. I wondered how people managed to work comfortably inside the space for any length of time, until I spotted the second Patrol guard wearing ear plugs.

We were directed across the bridge to the other side of the plant where the guard was noting down figures on a clipboard. He waved a vague hand in our general direction, but didn't attempt to speak. Tyler pointed out some of the equipment:

what I assumed were the turbines, a storage locker containing safety gear, various control levers and dials and a dashboard of sorts with a number of display panels. Then she ushered us back over the bridge and out through the gate, where we could hear her more clearly.

"The location of this plant was carefully selected before it was built. The river is at its widest point here and the hillside drops off quite steeply, which creates a rapid vertical flow of water. Did you see the turbines I pointed out, submerged in the river?" She paused to check that we had noticed them. "They are by far the most important pieces of equipment here. They are constantly turned by the water and are essential in converting the kinetic energy which is used to power so many things in The Beck. The job of the guard inside the plant is to check the equipment at regular intervals to ensure that all is working as it should be. We rely heavily on this plant for our energy. If it were to break down, we would all suffer."

I stopped listening to her and looked around. The guard outside the gates looked bored, glancing around as though the last thing he expected was any kind of attack. As far as I could see, there were only two guards required at any one time at the plant, and this patrol assignment seemed to me to be even more dull than defending the Solar Fields. I didn't relish the thought of six hours straight standing outside a gate which few ever entered. But at least from the outside there was a view of the goings on in the Lower Beck. The officer inside had little other than the flowing water to entertain him. I wondered if Patrol citizens had any control over which areas they were assigned to. If there was any way of controlling the assignments, I would certainly look to avoid guarding the power plants as often as possible.

My attention wandered further, to the activity in the Agric Compound. The citizens were currently harvesting potatoes in the fields closest to me. Potatoes were one of our staple crops, and we grew and harvested a huge amount every year. The barns at the rear of the Agric Compound were dark and cool, and two of the largest buildings were entirely devoted to the storage of our potato crop. Given the right conditions, we could make a good crop last almost the full year, until the next one was ready to be harvested.

I had never really considered how those crops were distributed, assuming their division to be equal. I knew now that this was far from the truth. Watching the Agric staff toiling away, digging up the harvest which they had diligently planted, watered, fed, protected and tended to for months made me angry. They did this, for the most part, with the faith that they were doing their part in contributing to the survival of The Beck. We all knew things were difficult, conditions harsh. But if we pulled together, we were told, we would survive. We could thrive in a world which had become difficult to live in. But it was clearly made more difficult for some citizens than for others. The thought of it made me sick.

I realised that Tyler had stopped talking and was staring at the sky, which had turned an odd shade of yellow. Hastily I refocused, hoping she had not noticed my lack of attention. After shooting a dark look at Cameron, she continued, more hurriedly than she had before.

"That's it really for the Hydro Plant. It's pretty simple. We are not required to do anything beyond the simple checks I have just explained. To begin with, as with any new Patrol Citizen, you will complete shifts here with a more experienced officer."

Cameron chimed in, "If there is a serious problem with the machinery here, you need to inform someone in Dev as quickly as possible. They will send an engineer over to look at it. Never let the plant stay idle for long."

"Now we just need to make one more stop before we return to base. The wall." Tyler nodded towards it. "Another asset The Beck has which requires guarding. And a lot of it."

I looked over at the structure looming dark in the distance against the yellow sky and remembered my final night in the Lower Beck with Cass and Harper. An almost physical pain lanced through my stomach at the thought. Blinking furiously, I attempted to control my breathing and remain calm, knowing I couldn't afford an outward show of sensitivity.

Luckily, Tyler began to lead us towards the wall, and the movement distracted the majority of the group. I wiped a hand across my face surreptitiously, relieved no one had noticed, until my eyes locked with Cameron's and I knew that he had. He was observing me carefully, seriously, but his gaze was neutral and displayed none of the confusion I had witnessed the night before. Hurrying on, my head down, I prayed that I would be able to sustain the distance I had so far kept between us for the rest of the day.

Within minutes we stood at the base of a ladder, much the same as the one we had scaled on my last night in Agric, only this one had number 18 painted on the wall at the base. Tyler reached for the ladder and began to climb. She was, as ever, lithe and agile and had reached the summit of the wall before the recruit behind her was even half way up. I stood and watched as one by one, we scaled the ladder. I realised from the murmurs and expressions that most of the recruits had not been on the wall before. Realising that I should never have been up here either, I quickly imitated them, staring around me as though the view from the wall was completely new to me.

Once everyone stood together at the top, Tyler set off again, walking along the wall top away from the Lower Beck area. The air was chilly up here and the wind whistled along the length of the wall, slicing through our overalls viciously. Any earlier sunlight had been completely obliterated by the dense clouds. Cameron had been at the front of our group for the majority of the morning, but as I watched, he began to drop backwards, slowing his pace deliberately. My heart sank. If he came to speak to me I had no idea what I would say. Watching Jackson tend to Mason's lacerated back this morning had brought the horror of the night's events flooding back, and I was still angered by the part Cameron had played in the torture.

Despite this, I found myself curious about our conversation. Why was it so important that I thought well of him? I didn't understand his constant hot and cold behaviour: one minute berating me for even seeking him out and the next desperate for me to think well of him. Whatever the reason, my heart was pounding in my chest at the thought of another potential conversation with him here, on the very wall where we had first met.

As I watched, he drew level with Davis and they exchanged a few words, but then he slowed even further, moving steadily backwards through our group. I found myself breathless now, dreading the moment when he would get to me. He stopped next to Mason, who was managing to move along fairly steadily towards the rear of our group. Jackson and I had deliberately stayed behind him in support, appreciating that he was finding it difficult to keep up with the group in his current condition. He looked pale and was sweating considerably, despite the chill in the air. Cameron spent quite a while talking to Mason, and eventually passed him a flask, placing something into his other hand as well. Another of the painkillers, I presumed.

Mason swallowed it without hesitation and passed the canteen back to Cameron. He nodded, said something else to Mason, and set off towards the front of the group where he resumed his conversation with Tyler. I paused, waiting for the relief to hit me, but was surprised when a sinking feeling settled in my stomach instead. I had to accept that, no matter how conflicted I was about the potential content of our conversation, I was disappointed that he had not come to talk to me.

I swallowed the hurt and marched on, retaining my position behind Mason so as not to draw attention to his lack of speed. We reached a juncture where the wall changed direction slightly, angling backwards towards the drainage ditches I had helped to dig. Tyler held up a hand to stop the group.

"The wall is The Beck's central defence, which protects us from flooding and any kind of attack." Tyler glanced again at the sky as she spoke.

"It requires many guards," Cameron continued, "in six-hour shifts, one posted every few hundred metres along its length. There will never only be one guard up here. You will always have back up. And when you're on duty you will have one of these," he held up his walkie talkie, "to communicate with both the officers on the wall with you and Patrol Base camp."

"The biggest threat of attack to our camp will come from the outside. It will come from across the water. When guarding the wall we always anticipate being attacked."

Davis interrupted before Tyler could continue, "Attacked? So you're saying there is something out there which could come from the water and hit The Beck?"

Cameron nodded.

"What? Other humans, like us? Or wild animals of some kind?"

Tyler and Cameron exchanged glances. I wondered what it was that could attack us which frightened those in charge so much.

"Humans. The Beck is not the only settlement in existence. There are others out there, but they live in very… well, very different ways."

"There are people out there who do not have a well-run, self-sufficient society like us. They seek to gain assets from The Beck that they could use for themselves. It goes without saying that we do not want them to gain these assets."

A sudden crackling came from the walkie talkie attached to Cameron's belt. He stepped away from us to listen to its message, but the panicked voice came through loud and clear.

"Extreme weather warning. Severe squalls approaching from the East. Adopt storm conditions throughout."

Tyler nodded at the sky, "That's what I was afraid of."

Cameron raised his eyebrows, "As some of you have probably realised, there's a large storm coming. We have been monitoring its progress and were hoping it would change its course, but so far it hasn't. It's now close enough to safely assume that it will hit us. We need to get down off the wall immediately and do everything in our power to assist those in The Lower Beck to protect the crops and livestock."

Tyler had already set off in the direction of the nearest

ladder, "Get moving. Now. When we get to the bottom you'll be given further orders about where your assistance is needed."

Cameron grimaced as he followed her, "Ready or not, your first official shift as Patrol citizens is about to begin."

Chapter Twenty-Four

We reached the lower Agric fields quickly and gathered with another small group of Patrol Officers who were waiting for instructions. Cameron and Tyler took charge, serious and business-like now that the storm was approaching. We often had rain in The Beck, but storms on the level which we were about to suffer were thankfully fairly rare. We had around four per year, and the damage caused by each one varied. The worst storm in my memory had come during my first year in Agric, when I was relatively inexperienced. The wind had ripped through the Agric greenhouses and torn up some of the crops.

After taking emergency action to protect as much of the harvest as possible, we had taken shelter in the Kennedy Building, considered the safest place in the Lower Beck. Hours had passed while the storm raged outside. We had little food, and nothing to do but wait. As night fell, we were instructed by the Supers to try and sleep, but few of us managed any kind of rest. Forced to retreat into the rear half of the building in the early hours of the morning, we cowered in terror as the storm pulled part of the roof away from its fixings. The storm finally blew itself out the following morning. We emerged to fields which had been ravaged by winds and flooded in many places by the excessive rain.

We were lucky that time, as a lot of the harvest had already been gathered and the barns which stored the crops, specifically built on higher ground, remained mostly undamaged. Any plants left in the fields were completely destroyed, either torn up by their roots or submerged in floodwater which was several inches deep to begin with and took over a week to drain away. The LS citizens had managed to move some of the animals to safe places, but a large number of sheep and cows had been trapped in the lower grazing spaces close to the wall and drowned. We had spent a lot of time hungry that winter.

And by the looks on Cam and Tyler's faces, this storm was set to be a bad one. Tyler was dispatching the more experienced Patrol Officers to different areas of the Lower Beck, instructions about barrier fixing and livestock movement ringing in their ears. Cameron was marshalling the Agric effort, conversing with a Super I didn't know and pointing at the group of us in front of him. Moments later, she raced away, a panicked look on her face, while he hurried over to us.

"Ok so Agric has a real problem as many of the crops have not been harvested as yet this year. We are extra staff – not accounted for down here – so we can make a huge difference to the Agric effort. I've agreed that we will help alongside the Agric staff and Patrol Officers already assigned to help out here, ok?"

We nodded as one, keen to get involved and help save as many of the crops as possible. No one wanted to go hungry.

"Strictly speaking, as you haven't yet taken the Patrol pledge, you shouldn't be out here with the Lower Beck staff. But, with the storm coming in, I don't think we've much choice. It goes without saying I hope, after last night's events," he turned and nodded at Mason, "that speaking to the Lower Beck citizens about the things you know is forbidden. You will obviously have to speak to them to help out down here, but keep it to essential information only."

"I don't imagine there will be much time for idle chatter," Jackson muttered beside me.

"You're right Jackson, there won't be, but I needed to make the point." Cameron's voice was firm and serious. Jackson flushed.

"Quin." Suddenly, for the first time today, Cameron was speaking directly to me. "You're from Agric. What will be most helpful down here? That Super said the greenhouses needed reinforcing. Can you direct us?"

I nodded, not trusting myself to speak. Beckoning to the group around me, I sprinted towards the greenhouses, amazed when they followed me without question. As I ran, I tried to make sense of what had just happened. From being a lowly Patrol recruit who knew nothing, I had become a kind of leader: the only one of the group who truly knew what we could do here in Agric to help.

After the previous storms, the Supers in Agric had worked with some of the Dev staff to put strategies in place which would protect us further in the future. Digging a number of ditches had been the first step. We had many of them now, surrounding the lower Agric fields which had always been badly flooded before. The greenhouses were a different matter, their fragile nature making them easy targets for the winds which tore through the Lower Beck during storms.

Whilst the glass of the greenhouses was essential for maintaining a healthy temperature for the crops housed inside, during a storm the main issue was protecting it. Within weeks of the last storm, some of the citizens from Rep had built sets of heavy wooden shutters which could be fixed to the outside of the glass panels when bad weather approached. It was hoped that the new shutters would save the glass inside the greenhouse window frames. With the major part of the Agric effort going into collecting crops, checking that the trenches we had dug were shored up, and setting up barriers to keep the water from some of the lower fields, the greenhouses would be left until last.

But without the greenhouses we would be missing out on the produce we relied on to keep our diet a little varied. Tomatoes, peppers, cucumbers, and sweet potatoes were all grown there at different times of year and helped to keep Beck citizens healthy. These crops would be ruined if the greenhouse glass shattered in the storm. I knew where the shutters were stored, and where to find the tools with which to fix them over the panels of glass. If only we could do it in time, we could prevent Beck citizens having to exist on an incredibly restricted diet over the coming months.

I stopped running when I reached the greenhouse doors and headed around the side of Greenhouse One to the wooden chests which had been constructed behind it. Hauling open the first one I came to, I put up my hand to stop the group, who gathered around me quickly and attentively.

"Each chest contains a set of wooden shutters. They are designed to fit over each individual window panel and be nailed in place. They can be easily removed and restored to their chests later, once the storm danger has passed. They're not light though."

I gestured to Davis, who stood nearby. He came over and

helped me haul out the first shutter. We positioned it over the first section of glass and I motioned to Jackson, who helped to hold the other side in place while I opened a smaller chest to gather the necessary tools. A moment later I had hammered in the first nail, and nodded at those around me to check they understood the process. I completed the job quickly, making sure I demonstrated the places where the nails needed to be put to avoid breaking the glass ourselves. The others watched closely, many of them moving closer to be sure they could see exactly what I was doing.

"There are six greenhouses. Each one has three chests like this one. All the windows need covering. Mason, Davis and Jackson, take this greenhouse and then go on to Greenhouse Two." I gestured towards it before moving away, as they set to work at once, even Mason seeming determined to assist as best he could.

I left them where they stood and moved with the rest of the group to the third greenhouse, where I put three more of the Patrol recruits to work. I repeated the procedure until all the recruits were occupied. Reaching the final greenhouse, I realised that there was only Cameron left.

"Shall we try to do this one together?" he suggested as I stared at him, angry at myself that I had not redirected him elsewhere earlier. He was by far the strongest of the people I had available and would no doubt make easy work of lifting the sections of shutter.

"But we need three people to hold the sections in place."

"Let's try it. If we lift them in place together I might be able to hold them while you get the nails in. You seem pretty expert with a hammer, so I don't suppose I'll be holding them for long."

CHAPTER TWENTY-FOUR

I looked to see if he was mocking me, but his eyes showed nothing but respect.

I stepped away, wondering in desperation what else I could do to avoid working this closely with him, but the clouds continued to roll towards The Beck in the distance and I knew we didn't have much time. Without another word, I bent to lift the first shutter from the chest. He followed suit, mirroring my movements with ease, his long limbs moving with a fluidity which belied the strength contained in his arms.

We propped the shutter in place and I let go with trepidation, expecting the section of wood to fall, but he held it in place, only a small grunt of effort giving away its weight. I quickly fell to work, slamming in a nail at each corner of the window frame so that he wouldn't have to bear the burden for too long. We made a good team, his strength and my skill with the tools meaning that we managed the job in less time than some of the others working in threes. At first I felt self-conscious every time I leaned across him to place the nails in the frame, painfully aware of the closeness of his body and the muscles straining in his arms so close to my face. Once we had secured two windows successfully though, the feeling dissolved. Instead, I lost myself in the physical nature of the task and eventually marvelled at how rapidly we managed to secure the first greenhouse and even move on to a second.

As we were completing the final windows, the initial clap of thunder rang out across The Beck, splitting the sky and echoing across the fields. Startled, I jumped and caught the edge of my finger on a nail. Wincing, I managed to hammer it in and backed off so that Cameron could let go of the shutter and rest his arms. He was by my side in a second, and had my hand in an iron grip, examining the wound closely. Before I could react, he had torn a strip from the bottom of his overalls and bound up the finger.

"It isn't that bad." I tried to pull my hand away but he held on.

"Can't be too careful. Keep it covered. We both know how dangerous infection can be." His face reflected concern, and something else I couldn't identify. As the others approached he let go of my hand, almost reluctantly. They were all looking to me for further instruction, and I felt my face flushing.

"What next Quin?" Cameron nudged me, to jolt me out of my reverie.

I considered the options left to us: most teams had been directed to the lower fields, where they would shore up the ditches and try to gather as many last-minute crops as they were able to before the storm hit. Already, they had brought back several wheelbarrows full of potatoes, which they had unloaded by the side of the greenhouses and returned for more. Often storms temporarily flooded the lowest areas of The Beck, meaning that any crops growing there were dead by the time the waters had subsided. By bringing as much of the crop in now as possible, the Agric citizens were literally saving us from starvation. I looked across at the upper fields, now deserted, and spotted another task.

"Collect and store the crops already gathered in the upper fields."

"Sorry?" Cameron looked confused.

I pointed, exasperated by his slowness. "The Agric staff are trying to protect the lower field crops but in doing so they've abandoned tools and crop stores up here. We don't really have enough time to get down to the lower fields to help, but we can pack away what's been left out up here. Prevent tools rusting or getting lost, avoid wasting crops which have already been harvested."

I had already began hurrying towards the closest field and was again surprised to find the entire group moving with me. I stopped and considered the number of fields, the amount of Agric staff who I estimated had been at work down here, and the areas they had been covering. Then I looked at the group standing in front of me, awaiting my instruction.

"Cameron and Jackson," I began, "get to Field One – the one just ahead of us. Collect up any tools and bring them back here. If there is any sign of crops which have been harvested and left lying around then place them in the barrow at the head of the field."

The two set off without question. Was this what it was like to be an Agric Super? I felt a rush of something unfamiliar inside my stomach. It felt good to actually know what I was talking about for a change.

I quickly dispatched the remainder of the group to the fields which I knew had been occupied today, keeping Mason with me. I knew once the recruits began bringing back tools and abandoned potato yield I would need to get them into safe storage fast, but it was a job I could probably manage alone, which would give Mason a break. I motioned for him to sit on the ground and rest while everyone else was away, and he smiled in gratitude.

The wind had picked up pace and was already rattling the newly fixed panels on the greenhouse windows, though they seemed to be holding. Large clouds loomed on the horizon above the wall and the sky was leaden. I made some quick calculations, realising that the storage barns were too far away to make more than a single trip. We could store the tools in the greenhouses, the reinforced windows providing a decent amount of shelter for the equipment. After that, we'd have to carry what we could manage of the potato crop to the barns on our final trip to shelter.

I marvelled at the purposeful activity taking place in front of me. Already, two of the recruits from Barnes' group were returning, their arms loaded down with tools. I could see the other Agric staff in the distance, also heading back with barrows filled with potatoes. I knew we'd never manage to get them all up to the barns in time. Glancing around, I was struck by an idea. I pulled the lid off one of the storage trunks which had previously contained the window shutters. They were empty now, but made of stout wood, and there was plenty of tarpaulin in the greenhouses.

"Mason!" He looked up at me, weak and weary but his eyes alert. "Do you have enough energy to move?"

He nodded, "What do you need?"

"We need to get as many of these potatoes into the empty trunks as we can. That way they stand a chance of being protected. A far better chance than if they sit out here in the wet while it pours down. And it's going to pour down."

He stood up slowly, wincing a little, but then moved towards the pile of potatoes and began lifting them towards the closest trunk. He quickly got into a rhythm, shifting several potatoes at once, but placing them carefully inside the wooden box, being gentle so as not to bruise them.

"You'd have made a good Agric citizen!"

He smiled absentmindedly at the compliment. I yanked open the trunk closest to the greenhouse door and began working backwards and forwards, ferrying the potatoes over the longer distance to save Mason the strain. As the Patrol

202

recruits returned from their assigned fields they followed suit, so that by the time the other Agric citizens came back with the additional barrows, the pile of harvested potatoes had greatly reduced. I instructed Cameron to fetch the tarps and he and Jackson set to work covering the filled trunks tightly with the waterproof material. We could only hope that the boxes would remain weatherproof.

The other Agric staff had begun to gather by the green-houses now. Turning abruptly, I found myself face to face with Grady. She glared at me and tried to walk past without comment, but once she realised that half the crop was missing she turned back towards me, a venomous look in her eye.

"Where's the rest? We had more yield than this."

I motioned silently to the boxes. "We would never have had the manpower to get all this crop into storage before the storm hit. I thought our best bet was to try and protect them in these." I faltered at the look on her face, "Better than them just lying out on the ground while it rains."

She grunted and turned away, "On your head be it."

She motioned to the rest of the Agric staff and they moved off in the direction of the barns, each taking a barrow with them. I felt the first drops of rain begin to fall and knew that we didn't have long. Turning to look at my own group, I realised that the pile of potatoes was now almost gone and every trunk was filled to capacity and bound up with a tarpaulin. The Patrol citizens watched me closely, awaiting my next instruction.

"Gather what's left in the remaining barrows and let's get to shelter."

Davis and Jackson began loading potatoes into the boxes and barrows we had left. The others followed suit. Within minutes we had loaded almost every potato left into some kind of receptacle and were ready to go. I pointed in the direction the rest of the Agric staff had taken, and we moved off together. As we reached the Agric gates, I heard a voice calling my name and turned to look, wondering who had been left behind.

The rain was pelting down in earnest now, and I had to squint through the slanting drops to see. A lone figure was racing towards me. Before I could focus on the face, a body launched itself towards me, hitting me hard and almost knocking me to the ground. And as the arms closed around me, my heart leapt.

"Cass!"

Backing away slightly, she grabbed my hand and began pulling me in the direction of the storage barns as she had done once before. The mud splashed up on to our uniforms, the green and blue both turning a dull brown as our feet pounded the ground in an effort to outrun the storm. As we approached the rear of the escaping group, Cass's hand firmly grasping mine, I remembered too late the warning about getting close to citizens from our previous Sector. The figure at the back turned as we approached and I saw Cameron's eyes fixed on us, a furious expression marring his previously calm features.

Chapter Twenty-Five

We reached the barns as the storm hit with full force. Lightning ripped across the sky. Cam held the door open and flung it shut behind us as we raced through. Automatically, Cass and I hauled one of the wooden beams from the floor and lodged it in place across the doors, our storm lockdown drills serving us well. The barns were filled with Agric citizens loading potatoes into darkened boxes on the wooden shelves which dominated the room. There would be no time to get to the Kennedy Building now, but we had put other strategies in place since the last storm.

All the barns now had reinforced walls, and there was even some underground space which we had dug out to the rear of the area. It wouldn't shelter us all, but at least some of the Agric citizens could hide out down there. For now, protecting the crops was our ultimate priority. If we survived this storm but had no crops left, we wouldn't live to see the next one. We would starve.

Cass and I headed for some shelving near the door which was not already being filled up by other Agric citizens. We fell into a rhythm built of many years of working together, Cass taking the potatoes from the barrows and passing them up to me so I could load them into the boxes with care and ease. It was a few minutes before I paused and looked around.

The rest of the Patrol team were hovering awkwardly inside the doors, unsure what to do with the stock they had brought up from the fields. I nodded to Cass and left her alone for a moment, heading towards them.

Jackson and Davis had been watching me and I could see open-mouthed admiration on their faces as I approached. Mason managed a weak grin, clearly feeling the pain of his injuries. Cam's face was still thunderous. I ignored him.

"We need to get them all loaded into the empty boxes. Find one which hasn't already been stocked up and place the potatoes in it. They need to be handled carefully: dried off and stacked in layers with sacking in between each one. Otherwise, they'll rot." I gestured with a hand towards the sheets of sacking which we used to separate the potatoes. "Understand?"

They nodded as one.

"Then what?" It was Mason making the enquiry.

"Then we retreat to the rear of the building and wait. It's been reinforced since the last storm. There's a small latrine, emergency equipment, and a bunker which has been dug underground for additional protection, but it won't hold us all."

"I suspect since we're the last ones here, we won't get a place in the bunker," Cass had finished unloading and joined us without me noticing. "But there's plenty of space. We've worked hard to double insulate the walls since the last time, haven't we Quin?"

The others exchanged looks. For the first time since our arrival in Agric, I felt unsure of myself. Cam's face was as dark as the sky over The Beck, and I knew I had to be careful how I interacted with Cass in front of the others.

"We did. Cass, we need to get on with unloading the rest of this," I gestured to the boxes and barrows of potatoes around us, "so if you want to get back to your pod, we'll get busy."

"I'll help you." She stooped and grasped the handles of a nearby barrow, beginning to move back towards the racks she had previously been stocking.

Cam's frown deepened and he gave an almost imperceptible shake of his head. I knew he was angry and thought any contact with Cass would go against me. After Mason's midnight beating, I didn't want to risk any trouble.

"Leave us to it, Cass," I stumbled over the words, knowing how she would react, "We can manage from here."

She stopped, her back to me, but I saw her stiffen. I walked across and took the handles of the barrow out of her hands as gently as I could. She relinquished them, but refused to look to me. I tried to show the regret I felt in my eyes, desperate for her to understand why I was acting so coldly, but it was useless. Cass was the most stubborn person I knew. I understood the hurt that lurked just below the surface, but she was too proud to show it. Straightening up, she stepped back and stalked away to the rear of the barn, where I could see Grady registering the Agric citizens to check they had all made it back from the fields.

Biting back the tears, I motioned with a vague hand to the row of shelving I knew had yet to be stocked. The others followed me without question again, and Cam's face had relaxed somewhat, but I had lost the thrill I'd felt earlier when I had taken charge. Yes, the others respected my Agric knowledge and ability, but that experience had been gained through years of working hard alongside Cass and the other Agric citizens, and now I had to deny that heritage, as if I had never been close to these people. I wondered what the eventual cost of my transfer to Patrol would be.

We spent some time unloading the potatoes safely onto the shelves, and eventually I led the rest of my exhausted group to the rear of the barn where there was a larger area, free of shelves. We usually took stock here, had occasional meetings, and it was this area that was easier to settle into as a group. It meant we weren't separated by the floor to ceiling shelving units which could potentially topple over and injure people if the storm became too fierce. The area was already full when we arrived, and none of the Agric citizens looked very welcoming once they recognised the Patrol uniform.

I led my group to one side of the barn, where there was still a little space left. It was closer to the shelves than I liked, but we didn't really have any choice. We settled down on the floor and tried to get comfortable. I noticed Mason selecting a space next to Jackson, where he winced as he lowered himself to the ground. Cam sat on the opposite side of the area, his back to the shelving facing away from me, as though he wanted to avoid my gaze. Davis settled down next to me, a little closer than I was comfortable with. Shifting slightly away, I couldn't help but notice the look of hurt cross his features, no matter how quickly he hid it.

A cold wind was now ripping through the walls of the barn ferociously, and no amount of insulation seemed to prevent its bite. I shivered. The barns did contain some provisions for storm conditions, but these would be very much under the control of the Agric Supers. I wondered whether we would see any of the blankets and rations I had helped to store in the trunks at the back of the barn.

The unmistakeable noise of hammering fists on the door

suddenly startled us all. Glancing automatically at Cameron, I was surprised to find him staring at the doors, an almost panicked look on his face. A figure came from the main area of Agric citizens, and I recognised the figure of Grady marching past.

"Wait!" Cameron sounded agitated.

Grady barely glanced in his direction, the sneer on her face saying she didn't have to listen to him. He was invading her Agric turf. For once, I admired her spirit.

She reached the door and seemed to have a slight change of heart. Pausing for a moment and glancing back at the rest of us, frozen, all eyes fixed on the door, she seemed to wait for something.

"Cass!"

A moment later my old friend was also striding past me, a similar expression on her face. I hated the idea of Cass and Grady in league with one another, but since I didn't belong down here anymore I supposed I couldn't really say much about it. Once there were two of them at the door, they began to lift the heavy beam from across it, preparing to let in whoever was still banging on the other side.

But Cameron had sprung to his feet and was also headed for the door. I didn't understand what was making him so restless. Surely he would want anyone left outside to be let in as quickly as possible, given the racket being made by the storm. Why would he want to stop them? I imagined trees being uprooted from the ground and tiles flying off roofs. It couldn't be a pleasant prospect, the idea of staying out there in the driving rain and howling wind. I knew that I'd be battering the door down myself if I was stuck out there.

Looking at Cameron again though, I was worried. He wasn't

generally one to panic, in fact he was one of the calmest people I had ever met. He was now standing a few paces behind Cassidy, his eyes glued to the door. In his left hand he held the knife I had been practising throwing only the day before.

Easing myself into a standing position, I edged closer to him. When I stood directly behind him, I reached out and tapped him on the shoulder. He jumped and spun around, his hand slicing out defensively, stopping only when the blade of his knife was inches from my face.

I gasped, frozen to the spot. Cameron's eyes blazed and he did not retract the weapon.

"What the—?" I managed to stammer, "What are you doing?"

He leaned even closer, the knife still poised for action, "Do not sneak up on me."

"But why are you—" I paused, wondering if I wanted to ask the question, "Why are you so concerned about who's at the door? Surely it's only someone who didn't make it back before we shut the door."

I had intended my words to have a calming effect. If anything, he glared more fiercely at me.

"Look around," he muttered in a low tone, "All the Agric citizens are here. Registered. Accounted for, or someone would be looking for them."

"But it could easily be citizens from a different Sector – LS? Sustenance? Some Rep citizens caught in the storm on their way back from the wall? Governor Adams? It could be anyone."

"You're right," he almost spat the words at me, "It *could* be anyone."

I stared at him, wondering if he had gone mad.

He sighed and lowered the knife slightly, dropping his voice as he continued to speak, "Last time there was a storm we had some visitors. Unwelcome visitors."

I continued to stare at him, no wiser for his words.

"Invaders from outside. They took advantage of the lack of Patrol guards on the wall to try and enter The Beck. We are fully expecting them to try again this time."

"They must be mad! With the storm raging out there? They could end up dead."

He nodded seriously, moving back from me completely now, "Yes, but they're desperate. They'll try anything."

He turned back to the door again. Grady and Cass had managed to lift the beam away from the door and as it swung open, I could feel Cameron tense again, his knife at the ready.

"Does no one else know about this?" I deliberately kept my voice at a whisper, not wanting to further annoy him now he was confiding in me. He shook his head, his eyes fixed on the door.

"And that's why Grady and Cass aren't concerned?"

He glanced briefly at me, "Grady and Cass?"

I nodded at my old colleagues, watching the understanding dawning in his eyes.

"Ah. No. The Supers in Patrol are the only ones who know. Apart from those in Governance of course."

As the door swung open, sheets of rain showered in and Cass had to strain to keep it from bursting fully open. A single dark figure staggered through and collapsed onto the floor, panting.

I felt Cameron relax beside me. One person, couldn't be much of a threat. I watched as Cass bent over the figure, checking to see if they were injured. A moment later she stepped back, almost disgusted. She nodded at Grady and they went back to replace the beam across the door, shutting out the elements again. The two of them returned to their original places at the rear of the barn, ignoring us completely.

When I looked back at the figure on the floor, it had begun to rouse itself. Cameron was heading towards it and I realised as he did that it was dressed in Patrol colours. That explained Cass and Grady's sudden lack of interest. After a moment's hesitation I followed Cameron to the door to find him bending over an exhausted-looking Tyler. She was sitting up but looked drained.

"Some LS pods collapsed. Three gates already blown down. I was cut off."

She glanced over at me as I approached and I thought I saw her grimace. Cameron helped her to her feet and half carried her through the shelves to the space we had made our own. She allowed herself to be helped into a corner and promptly curled up, her body a shivering heap.

"Blankets," Cameron said.

Nodding, I turned around and moved towards the area I knew Cass occupied, knowing the reception I received would not be warm. She didn't even look at me as I approached.

"Are there any blankets?" I deliberately kept my voice neutral.

She shrugged, "Not sure we have any spare for Patrol. You're not supposed to be here."

"We helped you gather the harvest. Protected the greenhouses. Saved quite a portion of the crops."

Her eyes remained stony, firmly fixed elsewhere.

"Please Cass," my voice was a whisper now, not wanting Grady to overhear and join in. "She's soaking wet. She'll freeze."

Sighing, she reached behind her and pulled a box from the shelf. When she passed it to me I knew from its comforting weight that there was more than a single blanket inside it.

"Thank you."

There was no response. I waited a moment to see if there was any sign of the Cass who had flung herself at me when she first saw me, but she seemed to have retreated even further from me than before.

"Cass – I'm sorry. I just can't..."

I let my voice trail off. What could I say to comfort her, to explain? Nothing, without giving away things I was not permitted to discuss. Instead, I backed away slowly and carefully, the precious box clutched in my hands.

When I reached the rest of my group I opened the box and returned to my role as experienced, capable Agric citizen. Giving the first blanket to Cameron for Tyler, I handed the rest of them around and shared out oat biscuits and water. By the time I had finished, I had regained some sense of control and calm. Finally I went across to check on Tyler. She was still huddled on the floor, struggling to manipulate her shaking fingers. I helped her to lie down and wrapped the blanket firmly around her trembling body. In the back of my mind I realised that I should really rid her of the wet clothes, but knew she would never allow me to.

She let me cover her up at least, and managed a small smile of gratitude. Cameron had remained by her side and now lifted her, positioning himself underneath her slightly so he could cradle her head on his lap, making her more comfortable and sharing his warmth. I knew that this was a sensible move on his part, but as I walked away from them I felt tears pricking the backs of my eyes again without knowing why. I settled back into my place next to Davis, huddling under the shared blanket with him, and listened to the storm raging around us. As I drifted off to sleep, I saw visions of dark-clad strangers scaling the walls of The Beck, knives clutched in their fists as lightning split the sky behind them.

Chapter Twenty-Six

Everything was still when I woke and the barn was filled with an eerie half-light. I guessed that it was still early, but the comforting silence told me the storm was over. The vaguely unpleasant scent of damp bodies filled the air and the only sound was that of the shifting sleepers and their slow breathing. I tried to stretch and realised that something was preventing me from moving. Wriggling sideways a little, I discovered an arm flung protectively across my body which was now deadened in sleep.

For a moment I thought that the limb might belong to Cameron and found myself relaxing beneath its weight, but then I opened my eyes and found myself looking directly into his. Seated about ten feet away, he was staring straight at me, his eyes filled with a pain I couldn't identify. He was propped up against the shelves in the same place he had been the previous night, with Tyler's sleeping form sprawled across his lap. I felt like he had been watching me for a while. Realising that I was awake, he jerked his gaze away instantly, his face colouring.

Shifting my attention back to the figure with its arm around me, I cast my mind back to the previous night and realised it was Davis. Feeling quite different about the arm now but unsure how to act in this strange situation, I glanced back across at Cameron, who was still staring determinedly at the floor of the barn. As I watched him, he shifted uncomfortably and eventually dragged his gaze back towards mine. We stared at one another for a few moments, regarding our mirrored positions. I felt somehow vulnerable with his eyes on mine.

His expression changed as I watched him, the frustration dissolving, replaced by what looked like embarrassment. Taking a chance, I rolled my eyes at him, knowing my own face must be similar: I felt so awkward being this close to Davis. As I did, Cameron's face broke into a smile I hadn't seen before. Grinning back at him, I felt inexplicably happier than I had in days. He motioned with his free hand to Tyler's sleeping form and shrugged as though he were trying to tell me something, although I wasn't sure what.

All the same, I nodded at him slightly, as though I understood his message. A moment later, we were still looking at one another when Davis's arm moved as though he were waking up. Immediately, Cameron looked away, glancing around the barn as if assessing the situation this morning and the necessary actions which would need to be taken next.

I missed the warmth of his gaze the moment it was gone, and found myself inexplicably angry with Davis for shifting and causing Cameron to redirect his gaze. For those few seconds where we had quietly regarded one another I had forgotten all my fears, feeling something altogether more positive for a change. I realised with surprise that I had desperately been wishing that it had been myself, rather than Tyler, who was curled up in his arms, and for a minute, experienced a fleeting thought that perhaps he was thinking he would like to switch places with Davis.

Hoping that Davis wasn't quite awake just yet and longing

to prolong the moment, I shifted out from under his arm and crawled across the small space towards Cameron. He looked a little surprised, but smiled at my approach.

"Morning. Sleep well?"

He cocked an amused eyebrow at me, motioning to Tyler. "Sleep at all then?"

"Not really. I tried to stay awake. Keep watch, you know."

"Oh." I suddenly felt very selfish, "You should have asked us to take shifts. It's not fair that you had to watch all night alone."

He smiled, "I was hardly alone. You lot are noisy sleepers. You know, snoring, grunting, sleep talking... I'd rather have been alone!"

It was the first time I had heard him crack any kind of joke and I smiled in appreciation.

"So who talks in their sleep?"

He smiled again, mysteriously this time, "That's for me to know."

"Spoilsport!"

I swatted him on the shoulder before I could stop myself and instantly regretted it as his expression changed again. His gaze became challenging, teasing, and he leaned closer to me to whisper the next few words.

"Maybe it was you."

I backed away, suddenly feeling uncomfortable. What might I have said in my sleep?

He chuckled softly. "Don't look so worried. You're a very peaceful sleeper. You hardly stirred at all."

"You were watching me?" I knew the question was a loaded one, but I couldn't stop myself from asking.

He coloured again and shifted a little against the shelves, "I was watching everyone."

I looked away, feeling disappointed for no good reason.

"So Davis – you're close?" Cameron's gaze brought back the discomfort I had felt a moment ago in full force.

"What? Oh…no! I barely know him." I knew my face was flooded with colour and looked away, unsure what he was suggesting.

He nodded, looking satisfied about something. Then he was all business. "We'll need to wake everyone soon. Time to get up and out. You've still got training today, despite the storm."

I didn't have time to respond before Tyler began to stir and opened her eyes to stare at Cameron. She managed a tired smile.

"Morning. How are you feeling?"

She nodded, "Better thank you. All the better for waking up with you."

He looked instantly uncomfortable, his gaze flicking to me before moving across to the Agric citizens who were beginning to wake and regroup. Tyler caught his look and turned until she was staring directly at me. Her face instantly flushed and she hurried into a sitting position, straightening her overalls as she did so.

"I didn't know we were all awake."

"We're not." Cameron nodded at the rest of the Patrol group, who were yet to rise.

I looked at the rest of the group for the first time, noticing with a stab of envy that Jackson and Mason were curled in a similar position to myself and Davis, yet their faces were a picture of peace and security. I made a mental note to ask her about it later, and turned my attention to Cass. She was awake and also looking in our direction, but diverted her gaze the moment she saw me looking.

"Get everyone up will you Quin? We need to get going. I'll check that the Agric citizens don't need us for anything before we go."

Cameron slid out from behind Tyler and stood up in one fluid movement. He was gone before either of us could comment. I looked at Tyler to find her looking troubled.

"Are you worried about invaders too?"

"What?"

I felt uncomfortable under her heated gaze. "Cameron mentioned that during the last storm we had some unwelcome visitors. He was concerned."

I remembered that the information was classified as I saw Tyler's horrified expression, "And why did he think it was a good plan to let you in on that information?"

Grasping for an excuse, I stammered my answer, "I was too eager to want to open the door when you knocked last night. He had to tell me. He needed to make me understand the need for caution." As I said the words I knew they sounded weak.

She looked back at Cameron, "Well I suppose he knows what he's doing." She pulled herself to her feet, "Come on. Lots to do."

Once we were all grouped together and Cameron had returned with the report that the Agric Supers had said they could handle it from here, we began to head for the door, a little unsure of what we might find outside. I was the last one to leave, and hung back to check that we hadn't left anything. Our area was clear, but as I turned to go I gave a last glance at Cass, who had busied herself with jobs from the moment she had caught my eye and refused to look over again. I paused, deliberately waiting to see if she would notice us leaving, but after several moments of nothing, I gave up and followed the others.

"Are you close to her?" It was Jackson, noticing my hurt expression.

"I was. She was one of my two best friends down here."

Jackson nodded sympathetically, "There's bound to be some tension then. I can't imagine the Sustenance Crew receiving me with open arms now that I've abandoned them."

I shook my head, partly to clear away the tears that were heavy in my eyes.

"So where's your other friend?"

I looked at her, confused for a moment.

"You said two best friends."

"Oh. She's… well she's…" I faltered.

"Clearance?"

My look was all it took to tell Jackson the truth. She squeezed my arm awkwardly as we reached the door. Cameron checked that we were all present before effortlessly hoisting the wooden beam from across the door and lowering it to the floor. I recalled Cass and I doing it together the previous night with a smile. He paused before swinging open the door, as though preparing himself for something.

As we stepped outside there was a low sun rising in the sky, a fairly common occurrence once a storm had cleared The Beck's usual clouds away. I heard gasps as the others contemplated the destruction which had befallen the Lower Beck area during the storm. I could see the lower fields were flooded, and there was a lot of debris scattered around the fields which lay on higher ground. Slats of wood and broken tiles lay stranded on paths and fields and a lot of the green plants which had been growing sturdily the previous night had been torn up by the wind.

"Are you sure they don't want help clearing?"

It was Tyler who had spoken and she was looking back towards the barn. She was right. They would certainly have to spend a lot of time clearing up after this and attempting to rescue the crops which had not been completely obliterated by the winds or drowned by the rain. But I knew Grady or Cass would be too proud to accept any help. Cameron shook his head before moving on swiftly.

As we passed the greenhouses I was pleased to see that for the main part they remained intact. A little care and attention would see the majority of the crops inside protected, and I knew that Cass would make sure that this was done early on, to prevent any additional damage to the one greenhouse which had suffered a small roof collapse.

"You did a good job," a voice whispered to my left.

It was Davis, again coming a little too close for comfort. I liked him, his pleasant friendly nature and happy smile, his devotion to his friends, but was concerned that since my intervention the night of Mason's whipping, his feelings towards me had changed.

"Thanks." I smiled and continued walking, keeping a little ahead of him for now. As I did, I noticed Cameron watching me again, the same strange look on his face I had witnessed this morning upon waking up.

"How are you feeling this morning, Mason?" Tyler asked.

Mason nodded, looking a lot brighter than the previous day, "Not bad. Most of the wounds have started to heal a little. I'm not as sore anyway."

"Think you can cope with picking up the pace a little?"

"Try me!" The old Mason seemed to be back, and he began to run ahead, as if to prove he could do it.

"He's tough," Jackson was back beside me, admiration clear in her tone. I wanted to ask her about Mason, but with Davis still so close I decided to wait until later.

"Right. Let's pick it up then. Things to do today which won't wait. You ready recruits?"

And Cameron took off, not waiting to find out if any of us were following. He had caught Mason in no time, and as he moved into the distance we all began to run, gathering speed even as we moved up the hillside. We reached Patrol in record time and piled straight into the canteen for breakfast. Up here in the hills there didn't seem to be as much damage. We had seen some trees in the woods which had been torn from their roots by the wind and had to divert our course a few times, but there was no flooding up here and where some of the pods had been damaged, rapid repairs were taking place. The Annexe, canteen and Jefferson Building seemed mostly untouched. We were starving, having missed a proper meal the night before, so everyone was quiet, focused entirely on consuming their food.

Towards the end of the meal a sudden change came over the room. I felt rather than saw what happened, my face bent closely over my porridge. Looking up, I noticed that the platform at the front of the room was occupied by three figures for the first time since I had been in Patrol. I was startled to recognise Governor Adams and Superintendent Carter, who I had not seen here before now. Behind them was a figure whose very presence made me shudder. Director Reed. I couldn't look at him without seeing Mason's agonised face.

The room, which had been quiet, now fell completely silent. The governor stepped forward to address us.

"Good morning," he began, "not that it's a very good one here at The Beck since the storm last night. I wanted to speak to you all this morning about a matter of great importance. Last night during the storm, a group of our enemies attempted for the second time to enter The Beck."

There was a collective intake of breath at these words.

"I know that many of you are aware that this is not their first attempt. They tried once and succeeded in stealing some of our food stores, but not much else. Last night they were not even that lucky. Just after daybreak, two bodies were found trapped under a fallen tree in the woods leading up to the Patrol Compound. A further body was discovered floating in the flood water in the Lower Beck fields. They had all managed to scale the wall and were clearly making their way up through The Beck in search of supplies or equipment."

All eyes were glued to Adams' face as he spoke.

"We were lucky," he continued, "that they were unsuccessful in their attempt to infiltrate our camp. In the past they have not made it further into our community than the Lower Beck area. This time, they were far closer to the upper areas of our society, and this is worrying. Yes, last night's particular invaders are no longer an issue, the storm took care of them for us, but we need to put measures in place for the future to ensure that this kind of invasion isn't possible again."

Adams stepped away and nodded to Reed, who came forward to take his place.

"I have assured Governor Adams that we in Patrol will increase guard levels in all vulnerable areas, as well as completing further investigation into the origins of these invaders.

They are not welcome here and come only to cause trouble. We will be looking to recruit more Patrol citizens sooner than the next Assessment and making sure that during the next storm there are more citizens trained specifically for storm guard duty."

He glared around the room, his eyes boring into us, "We have been lax for too long. The invasion this time was too close for comfort. We must take more action, and I know we are ready to do this. Please await further instructions over the next few days which will alert you to more training and new guard rotas."

As suddenly as they had appeared, the three officials left the stage. The room remained quiet while they left, and then a storm of whispered comments swept around the room, shock apparent in the chorus of anxious voices. I looked around at my companions. We would clearly not be the new recruits for long now. Davis and Jackson looked afraid. Mason looked angry and rebellious.

Glancing down at the end of the table, Tyler and Cameron were deep in discussion, concern etched into their faces. Barnes, seated next to them, was not speaking to anyone, but looked strangely excited. I had no idea what my own expression might convey. Three people coming into The Beck didn't seem like much of a threat, but Adams had seemed extremely concerned by it. I was appalled by the way he had almost celebrated their deaths, as if their lives were of no importance at all.

I wondered who they were, where they were from. Could they live in another society like The Beck? Or another society which was not like The Beck? I didn't know which was worse. Had we tried to speak to any of the people from this other society? Could there be more than one? Reed had spoken of investigating the existence of the intruders, as though there were some Patrol Officers who had been looking into who these people were. I wondered how much we knew about them and if we had ever tried to talk to them, to see what their society was like, whether we could learn from them or cooperate in some way. It seemed incredibly harsh to rejoice in their deaths simply because it meant that they had not been able to steal from us.

As most of the Patrol Officers left the canteen to help out with the clear up and attend to their ordinary duties, we remained behind, awaiting further instructions from our trainers. I watched as Cameron stood up from the table and nodded his goodbyes to Tyler and Barnes before heading out of the door without a backward glance. It seemed we were stuck with Barnes again. I realised with a wry smile how much my feelings had changed since the previous day, when I had been dreading Cameron's company.

Moments later they made their way to our table.

"Time to head out," Tyler began. "Big day."

I turned to look at her, unsure of what her words meant for us all.

"This will be your last full day of training before your Pledge Ceremony tomorrow. The Governor has agreed to bring it forward by a few days because of last night's events. You'll soon be one of us for real."

"Where are we going today then?" Mason's whipping had clearly not made much of an impression on him, he was still asking dangerous questions.

Barnes glared at him, clearly resenting his audacity, but Tyler sighed and answered him.

"Get ready guys," her voice was solemn, "You need to prepare yourselves."

She had all our attention now. Every eye was fixed on her.

"Today," she paused once more and looked around at every face in the group seriously, "we're going to take a tour of Clearance."

Chapter Twenty-Seven

A jolt went through my body at her words. Clearance. That meant the possibility of seeing Harper. After all I had learned, I wasn't sure that I was ready to discover what had happened to her, but it seemed I had little choice.

Within minutes we had gathered equipment and were on our way. My feet felt heavy as we made the trek towards the mountain which hid Clearance from view. The meeting with Governor Adams had infuriated me, and I was finding it more and more difficult to simply accept that The Beck Governance had our best interests at heart. After being desperate for so long to find out what secrets Clearance held, I was terrified that what we discovered over there would only add to my growing hatred of the system.

Today we were hiking rather than running, and carried heavy packs on our backs. Supplies for the Clearance citizens, we had been told. The initial part of the journey through the woods was cool and damp. Our group emerged at the base of the mountain pass, flanked either side by two Patrol guards I didn't recognise. As we began the steep ascent I soon found myself too hot, and by the time we neared the top, sweat was dripping round the back of my overalls.

Jackson and I had exchanged several nervous glances prior to setting off up the mountain. I knew that she, like me, was dreading witnessing first-hand what went on in Clearance. Fin was there, and Harper, and, though I hadn't known her well, Miller. It seemed extremely likely that we would find them in terrible circumstances. Yet we would not be allowed to react as the friends that we were. I wondered if this was another sort of test: one of our loyalty to The Beck over those we held dear. They were all considered rejects now, and any sympathy shown towards them would not be tolerated. Yet the notable difference in the treatment of citizens in the Lower and Upper Beck only led me to dread discovering how the Clearance citizens fared.

The path grew steeper and the silence which had fallen over the entire group lay heavily on us all. Even Barnes and Tyler, more used to conversing comfortably with one another, were quiet. Jackson and Mason walked close to one another, grim expressions on both their faces. Davis was close to the head of the group with Anders, and I was grateful for his absence, the awkwardness of waking up next to him this morning not far from my mind.

After working closely with Cameron for the past two days, I realised that I missed him. His strong stride as he moved through the forest. His broad back straining as he lifted a heavy load or lined up his knife with its target. And his voice. Even when delivering orders to the group, it was appealing, commanding, trustworthy. Now he wasn't here, I really felt his absence.

Eventually we reached the summit of the hill and for a moment it looked as though we were approaching a sheer, impassable rock face. As we neared it, the path twisted sharply to the left and became more difficult to follow because of the thick roots which twisted across it, like a nest of tightly coiled snakes. Beyond this, it disappeared into a dense outcrop of unusual-looking trees with many trailing branches. Most of us stopped short, wondering why we had been led towards a dead end, but Barnes stepped into the foliage and held the fronds back, revealing a far narrower continuation of the same path.

We continued on, now fighting our way through the branches, our progress much slower. Finally we emerged on the other side, our arms aching from the effort of fending off the attack of the long, sticky leaf fronds. Tyler was the last one through, and as she dropped the final branch back into place, I marvelled at how the trees on this side mirrored those at the Patrol entrance, creating a completely secret entrance on this side of the pass too. I realised how well hidden Clearance was from the rest of The Beck. It didn't seem like Governance wanted anyone who wasn't supposed to be in Clearance to find their way here. The thought made me shudder.

The path in front of us now began an equally steep descent of the reverse of the mountain. To begin with, the view down into the valley below was hidden by another dense thicket of trees, but as we continued to march, there were glimpses of some kind of civilisation. At first glance it seemed similar to the rest of The Beck: groups of pods were constructed around a central area and there were two buildings, one long and low, the other much smaller and more rundown, in the centre. Behind these was a small, single field of solar panels. The citizens here were supposed to manufacture all the uniforms and pod materials for the rest of The Beck, which was presumably done from the larger building in the middle, utilising the power provided by the solar panels.

As we emerged from the trees and the layout of the area

below became clear, I could see that it wasn't actually a valley at all, but a fairly limited area of land which sloped down toward a shore of sorts. All the pods were housed on higher ground, but the land sloped away, gently at first and then more steeply, to a rocky beach which was flanked by grey, murky water. There were no fields, and little seemed to grow here, other than the strange trees, which looked like the only living things to survive in the challenging soil conditions. The absence of a wall on this side of The Beck surprised me and I wondered how we were able to defend ourselves here, but reasoned that the land was far less appealing on this side of the mountain. Perhaps our potential invaders understood that all our valuable commodities were contained in the valley we had just come from.

As the thought came into my head I felt instantly ashamed. My friend, Harper, was here in Clearance, as were countless other citizens. Their lives should count for just as much as those citizens on the other side of the mountain. But the way that those in charge had set up The Beck was obvious to me now. All things of value: the fields full of crops, our energy plants, the citizens who were able to work to earn their keep, were situated in the valley we had travelled from. And everything which was considered to be no longer of use was right here. Transferred to the other side of the mountain where nothing grew. Abandoned, as if for disposal. The thought made me shudder.

The storm had had an impact over here as well. The area didn't look like it was well maintained in the first place, but the higher pods looked particularly damaged, as though they had suffered a battering in the high winds of the previous night too. I spotted a few skeletal figures huddled over them, attempting some kind of repair. As we descended from the hillside I could see that the pods here were in fact quite different from those I had known previously. Both the Agric and Patrol pods were constructed from tough tarpaulin which withstood the weather fairly well, and I had been in Agric long enough to know that the tarps were replaced every year with new or re-strengthened ones manufactured here in Clearance. This meant that, despite being chilly in the winter, we were always protected from the wind and rain, and I had always felt safe sleeping there.

But here in Clearance it seemed that the pods were covered with older, more flimsy material, much of which had been badly damaged in the storm. Large holes were torn in the sides of some of the pods, meaning the inhabitants would freeze on a cold night and be soaked during any kind of rain. Even the pods which were still intact seemed patched and worn, providing little in the way of shelter from the weather. The citizens who were fixing them seemed to have limited materials to help them. They appeared to be painstakingly pinning and sewing the material back together by hand, with stiches I doubted would hold for long in any kind of bad weather.

But more shocking was the state of the people engaged in fixing the pods. There were four or five citizens, all male, and what struck me about them was how thin they all were, and how poorly dressed. Considering that Clearance made the clothing for the rest of The Beck, the sturdy overalls for the Agric and LS citizens to work in, the tough, smart Governance uniforms, the protective coats of the Dev workers who needed shielding from potential chemical spillages, their own costumes appeared flimsy and patchwork. A poor man's rainbow of washed out colours, the clothes seemed to have been sewn together from bits of discarded overalls when they had been used to the point of rejection by citizens from the other Sectors.

Our group had reached the upper circle of pods now and, as we passed, we were able to see straight inside them due to their poor repair. All were empty, but instead of the camp beds I was accustomed to sleeping in, the citizens here each appeared to have a single blanket which lay on the groundsheet of the pod. There were no other possessions in view. Continuing down the path, I noticed a couple of pods which were larger than usual. They had a coloured rag tied on the outer side of the front entrance, which was closed over. We came to a stop outside the first of these.

Tyler cleared her throat before addressing us, seeming uncharacteristically uncomfortable. "This is Clearance. At the moment you will only be asked to supervise the entrance to the pass which we just came through, however we like to give all Patrol staff a tour so that you are aware of what you are guarding. The pods where the citizens sleep are much like your own," she gestured at the pods we had just passed without much conviction. "These larger pods house those Beck citizens who are sick. The long building just below us is The Warehouse, where the majority of the Clearance citizens work."

She walked ahead of us now, passing the larger pods without further comment. Davis nudged my shoulder as he caught up to me, hissing quietly in my ear, "Why give us a tour but not show us inside? I wonder what state those people are in."

I didn't respond, but my thoughts echoed his. I wondered where Fin was. She had been sent to Clearance with a leg injury which had looked severe. Was she lying the other side of that canvas in agony? I could tell that the same thought had crossed Jackson's mind as she hurried past the sick pods with a concerned glance. I noticed Mason, who never seemed far from her side now, reach out to squeeze her hand for a moment before they continued down the path.

As we reached the lower level of the camp a sustained, high pitched whining sound assaulted our ears. The closer we came to the building Tyler had called The Warehouse, the louder it became. Tyler put up a hand to stop us as we reached her and we stood waiting for further instructions, my brain dreading what we would find if we were allowed inside the building in front of us.

"The Warehouse contains machinery which assists the Clearance citizens with the production of all our clothing and other materials. The noise is made by the machinery the citizens use to create the different garments. We will walk through the building, but not stay there for long, as the sound can damage your ears. Leave your packs out here for now."

"What about their ears?" Davis whispered, as we shrugged the heavy packs from our backs and leaned them against the wall of the building. I shrugged, not trusting myself to speak.

Barnes opened the door and the noise grew to an almost unbearable level. Beckoning to us to follow, he marched into The Warehouse. Once we were all inside, Tyler shut the door behind us and I felt like I had been sealed inside hell. The room was unbearably hot, the heat created by the working machinery and the hundreds of bodies crammed into the space. Seated at intervals along a series of long, narrow tables slumped a number of figures, each one operating the machine in front of him or her. Around each work station crowded more Clearance citizens performing a number of other tasks: transferring materials to other sections of the room, folding and packing up the garments as they were completed, hand operating some of the machinery, or perhaps simply waiting to take over when the citizen at the work desk collapsed from exhaustion.

The whining noise had quickly become unbearable and I tried surreptitiously to block my ears. I noticed several other recruits doing the same. I remembered the ear plugs provided to Patrol citizens on duty in the Hydro Plant with anger. The Clearance citizens did not attempt to cover their ears. Terrifyingly, they seemed to have become accustomed to the sound levels in the building. The heat created by the whirring machinery was also horrendous, and I wasn't sure how much time I could spend in here without passing out.

Thankfully it looked like Tyler was simply going to walk us through the building from one end to the other. A heavy fog hung over the machinery and enveloped the citizens seated at the machines, but here and there I caught a glimpse of their faces. Most were thin and pale, many simply focused their eyes on the work in front of them, their expressions glazed and dull. One or two of them looked up as we came in, but most simply nodded at our group, as if they were used to being observed like lab rats, and continued with their work.

As we reached the end of the final row, a group of women at one station looked over at us. I tried to smile, not knowing how my face appeared to them, but desperate to convey that I didn't like the way they were being treated and that I wasn't a part of the terrible way they were forced to live. The woman at the machine glared at me fiercely, and I could tell from her expression that she saw me as part of the system which had abandoned her here to rot. I found myself unable to meet her gaze for long, guilt making me look away, shame flooding my body even though I had no control over her fate.

As I looked at the others working around the same machine, unable to bear the woman's wrath any longer, my eyes met another girl's and a bolt of electricity tore through my body. She was paler than I had last seen her, thinner than I could have believed, but I would have known those gentle eyes anywhere.

Chapter Twenty-Eight

She looked weak and her skin was almost translucent, but it was Harper all the same. Her eyes looked into mine blankly, at first not seeming to know who I was. I continued to stare, my eyes burning with the effort of getting her to recognise me. Tyler began to move our group along, sensing that most of us were getting restless, but I found myself rooted to the spot as the rest of our group began to leave.

Only Jackson remained behind, seeing that I hadn't moved yet. She nudged me gently, signalling that I needed to start walking. The others had almost reached the door now, and Barnes had noticed our absence, frowning when he realised that not everyone had followed. As I started forward, my feet reluctant and my eyes filling with tears, the expression on Harper's face changed. A small smile spread across her features, making her look more like her old self.

I smiled back, unable to help myself, and bit my lip to stop the tears. She shook her head at me, seeming to instinctively understand how I was feeling and knowing that crying would not help our situation at all. Jackson steered me from behind, also realising the disastrous consequences of being caught associating with a member of Clearance. After Mason's punishment for visiting his old LS friends, I dreaded to think what the sanction for associating with one of the Clearance citizens would be.

Somehow I managed to shuffle forwards, and we reached Barnes without him working out why we had stopped. Jackson moved in front of me and mimed tying a loose bootlace, which he seemed to accept without question. Within moments we were outside the door in weak sunshine and relative peace. Tyler stared at me questioningly and I was sure she hadn't been fooled by the bootlace story. I moved past without returning her glance, stumbling towards the smaller building behind. Once there I leaned heavily against the wall, trying to control my racing heartrate and rapid breathing.

"Right. We need to take the packs down to the harbour. That's really the last stop before we eat and then head off. No use getting stuck over here as it gets dark. It's a long hike back."

Tyler set off again, looping around the building to the front entrance. Once we had all collected our packs we continued to follow the narrow path as it snaked between some more pods and then sloped sharply down through some bare scrubland to what appeared to be some kind of harbour. It was small, consisting of two small jetties where four shabby-looking vessels were moored up. Other than that, there were a couple of storage huts on one side of the rocky beach and nothing else. They were guarded by two Patrol Officers wearing a strange version of the Patrol uniform, which was black in colour.

"What are they?" Mason's voice hissed in my ear.

I shrugged, not knowing how to answer.

"They look like Patrol, only different."

We were saved from any further debate by Tyler, who had stopped at the top of the beach to deliver further instruction.

"We're taking the supplies to the storage base over there." She nodded at the guards. "Campbell and Tench are members of the Shadow Patrol. They are specially trained to work in Clearance and have a specific position over here, unlike most Patrol Officers who take a more general role."

She set off again, without offering any further explanation. Puzzled, the group followed behind her, where she didn't stop again until she reached the storage hut.

Campbell and Tench stared at us. Neither of them smiled. They simply nodded, and one of them unlocked the door to the hut behind him and motioned us to go inside. Tyler led the way and moved to the rear of the hut, stopping by some shelving at the very back, many of which were already stacked with the same kind of packs we had carried over from the other side of The Beck. There must have been close to forty back packs lined up on the unit, yet there was still space for more. I wondered again what they contained. Tyler motioned for us to put the packs down, and I gladly relinquished the weight after so long carrying it.

"Ok that's it for the packs, just put them up on the shelves with the others over there. Next we need to go back up the hill to..." her voice grew suddenly shrill, "Stop! Stop that now!"

We all jumped as she shouted at Davis, who had begun to unzip his pack, perhaps thinking he would unload its contents. Some kind of strap had slipped out. In seconds, Tyler had grabbed it and thrust it back inside the bag. More flustered than I had ever seen her, she yanked the zip closed and turned to face us.

"They'll be unloaded by Tench and Campbell later. Not us."

Davis looked startled. "Don't we need to take the packs back?"

"No." Tyler motioned at the others left on the shelf. "They can stay here for now with the others. They'll be brought back later, don't worry – they'll be empty by then."

Smoothing her hands over her overalls, Tyler took a deep breath. I had never seen her look so uncomfortable.

"So let's just... just stack the packs here. Leave them for the Shadow Patrol." She gave a shaky laugh, "Why not make them do the unloading?"

Her laughter was forced and she did not convince me with her falsely light tone. I glanced at Jackson, careful to keep my face neutral, while Tyler supervised the unloading of the backpacks closely and directed us back out on to the beach where Barnes had remained in conversation with Campbell and Tench. Tyler didn't say a word to them, simply nodding back over her shoulder as she passed.

She headed towards the path without further comment, making no attempt to explain the purpose of the boats floating next to the jetties. After a few strides she paused and turned to find that Barnes was still deep in conversation with either Tench or Campbell, the other officer having disappeared from view. Looking annoyed, she put a hand up to halt us and headed back down the hill.

"Stay here." The comment was directed backwards over her shoulder.

We stood huddled together, uncertain of what to do next. Mason stepped off the path on to the yellowing grass at the side and sat down. After a few moments, Jackson followed him, as did most of the group, seating themselves in small clusters watching what was happening down on the beach. Tyler appeared to challenge Barnes, more fiercely than she had previously. I had seen her tease him before on numerous occasions, even rail at him when he did something she disagreed with, but never actually fully attack him like this. I could see from her furious gestures that she was very frustrated, but failed to see how him not following the group immediately had angered her so much.

"I wonder what the boats are for," Jackson mused from her position next to me.

I shrugged, "It's weird. They must use them for something."

"But what?"

Mason pointed off into the distance, where some other hills were faintly visible along the horizon. "Do you think there are really other people out there? People like us, who want to attack us or steal from us?"

Davis shrugged. "Maybe."

"Why do we automatically assume they want to hurt us?" I voiced my own thoughts hesitantly, "Maybe they aren't all so terrible. Don't you think it would be better if The Beck tried to work with them rather than actively keep them out?"

"Why?" Davis sounded incredulous.

I hesitated, "We might achieve more."

"D'you really think Adams and Carter would see it that way?" Mason's voice was low and steely.

"He's right," Jackson sighed, "Less land means less space. Too many people means not enough supplies. We can't fit anyone else here in The Beck. That's one thing they haven't lied to us about. That's just a fact."

"I agree, but maybe these people don't need to come and live here or take our supplies. If there are people out there, then they're already living on some kind of land." I gestured with my hand at the mountains in the distance, "We could work with them, trade with them."

"But what if their land, their society is in a worse state than ours, Quin?" Jackson's voice was soft, but reflected her fear, "What if the people out there are coming here to steal our supplies because they're struggling too? Struggling even more than we are here?"

Mason snorted, "You're basing everything on what we've been told. How much of what Adams says do you trust anymore?"

I fell silent at this. I wasn't sure I trusted anything anymore. Mason was angry, but perhaps he was also right.

"What about what was in those packs? What have we just carried over here?" This voice belonged to Davis. "You saw the strap inside the pack I opened. Some kind of harness maybe. But what for?"

I shrugged, "Climbing steep areas on the mountain?"

"But they were so heavy. Who makes a safety harness which weighs a ton? Most harnesses are lightweight."

"Depends what they're for."

A noise from further up the hill prevented the discussion from continuing. The Warehouse door slammed suddenly open, the increased volume of the whining machines attracting our attention, and we all spun round to look. A thin figure came flying out of the machine rooms, followed by a tall man in Shadow Patrol uniform. I realised the figure seemed familiar, but couldn't place her. She was running, quickly, her power and speed belying the brittleness of her thin shape. The officer lunged after her, shouting incoherently.

Startled, our group stumbled to its feet, all well aware that the route being taken by the girl led straight towards us and instinctively knowing not to get in this girl's way. She didn't slow her pace at all as she ran full pelt down the hill, unconcerned by the steep slope and the dangers this could pose for her. The Patrol Officer chased her, his size making him slow and preventing him from catching her. For a moment my heart raced with the potential triumph of her escape, but it was clear that there was nowhere for her to go. Before her lay only the rocky beach and, beyond that, the water.

It struck me that escape from Clearance, should a citizen wish to attempt it, was pretty much impossible. The path up into the mountains was difficult even if you were strong and fit, but most of the citizens here in their weakened state would find it an insurmountable obstacle. And on the other side there was only a forbidding expanse of water.

Davis was still standing on the path watching the girl's progress, completely transfixed. Jackson and I managed to pull him back out of the way as she bore down on us, the officer hot on her heels. As the path curved towards us and she was metres away, she risked a glance back over her shoulder and her foot struck a boulder awkwardly. With a brief scream, she twisted sideways and landed hard on the rough gravel of the path, scraping her face.

Jackson cried out and Mason ran forward to help her just as the Shadow Patrol officer reached them. He held out a hand which froze Mason in his tracks. We all recognised the electric cattle prod, and no one wanted to challenge a man wielding one. My eyes travelled back to the girl lying on the ground, her head down, and my blood ran cold at the thought of what might happen next. As I watched, her head came up slowly, blood streaming from a large gash on her cheek. Her eyes were still fiery though, and I had to admire her spirit.

And suddenly I knew why I recognised her. My mind

flashed back to the assessment room, rows of desks laid out, girls sitting ready to take the written test. And an Agric girl being hauled to the front, her sleeve peeled back to reveal line upon line of figures inked on her arm. It was Miller. The girl who had been caught cheating. And here she was, yet again proving her refusal to accept her fate, rebellion stamped across her features.

The officer loomed over her, the cattle prod close to her face.

"Get up."

She stared at him, unmoving, her eyes blazing.

"Get. Up."

I expected her to clamber to her feet, terror at the prod clear in her expression, but instead she looked away from him and directly at Mason.

"They won't let you go you know. Disobedience will not be tolerated."

The officer inched the weapon closer to her, the threat clear in his stance.

"Not tolerated!" She laughed suddenly, shrilly.

I couldn't see what was funny. We all stood, frozen in the moment. Out of the corner of my eye I could see Tyler climbing back up the path towards us. Miller continued to laugh louder and louder, the sounds echoing up the mountainside. I willed her to stop. Didn't she know it would be worse for her if she continued? But she didn't seem to know or care what the consequences of her actions would be.

She stopped laughing as quickly as she had started and screamed up into the officer's face. "There's too many of us here. Too many! Do you hear me? There'll be an accident soon. An accid—"

The officer lunged forwards and thrust the prod into her arm. Her voice, cut off mid-sentence, fell silent and then she slumped to the ground again, a yelping sound escaping her mouth like that of a wounded animal. Her face plainly showed the agony of the volts of electricity lancing through her, and I was reminded of Grady sticking Cass with the same weapon so long ago. But Grady had only pressed the wand to Cass' leg for an instant. The Patrol Officer held it in place against Miller's arm for much longer, until the yelping subsided and she lay twitching painfully on the ground.

I found I was biting my lip to stop myself from screaming, and when I could look at Miller no longer and stared down at my own hands, I realised that I had dug my nails into my palms so deeply that I was bleeding. Rubbing them together to numb the pain, I forced myself to look up again and face what was being done to a fellow Agric citizen. Miller lay still now and I wondered for a moment if the officer had killed her, but then her head twisted slowly to face her attacker and I could see her eyes, now glazed with the agony the weapon had caused her.

"Please." her voice was barely a whisper now, "Please. Just stop."

The officer stooped down and took hold of her arm, dragging her roughly to her feet. She sagged at his side, her legs clearly unable to hold her weight after the vicious attack. Eventually he leaned over and scooped her up like a rag doll. Throwing her over his shoulder, he set off back up the hillside, striding back to the sick pods rather than The Warehouse. She was clearly incapable of working for the rest of the day. As he made off up the path, Miller raised her head one last time, her eyes filled with tears of terror and desperation.

I closed my eyes and looked away from her towards the beach. I knew I would not forget that expression in a hurry, no matter how hard I tried.

Chapter Twenty-Nine

Once Miller had disappeared, Tyler and Barnes seemed anxious for us to move on. They ushered us back towards the building behind The Warehouse, which appeared to have multiple functions. We entered through a rough-hewn wooden door and were faced with a room sparsely furnished with a few tables and chairs. It was a canteen of sorts, but there did not appear to be much in the way of cooking going on, and there was no serving hatch linking to a kitchen at the far end. In fact there was no sign of a kitchen at all. There were certainly no Clearance citizens present in the room, and the only sign of life came from a single Shadow Patrol Officer who was taking supplies from a box at the front of the room.

We made our way towards him and received a bread roll and apple each. Sitting ourselves down at the tables, we ate in relative silence. Most of us seemed to be disturbed by the scene we had just witnessed. Tyler and Barnes sat together, stony-faced, and consumed their rolls with only a small amount of muttered conversation, their earlier disagreement seemingly still affecting them. Eventually, Barnes got to his feet and left the room with the Patrol Officer who had handed out the food.

I found myself biting back tears again. My previous knowledge of Miller's rebellion had made her into a kind of hero figure in my head and to see her cut down so brutally right in front of me had been distressing. Added to the sad sight of Harper earlier, it was all I could do to keep breathing and avoid a flood of tears from betraying my feelings. I chewed the bread slowly and methodically, knowing that despite my lack of appetite, I needed the energy to help me through the journey back to Patrol.

I was beginning to see what Cameron meant about surviving The Beck. Open rebellion was simply not tolerated, and any kind of public objection to the way things were run here, however peacefully expressed, was a rapid ticket to expulsion from Beck society. Perhaps Cameron's own brand of rebellion, small though it seemed on the surface, was the only kind which stood any hope of success. Helping people silently, secretly, was perhaps the only way to avoid being discovered and potentially obliterated for betraying The Beck authorities.

Jackson seemed to become more and more worked up throughout the meal. Towards the end, as most of us were finished, she rose and began to walk slowly towards Tyler. I started at the sight, concerned what kind of trouble my friend might end up in by speaking out of turn to Tyler, but there was little I could do to stop her. As she approached, Tyler looked up, surprised.

"I was wondering if there was any way we could see the patients in the sick pods. Not the one where that girl was taken before." She hurried on, "We won't be fully aware of conditions here unless we see everything. If this is where Governance send those who are sick, then they make up a large part of the population here, but you haven't let us see any of them."

I was glad that Barnes wasn't here to witness Jackson's

boldness. There was a collective intake of breath as Tyler considered her answer.

"I don't think you want to look inside those pods. The people who are ill over here and don't recover within a week or so are pretty much done for."

Jackson persisted, "All the same, I think we should."

Again, Tyler hesitated, "I understand why you want to, but I'm honestly trying to save you from the experience. It won't be pleasant."

I shuddered, remembering Fin's leg and wondering how it might look now. It hadn't been the kind of injury which looked like it would heal well. But Jackson's interest in the sick pods had to be linked to her old Sustenance colleague. Her determination to see them was clear. I watched as her face changed, seeming to waver slightly, but then she steadied herself, resolute.

"I understand, but I'd really like to."

Tyler took a deep breath before continuing, "I'm sorry Jackson. I can't permit you to go into the sick pods."

"Why not?"

"There are citizens in there with all sorts of diseases and illnesses. We can't risk them being passed on to you and carried back across into The Beck."

"Then I won't go inside. Just let me look from the doorway. I'll wear a protective suit. A mask. Anything."

"No. You can't. I'm sorry."

Tyler's voice was not harsh. She didn't seem to enjoy refusing Jackson's request. I felt a real understanding in her face, as though she knew why Jackson wanted to go to the pods. The way she had changed her reasoning suggested that she had tried to put Jackson off gently and avoid upsetting her further. Something was preventing her from granting the request though. Watching Jackson closely, I could see she still wasn't finished.

"I'm prepared to follow any guidelines you provide to keep myself and my fellow citizens safe. I would just really, really like to see inside one of those pods."

Tyler's face hardened. She turned her back on Jackson and began rifling through the pack which sat on the bench beside her.

"Don't ignore me. I'm asking you a question."

By now all the eyes in the room had settled on Tyler. After a lengthy pause, she swung round to face Jackson again and tried a different tack, her voice gentle.

"I know why you want to go. I understand that you want to see what has happened to your friend."

Jackson nodded, her eyes filling with tears at Tyler's sudden understanding.

"But it's useless. You can't be sentimental. The moment Fin fell and broke her ankle there was no going back for her. I think you know that."

The tears began to fall down Jackson's cheeks, unbidden. I knew she would hate to cry in front of Tyler, Mason, even me, but the pain etched into her features showed that she was helpless to prevent them.

Tyler continued, "Seeing what happened to Fin is not going to help you. Or her. You have to find a way to put it behind you. You've forged bonds with the other recruits, I can see that." She nodded at Mason, at me. "They will become your allies now. You have real potential as a Patrol Officer, Jackson. But you have to get past this."

Tyler stood up, lifting her pack and stepping over the

bench. She walked away purposefully, her head down, clearly signalling an end to the exchange. Jackson wiped a hand across her cheeks, ridding herself of the tears, and called after our Super.

"Tyler?"

I wondered if our trainer might ignore Jackson altogether. But she faltered and a few steps later came to a halt. Jackson waited for her to turn around but she didn't. Instead, she waited, statue-like, for Jackson's question. When it came it was barely a whisper, but it carried in the silent room.

"Is she– is she still..."

"Alive?" Tyler's voice was a little unsteady. "Yes, Jackson. She's alive. For now at least."

In the silence that followed, Tyler forced her head up and strode from the room. After a moment, Jackson returned to our table looking shaken, but resolute. I was surprised by the determination on her features.

"I will see what happened to her. I have to."

"Are you certain you want to?" Davis sounded doubtful.

"Just because you don't want to face it, doesn't mean the rest of us are cowards." Davis' face fell as Jackson continued, her voice harsher than I'd ever heard it. "She was my friend. I can't be this close and not find out what happened to her. Even if I can't help her. I need to see what The Beck does to those citizens who are no longer useful." She paused, looking around the rest of our little group and lowering her voice, "I'm coming back later. By myself if necessary."

Her words did not surprise me. I had seen a new side to Jackson in the past few minutes. A side I admired, but which also frightened me a little.

"Who's with me?"

I looked at the others. Mason nodded immediately. I joined him quickly, unsure of exactly what I was agreeing to, but wanting to show my support to the girl who had unquestionably become my friend. Davis was the last to respond. His face screamed how uncomfortable he was with the idea of such defiance, but he clearly didn't want to be the only one not to.

He turned to me. "Quin, when I tried to stand up for Mason the other night you stopped me. Why is this any different?"

I answered with no hesitation, "Because it's not public. Because, if we're careful, we can do this without being discovered. And because I hadn't seen what Clearance was like yesterday. And now I have, I want no part of it."

He stared at me for a moment before nodding.

"Alright then. But we have to be careful. If we get caught we'll all be sent here."

A noise from the doorway startled us into silence and we turned as Barnes burst in through the door.

"Right. We're heading back."

He motioned for us to stand and ready ourselves to leave. It didn't take long. We were outside within minutes, and I felt guilty at the relief which flooded through me at the prospect of leaving. Tyler was nowhere to be seen. Instead, the two guards from the harbour stood there, looking as fierce as ever.

"Campbell and Tench will provide an escort for us up into the mountains and leave us at the pass." Barnes nodded for the two hulking figures to set off at the front of the group.

We began to walk, following the Shadow Patrol officers silently. I wasn't sure why we needed an escort out of Clearance: we hadn't had one coming in. Either they were concerned that we would cause some kind of disturbance on the way out, or that the Clearance citizens might attempt to communicate with us further. Miller's tirade had been directed at Mason, and it was very clear that we were not supposed to see the full truth about what went on in Clearance.

I desperately wanted to speak to Jackson and Mason, but didn't dare. It might well be that we were permitted some small amount of conversation, but the topics I wished to discuss with them were not ones I wanted overheard. So I said nothing and carried on putting one foot in front of the other, trooping up the mountain to the top. The trek was easier than it had been earlier as we were free of the heavy packs, but my heart was heavy with the horrific reality of the situation in Clearance.

I wondered at Miller's words. She had screamed that there were too many. And The Warehouse had seemed overly full of people. We had no idea how many citizens were contained within the sick pods, but I feared that it was a larger amount than it should have been. So what did Clearance do about it? More people meant less food rations and living in more cramped conditions. I knew that the Clearance citizens were sleeping under thin blankets on the ground in their pods. There had appeared to be little provision for food preparation, which suggested that the rations here were extremely simple. How could hot food be prepared if there was no stove? Was the food consumed here all cold? How much of the food grown on the other side of the mountain actually made it over here?

And Governance kept sending people over. Fin had been a new addition, an unexpected one. People were sent to Clearance all the time with illnesses, but did they simply end up over here waiting for death? And what about those sent here for defying Beck rule? Were they beaten until they toed the line and got on with the monotonous work of The Warehouse? What happened to them eventually? Because I had never known anyone sent here to return.

We made our way past the lower pods, the perpetual shrieking of the machines in The Warehouse gradually fading into the distance. Tench and Campbell picked up the pace past the sick pods, clearly signifying that we wouldn't be stopping there. As we passed the final one, Tyler caught up and headed for the front of the line, deliberately averting her gaze from the rest of us. Close to the top of the slope, the path snaked to the right and I could see right down into Clearance. In the harbour, an alarming number of figures in the Shadow Patrol uniform had gathered and were busying themselves around the boats moored to the jetties. I wondered what they were doing.

Raising my eyes to the mountains in the distance, I wondered again if Governance sent boats out to other areas, reconnaissance missions to connect with or spy on other communities. Perhaps that was the reason for all the action around the boats. I recalled how a few weeks ago all I had wanted to do was to explore the rest of The Beck and the area beyond. Now the prospect terrified me.

We had reached the hidden exit now, where the path disappeared beneath the trees and Clearance would no longer be visible to us. Tench and Campbell nodded brusquely to Tyler and fell back, exchanging some words with Barnes followed by a punch on the shoulder which seemed altogether more familiar than the way they had bid Tyler goodbye. Darkness fell over the group as we began to push our way through the dense cover provided by the trees. I closed my eyes for a moment and thought of Harper and Miller and had to forcibly stifle a scream from escaping my throat.

It was worse than I had feared up here in Clearance. But perhaps if we returned to see Fin later I could also speak to Harper, and discover more of the truth about life up here. I felt slightly comforted by the thought as I focused on putting one foot in front of the other. As we made our way slowly but surely back up the mountain, I remembered that I would need to conserve some energy to make the walk over here for a second time tonight.

Chapter Thirty

The rest of the day passed in a blur. We returned to Patrol Base and ate, though the fairly hearty stew almost choked me when I thought about the starvation rations in Clearance. I didn't even brighten up when Cameron arrived, looking exhausted. He sat with Tyler at the end of our table in the canteen and wolfed his food like he hadn't eaten in days. He didn't look at me once throughout the entire meal, and my spirits sank even lower. The experience of waking up across from one another in the Agric barn seemed a million miles away.

Looking over at Jackson and Mason, who exchanged secretive glances throughout the meal, only made me feel worse. Davis, who had not spoken to me at all on the way back from Clearance, was now attempting to sit far too close to me for comfort and all I wanted to do was cry. As soon as I had forced down the last spoonful of the stew, I cleared my plate and left the building.

Once outside, I let the cold night air wash over me and slowed my pace as I walked back to the Annexe. Half way there I decided that I didn't want to be where there were others, so I changed my path and headed instead for the woods. We had been given the evening off to rest and prepare for the Patrol Pledge Ceremony tomorrow, and I knew that for now,

I wouldn't be missed.

Crossing the field where I had first entered Patrol, I wondered for the first time whether there was any kind of escape from The Beck. We had always been led to believe that there was no real life, no sustainable way of living, beyond the community we inhabited. But today, seeing the mountains in the distance from Clearance, seeing the boats which were moored up ready to take passengers somewhere else, I had to wonder. They had lied to us about so much. It struck me that they had probably lied to us to ensure that we didn't even begin to contemplate the possibility of escape.

I reached the woods as darkness began to fall. Wandering a little way in, I found a hollow tree and concealed myself inside it, knowing from this position that I would be difficult to spot if anyone passed by. I wanted to escape from people, but I didn't really want to be caught out here. It was growing colder, but the tree provided me with some shelter from the wind which was cutting through the woods. From my position I could just see the sky through the branches above. I tried to empty my mind as I watched it turn from slate grey to black.

I knew I had to be back at the Annexe within the hour. Jackson was planning to set off for Clearance as soon after lights out as possible. We couldn't leave too late or we wouldn't make it there and back in time without being caught. I was more scared than I could remember ever being, but knew that I couldn't let Jackson down now.

A rustling in the trees close by alerted me to a presence. Silently, I withdrew my feet until they were completely concealed and waited. The noise grew in volume, as though the person were coming closer. I wondered who else might be out here at night and not in the Patrol Compound, already eating or preparing for bed. Perhaps Patrol Officers heading back from a shift, but the person appeared to be travelling slowly, cautiously, as though the route was unfamiliar. I thought again of the invaders who had come during the storm. Surely they wouldn't risk another visit so soon, when we were on full alert? But anyone who belonged in Patrol would be striding up the path with a lantern, not skulking in the bushes.

The footsteps were much closer now, almost passing the tree. Strangely, I didn't feel fear. I knew that I was concealed and I was pretty good at staying quiet when I needed to. I figured that I would let the person pass me by and then sneak back into Patrol once they were well past me. It was only when the figure came into view that my heart began to pound. It was female and very familiar. And when she stumbled over a root in the darkness and whispered a curse under her breath, I was certain.

"Cass?" I hissed into the darkness.

She froze. There was a silence. Eventually, the feet shuffled closer.

"Quin?"

"Over here."

I reached out a hand and took hold of her arm which was easily within my reach now. Within seconds she was hunkered down in the hollow tree next to me, her body squashed against my side as it had been so many times before in the alcoves on the top of the wall. It was like coming home. But I was frightened for her too.

"Why are you here?" I knew my voice was harsher than it should have been.

I could feel her eyes on me, though I couldn't see her properly in the darkness. For a moment, she didn't reply.

I forced my voice to be more gentle.

"Cass?"

"I had to… had to see you. After last night… this morning."

I had never really seen her stumble over her words so much. She was usually calm, confident, assured. But not tonight. I waited to see what would come next, knowing instinctively how difficult this was for her.

"I wanted to say–" She stopped again, taking a deep breath, "…well… I… I'm sorry."

She blurted the final words out and let them hang between us. Her pause only underlined how difficult the words had been for her to say.

"I shouldn't have gone off at you. But without you… and Harper… it was harder than… than I thought. And when I saw you…"

The words came out in short bursts, as if she had been rehearsing them and now wanted to get them out as quickly as possible. I waited, knowing there was more.

"…you were so cold."

I couldn't bear the hurt in her voice. "Cass – we were told not to speak to you all. They threatened us… it wasn't safe. I thought you'd understand." I trailed off, unsure how else to explain it.

"I do… I did… when I thought about it. Too late then though."

I chuckled and felt her relax beside me.

"Once you'd gone and I calmed down… I knew it wasn't you. This Super job has been… well I've found out some scary things. I should've guessed you had too."

"I have. That was why I ignored you. Cass – I'm not sure who I can trust… I saw someone whipped for going back to their old Sector." I shrugged. "Seemed better not to speak to you at all."

"Yes. I just felt… like I was lost. Like you had new friends. Like you didn't need…"

She broke off, and I regretted the pain I had caused. Then, in the darkness, I felt her hand creep into mine. She was freezing.

"You know—you were brilliant."

I wrapped my hands around hers in an effort to warm them. "What?"

"You saved most of the greenhouse plants. And putting the leftover crops in the storage boxes–genius! You stopped tons of potatoes being washed away. You're kind of a hero."

I snorted.

"No really – in Agric anyway."

"Thanks." I managed a small smile at the thought of my old Sector, before remembering the day I'd spent in Clearance. "But I think we have more to worry about than coping with a storm."

"What do you mean?"

"I don't want to tell you. It's probably better you don't know. Safer." Feeling her stiffen beside me, I was quick to follow my words with some reassurance. "Cass – I trust you. Always. But I know things that put us all in danger. If you don't know, for now at least, you're safer."

Her body lost some of its tension. She sighed, but didn't reply. Silence fell between us again. The wind had dropped and an eerie stillness had taken over the woods. We were protected in the tree from prying eyes, but I knew that, sooner or later, I had to make my way back to the Annexe to meet the others for our trip to Clearance. I wrestled with whether or not to tell Cass about Harper, about Clearance, but decided that she was better off not knowing.

"I've decided I want to join Patrol." Cass' words flew out of the darkness like bullets.

"Why?"

She shrugged, "I miss you. I figure if I manage a Patrol Assignment at the next Assessment we'll work together again. I don't care about the Super thing anymore. It's okay here?"

I paused, not knowing how much to say. "I suppose."

"There's a rumour they're looking to recruit up here. I thought I could put myself forward..." she trailed off and I realised that she was unsure that I wanted her to join me.

"The rumour's true. You'd enjoy the work in Patrol, except—"

"Except what?"

"Except there's a lot you don't know yet."

"Like what?" Her tone had become belligerent and I could tell she was becoming frustrated again.

I didn't want to be the one to tell her. Not tonight anyway. "You'll find out. They'll take you. Just make sure you're ready."

"I will be."

Her tone was sullen and I knew I'd upset her again. She felt like I didn't trust her and desperately wanted me to. I tried a different tack.

"Where do the Agric citizens think you are right now? You know if you're caught up here you'll never make Patrol."

Her hand disappeared from my own. "I told you– I had to see you. My new pod– they're ok. Some of them are covering for me. I'll be back before anyone notices."

"You hope."

She shifted away from me, a task which was made almost

impossible by the narrow space available in the tree's trunk. As she resettled, we both heard something close by. More footsteps. We froze. The footsteps were coming from the direction of Patrol and were very sure of themselves. A faint light swinging this way and that across the trees signalled that the person approaching had a lantern. This was an experienced Patrol citizen. I grasped Cassidy's hand tightly and we held our breath, praying that the footsteps would pass us by.

Chapter Thirty-One

I wondered who else might be out here at this time of night, desperately hoping it might just be a concerned Jackson looking for me. As Cass and I crouched together, our fingers turning slowly numb from the fierce grip we had on each other, the footsteps continued to advance. I considered running further into the forest and taking Cass with me, but knew that the person was too close now and would certainly see us. Our only chance was to keep hidden and hope that whoever it was would pass us by. At first, it seemed like they might, but then the footsteps stopped. We held our breath collectively and waited.

"Quin? You out here?"

I sighed with relief. It was Cameron, who I was fairly certain would not betray me. Despite this, I was still torn as to whether to reveal our whereabouts. I felt like I could trust him, but didn't want to risk Cass's position as well. To find just me would be one thing. To find an Agric citizen who had sneaked up here to see me was entirely different. I held my tongue.

"Quin!" The voice was hushed, one which didn't want to be heard. I didn't think he'd been sent out here to look for me. He was trying to find me for his own reasons. An unbidden thrill swept through me at the thought.

I made to move forwards but Cass grabbed hold of my arm and held on, her grip like iron. As I glanced over at her, I could feel her head shaking intensely. She didn't trust Cameron. But then, she didn't know him. Brushing her arm away, I got to my feet and stepped out from the hollow tree into the clearing. Cameron, armed with a torch, spotted me instantly.

"You are here! What are you doing?"

I took a tentative step towards him. "I wanted… I needed a bit of space. Clearance was… well it was tough."

He paused, staring at me in the darkness. I prayed that Cass would have the sense to stay hidden. In the shadows it was difficult to see his face.

"Yeah. Clearance for the first time is hard. I spoke to Tyler. She still finds it difficult over there. She said Jackson was upset, but you seemed ok."

"On the outside maybe…"

"Did you see your friend?"

For a moment I thought he was referring to Cass and I froze, terrified that he knew.

"The one who was sent there after the last assessment. Remember? She tried to protect you when I first met you on the wall."

His voice was soft, tender almost, and I couldn't bear the understanding he was showing me. He took a step towards me and held out his hand as though he would take mine. Knowing Cass was so close, I jerked back instantly. The look of hurt that crossed his face was unmistakable, even in the near-darkness. I stared at the floor, not knowing how to reply without hurting Cass.

"Did you see her? I know she's over there."

I nodded silently, unable to speak.

"And was she ok?" He seemed to catch himself and gave a brittle laugh which had nothing to do with humour. "Of course she wasn't. No one in Clearance is ok. Who'm I kidding?"

I didn't get the chance to reply. Before I could open my mouth I found myself plunging to the ground, assaulted by Cass as she flew from her hiding place and launched herself at me. I could see the shock on Cameron's face as I crashed to the ground heavily, Cassidy pounding me with both fists.

"You saw her? You *saw* her?"

Cass was crying. Harsh, dry sobs which echoed around the clearing. I held up my arms instinctively, trying to fend off the blows she was raining down on my head.

Cameron had recovered slightly and rallied. Swerving his body behind Cass's, he hauled her off me and pulled her to one side. Then, with an expertise which came from years of Patrol combat training, twisted her arm behind her back. I had known he was capable of such violence. You couldn't survive Patrol without learning how to fight. But witnessing it was difficult. After a few moments of struggling, she lay beneath him, squirming but unable to break free.

"Cameron stop!" I wanted to scream but was too afraid of being overheard. Instead, my tone was whispered and hoarse.

He looked up at me and I felt rather than saw the dawning recognition.

"This is your friend from Agric right? The one who was trying to talk to you yesterday?"

I nodded, placing a hand on his arm.

"And you knew she was here." A hurt expression crossed his features as the understanding dawned. "You were trying to hide her from me?"

"Yes." I paused, "I'm sorry. I know she shouldn't be here. But please – just let her go."

"Why is she here? Is she spying?"

"No!" I knew my voice sounded as panicked as I felt. "She came to apologise. For earlier. She was angry at me for rejecting her but regretted it later when she realised I was trying to protect her."

He snorted and tightened his hold on her arm. She let out a short, terse cry and I knew she had been biting her lip to stop herself from making any noise.

"You're hurting her! Leave her – please Cam?"

I was surprised to hear the unfamiliar nickname tumble so naturally from my lips. I had only heard Tyler and a couple of other Patrol citizens I knew Cameron counted as friends call him that. As I spoke the word though, his grip on Cass loosened and he stared up at me, an uncertain look on his face.

Taking advantage of his hesitation, I knelt down at his side and put both hands over his own, gently working to relax their grip. He let me, but I could still feel the tension knotting in his arms and knew that, if he wanted to, he could easily have overpowered me. As he let go, Cass sprung to her feet, her eyes blazing.

"You saw Harper and didn't tell me?"

Desperate not to anger her again, I stood up and walked towards her cautiously. When I knew she would let me, I took hold of both her hands in mine.

"Cass. I wanted to. But she's in a bad way." I broke off, seeing the pained look on Cass's face. "I knew it would upset you. I didn't want you to feel like I do right now."

As I spoke the words I was reminded of Tyler saying almost

exactly the same to us earlier that day. Perhaps I was more like her than I realised. I could feel Cass shaking with anger as I held her hands in mine, but eventually the trembling subsided and she grew still.

"Alright. I get it. But you have to stop protecting me. If I'm going to be up here in Patrol, you'd better start to trust me with all the information," she looked at me meaningfully, "like you used to."

"You? Up here in Patrol?" Cameron sounded appalled.

Cass's eyes glittered at the challenge, "And why not?"

He paused, taking a deliberate step towards her. "I know you. You're hot headed. You've a temper you can't control. But you have to learn to hide your feelings up here, whatever it takes. Think you can do that?"

Cass stared at him defiantly but didn't answer.

I took a step towards Cameron, trying to further calm the situation. I knew that I needed to get back to the Annexe soon, or Jackson would leave without me. I had to persuade Cassidy to leave and get myself back to the Annexe without Cameron following me. My head spun as I considered possible courses of action.

But before I had a chance to act, more footsteps sounded close by. Glancing in their direction I could see the beams from two lanterns in the distance. This could only be Patrol officers returning from a shift in The Lower Beck. I turned to Cameron, my eyes pleading. We couldn't be caught now. But I didn't know if he would help us a second time. He hesitated for a moment, glancing in the direction of the footsteps, then seemed to make a decision.

In one smooth movement he thrust Cass back down into the hollow in the tree where she crouched, a mutinous expression clouding her features. Cameron pointed at her and placed a finger over his lips. She nodded begrudgingly. Standing up again, he turned to me. I fully expected him to push me down beside Cass, but instead he grasped hold of my shoulders and spun me around so that I had my back to her. Then he pushed me backwards into the hollow, ensuring that I remained in a standing position. As the footsteps bore down on us he moved closer to me until he mirrored my position, circling me with his arms and lining his body up so that it was exactly parallel with mine. Suddenly I was pressed up against him so close I could hardly breathe. He buried his face in my neck and I could feel his breath, his lips millimetres away from my skin.

"Close your eyes." His whisper was urgent.

I did as he instructed, glad of the distraction. His body was rigid with tension, the arms which circled me clamped me in place against him tightly. One arm snaked around the back of my head and tangled in my hair, pulling me even closer. The blood was pounding in my head and I found that the approaching footsteps accompanied the drum-like beat of my heart. When they entered the clearing, the footsteps stopped. Clearly they had seen us. I swallowed a scream, unsure of what Cameron's plan was; certain that Cass would be discovered at any moment. Then I heard a chuckle which was about as far from dangerous as I could have ever imagined.

"Hey Cameron! Getting to know the new recruits a little better?"

Cameron raised his head from my neck and glanced over his shoulder casually. The voice he used was unlike any I had ever heard from him and, belying the stress which held his body tense, sounded almost playful.

"Yep. Don't really appreciate the interruption guys!"

He turned his face back to me and buried it in my neck again. This time I could feel his lips moving, burning patterns into my skin. The two officers laughed again, but this time they continued walking, their footsteps picking up speed as they passed us and eventually fading into the distance. Only once they had disappeared entirely did his body relax, collapsing even closer to my own. My heart rate decreased a little, the fear of being discovered fading, but I couldn't quite calm it completely. I felt flushed and overheated, even in the cold night air.

Stepping away, Cameron motioned for me to step out of the tree hollow. His shoulders were taut again and the look on his face was far from calm. Avoiding his gaze, I turned and helped Cassidy up. Her expression was also unreadable and, for once, I had no idea what she was thinking. We stood in the clearing, tension crowding the spaces in between us.

"You need to go." This was directed at Cassidy, although Cameron refused to look at her. His voice seethed with barely controlled fury.

Cass stepped towards me and thrust her arms around me awkwardly in a brief hug. Turning on her heel and equally evading Cameron's gaze, she disappeared back down the path the way she had come. For a moment I worried about her return journey, but I quickly realised it was useless. She had arrived here ok and I could only trust that she could make the return journey equally successfully. Cass was tough and smart. But I watched her until I lost sight of her between the trees, before turning back to Cameron, unsure of what I would see.

He stood, also staring after Cass, his figure frozen and distant. I tried to make amends, my voice shaking slightly.

"Thank you." I stepped towards him, wanting to feel close to him again, but he held out a hand to stop me. When he spoke, I was stung by the anger in his voice.

"Get back to the Annexe. What were you both thinking, sneaking her up here like that? Haven't you learned anything in the past few days?"

"What? I didn't know she was coming! How could I have stopped her?"

He stared at me. "And now I've put myself on the line for you a second time. You have no idea how much we both risked then. And for what?"

I found myself biting back bitter tears. "For Cassidy. To save her from being sent to that hellhole I visited today. Because if she'd been caught, that's where she would have ended up, isn't it?"

"Yes. So she needs to learn from her mistakes and stop risking herself – and you!"

I stared at him, hurt by his anger, wanting to calm him but not knowing how to.

He looked away. "Just go."

I lingered for a second longer, but he wouldn't look at me. Seeing no other option, I took his advice. At least it would allow me to reach the Annexe without him trying to follow me. But it hurt. Brushing past him as I broke into a run, I remembered how close I had felt to him a moment ago. How thrilling his touch had been. Now all I could see in my head was his cold, hard eyes staring at my retreating form.

Chapter Thirty-Two

I arrived back at the Annexe close to tears and had to stop outside the door to gather myself. I felt drained, exhausted, and had no idea how I was going to manage the hike to Clearance again. A movement at the side of the building startled me and, fearful of what I might discover, I peered around the corner. In the shadows, way back from the Annexe entrance, stood a couple. They were locked together very much like Tyler and Cam had been in the woods, except this time both sides of the twosome seemed happy to remain entangled.

As I stared, they separated slightly and I recognised them. Jackson stood in the faint light cast through one of the Annex windows, her hand reaching up to caress the face of the boy who stood in front of her. Mason bent towards her again and for a moment I thought about the way Cameron had buried his head in my neck, but then he pressed his lips to Jackson's and held them there for a few seconds. As they parted, I ducked behind the building again, my heart racing. Silently, I opened the door to the Annexe and slipped inside.

Most of the recruits were already in bed. Others were settling themselves, packing up their rucksacks ready to move into the Patrol pods after the Pledge Ceremony. I avoided Davis's gaze as I passed his bed and quickly thrust all my own things into my pack. As I did, I secreted a warmer pair of overalls, a lantern and a pair of binoculars from my equipment stash and hid them under the covers on my bunk. After washing my face in the basin in the rear corner of the Annexe, I returned to my bed to find Jackson and Mason were back. Nodding at her a little awkwardly, I tried to get past and climb the ladder to my bunk without conversation, but she gripped my arm tightly and put her mouth very close to my ear.

"Mason kissed me." She sounded breathless, "I was upset about Fin... he was comforting me and well... it just sort of happened." She paused and stared at me, her face serious, "I'm sorry– I know after everything we saw today that it doesn't seem important. But I had to tell you."

I tried to smile. Things between Cameron and I were so difficult. Being the same status, as Mason and Jackson were, seemed to make things easier. No secrets. No lies. But I was happy for her and squeezed her arm to show her that I approved. A fleeting smile crossed her face, but then she was immediately serious as she leaned once more to my ear.

"Ten minutes. We'll wait until everyone's asleep and then go. You're still coming?"

I nodded firmly, "Wouldn't miss it."

She nodded and I climbed up to my bed. Lying in the darkness I found myself paralysed by fear and exhaustion. All I wanted to do was close my eyes and give in to the sweet relief of sleep, but I knew that I couldn't. To prevent the drowsiness from taking over, I shuffled around under the covers, changing into the warmer overalls. Within a few minutes I was ready, clutching my torch and binoculars. A hiss from the bunk below told me that Jackson was waiting.

I slid down the ladder silently, watching Mason and Davies do the same. The four of us crept to the door, praying that no one else would wake.

Once outside, Mason hauled something from underneath the Annexe porch. It was a pack and, from the way he hoisted it on to his shoulders, fairly heavy. I looked questioningly at Jackson as we set off towards the woods.

Jackson leaned closer to me as we moved into the fields away from the central Patrol area. "Explosives," she explained, "From Patrol supplies. Mason took them earlier."

I stared at her, "Explosives?"

"A distraction," she added, before jogging into the woods behind the boys.

We didn't dare turn on the torches until we were several steps in. With the light to guide us we moved fairly quickly, fear keeping us going despite our fatigue. We made good progress through the woods and arrived at the pass without issue. None of us had spoken since leaving the Compound. When we were within sight of the Clearance outpost, we stopped and took refuge behind some of the denser bushes. From here we had a good view of the guards on duty, and were surprised to see that they were Shadow Patrol guards rather than ordinary officers tonight. Their uniform rendered them almost invisible in the darkness.

Mason took something from the pack he carried and nodded at Davis. They dropped the bag at our feet and sneaked back off into the woods. Jackson and I held our breath and waited. The slight noise made by their movement died out quickly and we were soon crouching in complete silence, aside from the rustling of the trees in the slight wind. The guards at the mouth of the pass stood together, stamping their feet slightly in the cold. Their posture suggested they had been here for a few hours and they slumped over as though exhaustion was beginning to overtake them.

Moments later there was a loud explosion. Instantly the guards leapt into action, grabbing guns and racing off into the woods, straight past the bushes where we were concealed. They passed us without a second glance. Jackson shot me a look and gave a tentative thumbs up. The first part of her plan had worked, at least. Now the boys just had to avoid being seen and get back to us without the Shadow Officers noticing. We both sighed with relief as they approached from the opposite direction, having returned by a different route.

Wasting no time, we crept past the Patrol post and hurried on through the pass. As long as we could make it to the hidden entrance in the trees without being seen, I figured we were safe. Travelling in this direction anyway. The way back was a different matter. I wondered if Mason had enough explosives to repeat the process in the other direction. Or perhaps we could find a different way to distract them on the return journey. As soon as we dropped the curtain of fronds across the hidden Clearance entrance, I heaved a sigh of relief. We had made it this far without being caught. Maybe we could do this.

We continued along the path, more slowly now as we battled our way through the trees. When we emerged on the other side, a pale moon cast a ghostly light on the valley below. Jackson cursed softly under her breath. I knew she had been hoping for a cloudy night which would better shield us from view. There were muted noises coming from the area below us, which was surprising considering how late it was.

Clearance looked much the same at night, except the

machinery in The Warehouse was still and silent. The pods closest to us were dark and quiet too, but as we progressed through the woods alongside the path, I noticed that some of those further down had their canvas doorways propped open. Davis pointed at the flags attached to their entrances and I realised they were the sick pods. But the noises we could hear were not coming from inside.

Glancing down at the harbour, I could see a large number of Shadow Patrol guards. It looked like they were moving equipment, slowly and steadily, between the boats and the beach. A feeling of dread had begun to creep over me the instant we had emerged from the hidden entrance and it was only growing. I didn't want to be here. I'd felt frightened earlier, but it now was clear that something unusual was going on, and I was petrified.

I nudged Jackson and shook my head at her. She stared at me, the same look of determination in her eyes that I had glimpsed earlier in her altercation with Tyler. She was not going to be dissuaded from her mission and I knew I would never abandon her. I reasoned that at least the sick pods were quiet at the moment. The noise was definitely coming from the harbour area, which was a fair distance away from us. Maybe the fact that the Shadow Patrol were distracted would work in our favour. We could find Fin while the guards were busy on the beach and get out of here before they returned.

"We should go back. Something's wrong." It was Davis who spoke, but despite my attempts to reason away my fears, I found myself silently agreeing with him.

"No."

"But—"

"No. I need to see her. Once I have, we can go."

I put a hand on Jackson's arm, "Maybe we could come back another time. There's something going on here. We thought it'd be deserted."

"Well it isn't. But there's no one up here, is there?"

She was right. The sick pods were quiet and there was nothing unusual about them, aside from the fact that they were propped open. I sighed. We had to look.

Nodding my agreement, we crept forwards together, Mason leading the way. As we reached the first pod, we were assaulted by a stench like rotting meat. Instinctively, we covered our faces with the sleeves of our overalls. At first glance it was difficult to see inside the pod, but eventually my eyes adjusted and I began to make out the figures housed within the tent. It seemed that even here, in the pods which housed the ill and the dying, the citizens were not permitted beds of any kind.

The four of us stopped short just inside the pod. Almost the entire floor was filled with bodies. They lay, crammed in alongside one another, in the most devastatingly weakened state imaginable. There must have been more than twenty bodies crushed into the space, each one covered with a single blanket. Most of these looked filthy and some were stained with what could only be blood. The stench was clearly coming from some of the wounded, their injuries left untended. I had to fight to stop myself from retching, devastated by the horror in front of me.

Most of these people were sleeping, but a few seemed to be awake. They made little noise though, staring up at us as though they had no energy left to question our presence. I wondered how many of them might believe they were hallucinating the four strange figures entering their home.

I found myself backing away from the others. Everything about this: the smell, the heat of the bodies, the strange, stifled silence, set me on edge. Biting back a scream, I willed my body to leave the pod.

Once outside, I felt a little better. There still seemed to be a lot of activity coming from the harbour below, but the entire upper section of Clearance appeared deserted. I wondered if I dare venture further and find Harper, but was more wary of searching the rest of the pods where the citizens were not ill. Still, I reasoned with myself, I had come this far. I crept further down the hill. As I got closer, I could see a single guard on duty in the distance. Before I could make any further decisions, a rustling startled me and I darted further into the bushes, only to be joined by a breathless Davis.

"Couldn't stand it in there either," he hissed in my ear.

I nodded.

"Didn't want you going anywhere alone either."

I realised that I was actually quite glad that he had joined me and reached out instinctively to squeeze his hand. The gesture was supposed to be a grateful one, but I could see from his expression the moment I did it that he had read more into it. Snatching my hand back quickly, I turned away from him.

Before I could do anything else, I heard the sound of feet advancing up the hill. Clearly the officers from the harbour were on the move. Scurrying backwards, Davis and I headed up the path towards the sick pods and were met by Mason and Jackson almost immediately. But the footsteps of the Shadow Patrol were gaining rapid progress and we had little option but to retreat into the forest and hide until they passed.

The four of us scrambled into the trees, getting as far away from the path as we could. Mason waved a hand and motioned down the bank. If we stayed in the treeline close to the path there was a good chance we would be spotted, but movement further into the cover of the trees meant we were less likely to be caught. This meant we had to travel further down the slope towards the lower bay area of Clearance though. We crept slowly and silently down the hillside, until we found a dense area of bushes which easily concealed us all while still giving us some view of the path.

Jackson was crying silently, more distressed than I had ever seen her. Mason placed an arm around her, attempting some kind of comfort. She sank to the ground in the centre of the bush and crammed her hand into her mouth, as if she was stifling a scream.

"We found her," Mason whispered, shaking his head.

Jackson had regained some control and removed her hand from her face. "She's delirious. Her leg… infection… didn't recognise-" Unable to speak further, she clamped the hand back over her face and buried it in Mason's shoulder.

I looked back towards the path. An alarming number of Shadow Patrol officers were advancing up the hill. At the lower pods, some of them broke off and posted themselves by the entrance to each one. The remaining officers continued towards the sick pods.

"What are they doing?" Mason's voice was filled with horror as the disturbance inside the sick pods became clear. There was a growing murmur as we heard the citizens being roused.

Moments later, the officers began to emerge, bringing with them the people from inside the pods. Some of them walked independently, some stooped and supported each other. Those who could not walk were carried out on makeshift stretchers crafted from thick blankets. It looked like every single citizen in the sick pods was woken up and marched outside. Many of them looked like they hadn't seen the outside world for weeks, and were blinking and stumbling into the cold night air.

The odd procession made its way down the mountainside towards the harbour. Clearly the sick citizens of Clearance were being taken somewhere. But where? We watched from our hiding place in the woods, fascinated by the strange spectacle. My earlier feeling of dread intensified and, despite desperately wanting to distance myself from what was happening, I found myself unable to look away.

Chapter Thirty-Three

The group remained strangely silent as they continued down the hill, possibly confused as to where they were going in the middle of the night. Eventually all the citizens from the sick pods gathered in the harbour. Some took a seat on the beach; those on stretchers were placed in a separate group to one side. Others remained standing. These citizens had one obvious thing in common. They were all fragile. Even those standing looked as if holding their body upright was a challenge. The weakest and most 'undesirable' Beck citizens had been selected for whatever was about to occur.

Creeping closer to the harbour despite Davis's whispered protests, I could just begin to make out individuals within the group. With a shock, I spotted Miller standing to one side, exhaustion etched on her face. There was no sign of Harper as far as I could tell. Surely she was housed with the other 'healthy' citizens in the lower pods, which were still under heavy guard, presumably to prevent any of them from coming outside to see what was about to happen.

As we watched, some of the Shadow Patrol began to circulate around the group of people, barking an instruction which could not be heard from our position on the hillside. Their dark uniforms made them fearsome and completely anonymous in the darkness. I could not have identified

Campbell or Tench. Even their heads were covered with close-fitting black masks. At their command, the citizens bent down and began to remove their boots. One or two resisted, but found themselves quickly and fiercely dealt with, and were soon barefoot along with the others.

I looked again at the group of citizens on stretchers. Even they were having their boots taken from them. I managed to pick out Fin, her face twisted with pain. She looked as though she was about to pass out, and I tore my eyes away, not wanting to witness her agony.

Some of the Shadow Patrol had begun to gather on the jetties now, pulling down and securing the gangways on the four fishing boats which we had seen earlier. The decks had been cleared of equipment, I noticed. The Shadow Officers still on the shore began to herd citizens towards the jetties. The operation was carefully controlled: an officer standing at the entrance to each one, checking every Clearance citizen and handing something to them as they passed onto the narrow wooden walkway.

I realised with a start that they were being given a harness each. Jackson stifled a gasp by my side as she too understood that these were the ones which we had carried here in our backpacks this morning. Each citizen was securing the straps around their skinny waists as they moved down the wooden walkway to the boats. Another officer checked that the fastenings were securely tied and then directed them on to the deck of a boat, where they stood and waited.

"Where are they taking them?" Jackson's voice was low and tense, "And what's with the harnesses?"

"Why've they taken their boots?" Davis added.

I shrugged, "Who knows? Perhaps they're being transported

somewhere else? Somewhere they can get better."

Mason snorted, "You think they'd do anything to help these people? And why take their boots?"

Jackson nodded her agreement, "He's right. They wouldn't start to help them now."

"Perhaps they're selling them," Davis chimed in, "You know, to another society. Out there." He gestured with a hand out at the expanse of water ahead.

Mason's tone was grim, "What would they even be worth?"

I closed my eyes for a second and turned back to the operation unfolding below us. More than half the citizens on the beach had now been loaded on to the first two boats, whose decks were filling to alarming levels. Both were already packed, unable to take further bodies safely, yet still the officers continued to load them. They swayed dangerously with the constant movement on deck, sinking lower in the water with every new citizen that boarded.

The operation was still strangely silent, the only noise created by the shuffling of bare feet as the most vulnerable Beck citizens made their way on to the boats. Mason and Jackson were right. Something terrible was happening here. Where were they going? Giving them a harness on water made no logical sense. The fact that the citizens had no boots on only increased my feeling of dread.

The boats were loaded to overflowing. Every time I didn't think they could fit another body on deck, the officer at the head of the gangplanks would beckon someone forward and push them into the crowd. At one point I saw a man protest, stepping away as the officer took his elbow and tried to guide him on board.

After several unsuccessful attempts to persuade him to walk

into the depths of the seething crowd on board, the officer gave up and smacked him sharply over the head with a baton. The man collapsed instantly, and the officer was able to bundle him up and thrust him onto the deck. I fought against the tears streaming down my face as I watched him slowly disappear, held up at first by some of the individuals in the crowd, but then slipping from view completely.

I watched as Miller headed for the jetty, still struggling a little but seeming to have lost most of her fight. Fin was carried to the last boat on her stretcher and laid down close to the railing, but I lost sight of her as the deck began to fill with those who could still stand. Now the boat was swollen to bursting point, and I could feel Jackson sobbing softly by my side.

I put what I hoped was a comforting arm around her. I had no idea what else to do. Nothing I could say would help. It was abundantly clear that Fin would be trampled by the feet of those around her, simply because there was nowhere else to stand. My only hope was that the feet were bare and possibly not as painful as booted feet would have been. Or that Fin had already passed out.

The Shadow Officers loaded the remaining people, stowed the gang planks and unhooked the ropes. The engines spluttered into life and the boats began to move away from the jetties. Feeling movement to my left, I glanced down to see Mason and Jackson making their way further down the hill, closer to the landing area. There were still a few officers on the beach, but they appeared to be occupied with collecting up the boots and blankets left on the beach. Several had pulled the dark mask up to their forehead, but we weren't close enough to see their faces.

Tapping Davis' arm, I motioned for him to follow me and began to make my way through the remaining trees between myself and the sand dunes which flanked the bay. The officers left on land weren't looking for anyone; their focus was entirely on the boats out in the water and the abandoned belongings on the beach. We were able to get fairly close without being spotted, and crouched in a clump of bushes which gave us a better view of what was happening. The boats were far out on the open water now.

Mason sighed, "We won't be able to see them for much longer. We still have no idea where they're going."

Remembering the binoculars I had packed, I took them out and raised them to my eyes. At least we could track the direction they were heading.

"They've stopped."

Jackson's voice cut across our group, louder than it should have been. I glanced worriedly at the remaining guards, but they seemed untroubled by the noise. Hopefully the sound of the water had drowned it out. Looking back out to sea, I realised that Jackson was right. Around three hundred metres away from the shore, the boats had cut their engines and were simply floating.

"What are they doing?" Jackson breathed in my ear.

I shook my head, "Maybe waiting for something? Meeting another boat?"

But there was nothing else in sight.

"Something's wrong," Davis sounded frightened, "Maybe one of the engines has failed."

"But why would all four stop together?"

He shrugged. I peered through the binoculars again, trying to refocus them without much success. The boats had not moved, but there was definitely some kind of movement on each of the boats.

And then we heard it, cutting across the stillness of the night. A single splash at first, quickly followed by another, and another, until the sound became continuous, like the thundering of a waterfall. One by one, the bodies on board the boats were falling into the water. No, not falling. Being pushed. Because as the binoculars finally refocused, I realised what was happening. The Shadow Officers on board the boats were forcing their cargo into the water. Some were going willingly, seemingly surprised by what was happening. Others were putting up a fight, struggling to remain in relative safety on the wooden deck of each boat.

As panic spread and they realised what was happening, a noise rose above the sound of splashing water. Hundreds of citizens screaming, struggling to escape being tossed into the icy water like abandoned children's toys. I watched as a couple of stronger citizens tried to claw their way back on to a boat in desperation. This was met by a sharp prod from a pole brandished by the Shadow Officer on board, which pushed them back into the seething mass of bodies in the water.

Once those standing on the decks were in the water, the officers lifted the stretchers and tossed the others overboard as well. These were the completely helpless ones, those who had no way at all of struggling against what was happening to them. I knew that one of those stretchers contained Fin, and found myself struggling to even draw breath.

To begin with, the area around the boats was filled with bodies. The shapes in the water were a writhing mass of angry limbs, hands reaching upwards, fighting to stay above the water level. The prospect of impending death created a desperate strength in many of the citizens, yet eventually, the heavy harnesses did their job. Even those who might have stood a chance of swimming struggled against the added weight. I realised with revulsion that we had actually carried the tools responsible for the mass murder we were witnessing.

I imagined the cold numbing their bodies and the harnesses pulling them under. Eventually, the heart-breaking keening of the Clearance citizens grew softer. As the moments passed, the pale, struggling figures weakened, disappeared into the depths, and the water became still and dark again.

I finally tore my eyes away from the water and glanced at those sitting around me. There were tears streaming down Jackson's pale face, Davis had his head resting in his hands and Mason's eyes were fixed on the water, his hands balled into tight fists at his sides. They had all realised what was happening, without the binoculars to magnify the terror on the faces of those being murdered out in the bay.

We all knew that The Beck was not an easy place to live. We followed the rules, no matter how tough they seemed, because we believed that Governor Adams had our best interests at heart. But this abomination, this extermination of our weakest citizens: this we could not accept. Fin was dead. She had probably been dead before she hit the water, trampled by the feet of the other citizens around her who were simply trying to stay alive. A literal survival of the fittest.

And Miller? Well perhaps she had lasted a little longer. She had shown spirit and considerable strength. She had been assigned to Clearance to send a message to those who tried to fight the system, because she was dangerous rather than weak. Now the Shadow Patrol had put an end to her protests in the same way they had extinguished the lives of the weak and feeble.

I felt sick. Dropping the binoculars on the ground, I moved away from the others and found myself retching into the grass. I tasted stew again as the bile rose in my throat. Even once I had rid my stomach of its contents I couldn't stop myself heaving, feeling all the more frustrated because there was nothing coming up. It seemed like there would be no end to it. Waves of nausea rolled over me and I huddled on the ground for what seemed like an age, helpless in my agony. The others were no better.

I have no idea how long we sat there, waiting for something to happen. When I found I could finally sit up and gaze out to sea, the boats, empty of their cargo, were heading back into the shore. The water was dark and still, as though nothing at all had happened. The officers on the beach were now awaiting the arrival of their colleagues on the boats. Slowly, we began to move back up the hillside, knowing that we had to get back to base before anyone discovered we were gone. If we were caught here after witnessing the drownings, we were as good as dead ourselves.

Chapter Thirty-Four

We made our way back to the Patrol Compound in complete silence, lost in our thoughts. Getting back up the hill and out of Clearance without being spotted was not easy. We were more terrified of being caught now than ever, as the ultimate consequences of such disobedience were abundantly clear. We had been able to crouch in places, but in others had literally been crawling on our stomachs to ensure we remained hidden from the Shadow Patrol. The ascent was steep and took its toll on our already tired bodies. Travelling down had been far easier, without the burden of the terrible knowledge we now carried with us.

As we were almost clear, we had to duck and hide for several moments as two Shadow Patrol officers emerged unexpectedly from the hidden entrance. I crouched, my heart racing, as they passed by and headed down the path towards the harbour. Once we were sure they had gone, we hurried into the woods, for once grateful for the density of the trees which might hide us from view. Reaching the exit on the other side of the pass, Mason peered out through the tree fronds.

"It's empty." He sounded confused.

"What?" Jackson's reply was hushed.

"There's no one there."

"Do you think those guards who passed us were…"

Our voices were hushed, terrified. We hardly dared believe that there was no one guarding the pass, but if the two Shadow Officers who had just passed us were the ones who had been on duty here, then perhaps we were in the clear. It made sense that they were going to assist with the clean up after the drownings. We hurried on past the guard outpost and did not speak again until we had reached the relative cover of the woods closer to Patrol.

"All those people." Davis's voice shook.

"Fin." Jackson was past tears now, her voice dry and emotionless.

Mason's hands were still clenched in fists. He appeared unable to speak.

I shook myself, trying to rid my head of the disturbing images which floated unbidden into my consciousness like the bodies in the water.

"We have to do something. We can't just let it happen."

Mason barked out a short, humourless laugh. "Get real, Quin!"

I spun round and bit back at him, "You mean you're ok with sitting back and watching while they do this? To our friends? To those around us?"

"What exactly do you think we can do about it?"

I flew at him before I could stop myself, rage surging inside me. My hands battered against his chest, his face, his head and I found I couldn't stop myself, despite knowing that this was not his fault. He stood still, letting me hit him over and over, as if he knew how much I needed to vent my anger. He almost seemed to welcome the battering, as if physical pain might somehow ease his mental torture. Eventually the blows slowed and my entire body sagged weakly against his. He put his arm around me and patted my back awkwardly.

"Don't think I'm ok with what just happened. But we can't do anything about it without ending up on one of those boats ourselves."

"Look," Jackson spoke softly, but had regained some of her usual composure, "Let's get back to camp and try to get a little rest. Tomorrow we can talk... try to make some sense of..." her voice faltered but she continued, "Work out what we can do."

"We can leave."

"Leave?" I turned and stared at Mason, incredulously, "Where would we go?"

"We only need a boat and some supplies. We know there's land elsewhere now. Let's take a boat and go."

"What if it's further than we think? If we run out of supplies? Come across enemies?"

"Better than sitting here knowing what's really going on. Waiting until we slip up ourselves and get dumped over there." Mason's voice was bitter, cold even. He had made up his mind.

Again Jackson came to our rescue, the voice of reason. "Even that needs time and planning. Look, we have to get back before we're missed. We need some rest before the Pledge Ceremony."

Davis and I nodded and eventually Mason shrugged his shoulders and began to walk. We reached the final clearing at the edge of the woods and stopped dead as we heard noise in the trees above us. We waited, undecided on the best course of action. If we were caught now, that would be it. I was about to motion to the others to hide when the rustling stopped and a dark figure dropped out of the trees ahead of us.

"What are you doing here? Are you mad?"

It was Cameron. I felt a sigh of relief from those around me. I knew there weren't many people we could trust, but Cameron had intervened on my behalf too many times now for me to doubt his loyalty. He walked towards us slowly.

"I might have known it would be you. Patrol picks citizens with the strength to deal with the role, but fails to grasp how many of us object to what goes on here."

"So you object?"

His eyes blazed. "You think I approve?"

For a moment, I held his gaze, searching for any sign that he was lying. I wanted so much to believe him.

He broke eye contact and looked at the floor. "Many Patrol citizens hate it. We know the truth, we take the pledge, but we despise what goes on. The only ones who don't are those who want power… status."

I nodded, realising who they were. "Shadow Patrol."

He nodded. "Shadow Patrol. Few could do what they do, but those who do…" He trailed off, his meaning obvious.

Jackson choked back a sob, "I don't know how anyone could."

"And this goes right to the top?" Davis asked, his tone begging to be contradicted. "To Adams and Carter? They condone it?"

Cameron sighed heavily, "They created the system. The idea is that we can't sustain the amount of people we have living in The Beck, so there has to be a way to control the population. They do it at the other end too."

Mason shot a look at him, "The other end?"

"In Meds? They only allow births where there have been sufficient deaths to create room for new citizens to be born. But they have to time it right, which is easier said than done. Citizens need fourteen years before they can properly contribute. Fourteen years of taking food from the mouths of other citizens, without giving anything back. Adams resents it. And sometimes they get it wrong. There are too few or too many... then the problems begin. Too many mouths to feed, too few people working in the fields, with the livestock, preparing the food... You see how delicate the system is."

"No reason for murder though. Especially those who're ill because The Beck hasn't protected them." I fought to keep my voice under control. "Adams feeds them too little... they're starving... they don't have enough energy to work... they get sick... and he exterminates them? It makes me sick."

"I know." Cameron sounded sad. "It's horrendous. We're trying to... to stop it. There just aren't enough of us I'm afraid. Most are too frightened."

Davis looked up, "What are you doing?"

"Trying to marshall enough of us to fight. Tyler is part of it. But it won't happen easily. For now, we bide our time and wait, try to convert others to our cause."

"Wait? I say we just leave." Mason again.

"Leave? Are you serious?" Cameron's laugh was scathing.

"I am. Get a boat, save some provisions, get out of here."

"And leave all those you care about behind to die?" Jackson spat at him.

Cameron put a finger to his lips to quieten us. "There's no guarantee that you would survive. It's been tried before, Mason."

"And?"

"And I know of two attempts, one which failed completely – the bodies washed up on shore a day later. They didn't even make it out of the bay down there."

"What about the other?"

"We never heard from them again."

"So they made it."

"Not necessarily. The people who left were supposed to come back, to let us know what they found. They were part of our resistance. It was a year ago." He shook his head, "We've heard nothing from them."

"Maybe they made it, and what they found was so good they didn't want to risk their necks coming back."

"Maybe. We don't know."

Cameron paused and looked around at us all seriously, his gaze resting on me a little longer than the others. "Will you consider joining us? Or think about it, at least?"

Jackson was the first to reply, "Of course."

"No question," Davis added.

Finding myself unable to speak, I nodded fiercely.

Cam turned to Mason. "Look, you'd be a major asset, but I get it if you don't want to. Can you keep it to yourself though?"

Mason nodded slowly.

"Good. Now we need to hurry. The Shadow Patrol will come back this way pretty soon."

He moved off, setting quite a pace. Before long we were approaching the edge of the Compound, the Annexe in sight from the edge of the woods. Cameron motioned for us to stop.

"Be careful getting back in. You've about an hour left before wake up. Try and get some rest at least. You need to take the pledge convincingly tomorrow."

Mason and Davis nodded before taking off across the final clearing and crossing the courtyard.

Jackson remained behind for a moment. "Do we stand a

chance?"

He shrugged. "Maybe. If there are enough of us."

We turned to follow Mason and Davis, but Cameron took my hand, stopping me.

"Go ahead," I nodded at Jackson, who followed the others.

Cameron looked utterly defeated. He let my hand go, but continued to stare at me.

"I'm glad you finally understand, Quin. But I'm sad you had to know at all. The Beck's a terrible place once you know the truth." He shook his head.

"It is. I'm glad you want to fight it though." I paused and put my hand out, taking his in mine this time. He looked up, startled. "And I'm with you. All the way."

"Thanks." He smiled slightly, his expression filled with sadness. "You'd better go in."

I meant to leave, but instead found myself stepping towards him. He hesitated for a moment, before circling his arms around me and pulling me closer, far more gently than he had earlier. I felt the lean strength in his torso and let my head relax against his chest. All at once I felt warmer, more secure, as well as a little breathless.

"I'd like to kiss you," he whispered the words in my ear.

I froze, frightened, despite suspecting that I wanted the same thing. I knew that I'd only have to lift my head. For several moments, I couldn't move. I felt his hope, tense in every muscle of his body, slowly drain away as we stood there, immobile. Finally, I felt him exhale slowly, as if he'd been holding his breath.

"I understand. It's too much to take in. I wanted you to know how I felt though, now that you know everything. Now that you—"

I found myself leaning back, moving away from him slightly, angling my head so I could meet his gaze.

"Tyler."

He looked confused, "Tyler?"

"What about Tyler? It seems like you and her are... close."

Understanding slowly dawned on his face and he took a moment to answer. "Tyler and I... yes we're close. Good friends. We have known each other for a long time. But she's not..." he paused, his face colouring, "well she's not... you."

He stopped speaking suddenly as I moved my face closer to his, not entirely sure what I was doing. There was a pause as he considered my expression, a ghost of a smile on his face.

"Are you sure?"

I nodded slowly, not entirely certain what I was agreeing to. Slowly, he bent his head down towards mine, as if he were testing out what I would do. Now I was the one holding my breath, the warmth I had felt a moment ago intensified. It seemed to take an age, but eventually his lips came down to meet mine. They were soft and warm. Still, at first, simply resting against my own, but then beginning to move, gently, as if he feared I might bolt from his arms. I could feel his breath tickling into my mouth as I opened mine in surprise, the feelings coursing through me, completely unknown. When he broke away we were both breathless.

"Go get some sleep."

I nodded, "If I can."

"I'm going to have trouble sleeping myself too." His tone grew serious, "Try though, really. Tomorrow is a big day."

"I'm going." I leaned up once again and snatched another small kiss before breaking away and walking briskly across the field, my breath catching in my throat as I did so.

Chapter Thirty-Five

Later, I looked across the same field. Today it seemed very different: filled with benches and a platform, the majority of the Patrol cohort lined up to watch the new recruits take the pledge. It had been a matter of days since I had first entered Patrol here, full of hope that I might discover more about The Beck and the way it worked, be able to see more of it and make a difference to its society.

Now I knew too much. The burden of knowledge lay heavy on my mind as I stood between Mason and Jackson, ready to take my pledge. We had decided, last night when we gathered in the Annexe after returning from our conversation with Cameron, that we would stay. That we would learn to live under The Beck rules in Patrol. To appear as though we were reliable Patrol citizens. Discover as much as we could about Governance in The Beck and the way decisions were made. Work from within to combat the horrors which went on in secret. Try and save the weaker Beck citizens from Clearance. As many of them as we could, anyway. Learn from Cameron, and Tyler, and slowly change our society for the better.

I watched as Governor Adams climbed the steps to the temporary stage. He began to speak, his words heavy with lies about the importance of the Patrol pledge, how vital we were to ensuring The Beck society at large could thrive. I thought of

Cameron and Tyler, and their underground movement with its lofty aim of undermining the current system. I thought of Cass, slaving away on tiny rations in Agric, believing that she did a worthy job keeping The Beck fed. I thought of Harper, still trapped in Clearance. Working her already weak body into the ground on even smaller rations than Cass, all the while not knowing she was simply biding her time until Clearance became too full and she was disposed of. And finally I thought of Miller and Fin, already victims of The Beck's horrendous system. There was no way back for them.

I heard my name called and began to make my way to the stage to collect my Patrol pin, a symbol of the system which routinely murdered its weaker citizens and abused those who worked to maintain it. My voice recited the words of the Pledge, promising to defend Beck society, enforce its rules, and work to ensure the sustainability of its system.

Inside my head, I made a vow of an entirely different kind.

Author's Note

Thank you for reading Flow. I hope that you lost yourself in the world of The Beck just as I did when I wrote the book. I love building relationships with my readers. Quin and her friends will return in the sequel, but if you enjoyed Flow and would like to get additional free books please sign up for my mailing list below:

http://www.clarelittlemore.com/free-books/?signup=book-flow

Please note that if you sign up, you will not receive any spam. I will only send you occasional newsletters with details of my new releases, special offers and other bits of news relating to the Flow series and any other books I write.

And if you do, I'll send you the following freebies:
1. A copy of the haunting thriller novel, *The Search*.
2. A copy of the heart-breaking novella *Escape*, follow up to *The Search*.
3. An exclusive copy of the original prequel I wrote for *The Search*, which was edited out and is not available anywhere else.

About the Author

Clare Littlemore was born in Durham in the UK. Her parents were both teachers, and she grew up in a world surrounded by books. She has worked for most of her life as a teacher of English at various high schools in England, where she has shared her passion for books with hundreds of teenagers. In 2013, she began writing her own fiction. She lives in Warrington in the North West of England with her husband and two children.

You can connect with Clare:
- on Twitter at twitter.com/Clarelittlemore
- on Facebook at facebook.com/clarelittlemoreauthor

or send her an email at clare@clarelittlemore.com

Reviews

Liked this book? You can make a big difference. Reviews are really powerful. Being a self-published author, getting my books noticed can be difficult. If you enjoyed reading Flow, please consider spending five minutes leaving an **honest review** (it can be as brief as you like) on the book's Amazon page. I would be very grateful. Thank you very much.

Acknowledgements

Writing a book is not for the fainthearted. Stringing together 80,000 words is enough of a challenge without having to make sure that they make sense, are spelled correctly and, most of all, are entertaining. Flow could have never been what it is without the support of a number of very special people.

I would like to thank my editor, Beth Dorward, for her invaluable advice and support in making the Flow manuscript into the story you have just read. Without her corrections, suggestions, moral support and patience, the book would simply not exist in readable form.

Equally, I owe a debt of gratitude to my cover designer, Jessica Bell. I have never worked with a designer before, but Jessica made it an easy task. Tolerantly explaining how the process worked to my novice self, she was fantastic to work with and dreamed up a cover which was suitably haunting and intriguing. No matter how many changes I requested, she willingly adapted her designs until I was blown away by the finished product.

I also seem to have gathered a small but perfectly formed band of pre-readers, who each assisted in spotting typos, picking up on continuity errors, giving me feedback on the plot as it evolved and, of course, providing general encouragement to keep going...

So to my Mum: thank you for your eagle-eyed proofreading

expertise. To Linda, my mother in law: thank you for your honest and supportive feedback on the characters. To my Dad: thank you for checking the accuracy of my references to hydro-electricity, which I knew absolutely nothing about before I began writing! And lastly to Ria, Rachael, Allison, Lucy and Alison, thank you for all your kind and helpful comments along the way. I hope you will continue to assist me with the next book in the Flow series...

I'd also like to show my appreciation for my lovely children Daniel and Amy. They cheerfully put up with their mum obsessing over her book and also made suitably impressed noises over my daily word count whenever I shared it with them (which was fairly regularly). You don't get better kids than mine, though I suppose I'm biased...

A major thank you to my husband (and hero!) Marc, for his endless patience, unswerving belief in my ability to create a story other people might want to read, and last but definitely not least, his technical support. The amount of times I would have thrown my laptop out of the window whilst trying to get to grips with the latest technology available in the self-publishing world without him...

And finally, thank you to you, for reading this book. Without readers, a writer is nothing, and I'd like to say, entirely sincerely, how much I appreciate you reading Flow. I hope you will stick with me for many more books to come.